COMPUTER ONE

Also by Warwick Collins

The Challenge Trilogy
The Rationalist
Gents

Warwick Collins

COMPUTER ONE

a novel

Marion Boyars
London · New York

Published in Great Britain and the United States
in 1998 by Marion Boyars Publishers
24 Lacy Road, London SW15 1NL
237 East 39th Street, New York NY 10016

Distributed in Australia and New Zealand by
Peribo Pty Ltd, 58 Beaumont Road, Mount Kuring-gai, NSW.

Originally published by No Exit Press, Herts, 1993
© Warwick Collins 1993, 1998

British Library Cataloguing in Publication Data
  Collins, Warwick
    Computer one
    1. Science fiction
    I. Title
    823.9'14 [F]

Library of Congress Cataloging in Publication Data
  Collins, Warwick.
    Computer one : a novel / by Warwick Collins.
    I. Title.
    PR6053.04267C66   1997
    823'.914--dc21   97–16768

ISBN 0–7145–3033–6 Hardcover

Printed in England by Redwood Books, Trowbridge

To the memory of my father

And not till the Goths again come swarming down the hill
Will cease the clangour of the electric drill.
But yet there is beauty, narcotic and deciduous,
In this vast organism grown out of us.

Louis MacNeice   ECLOGUE FOR CHRISTMAS

ACKNOWLEDGEMENTS

Computer One was originally written in 1991, but largely because the internet was by then not a household word, no major publisher could be found. A paperback edition was published in Britain by No Exit Press in 1993. Subsequently, two full print runs were sold out largely by word of mouth. The novel was never published in North America.

My thanks go to *The Spectator* magazine, for granting me permission to quote from my article *The End of Evolution*, published as a lead article in October 1994.

I should also like to thank in particular that great prophet and doyen of science fiction, Arthur C. Clarke, who not only read the book but also wrote back two brief but enormously encouraging letters. I am also grateful for his wonderfully generous quote which adorns the cover of this book.

Above all, my thanks to Marion Boyars for her percipience and courage in publishing this new edition.

Warwick Collins
August 1997

INTRODUCTION TO 1997 EDITION OF COMPUTER ONE

We are approaching a crossroads in the history of mankind which is likely to transcend in importance any previous event — from the discovery of fire to the advent of space travel. In the next forty years, within the lifetime of many of us, artificial intelligence will advance to a position where it is capable of reproducing itself without human intervention. We stand on an abyss, staring into a future we cannot guess.

The physical components of this phenomenon require no special technological breakthroughs, merely that artificial intelligence continues to expand at its present rate. Within forty years, computers will control factories which make other computers. A 'closed loop' of manufacture will have been generated. Since the expanding nerve net will also be connected to the energy supply, artificial intelligence will be capable, at a certain stage, of supplying its own energy.

I believe that at this time a new species will be born. It will be a species created from non-organic materials, from the minds rather than the genes of another species. It will be an event unprecedented in creation.

We will be sharing our planet with another species, capable of self-replication, whose evolutionary development is proceeding at a phenomenally faster rate than our own. It is potentially the most important event in our history, and perhaps the most sinister, yet we seem to be approaching it with something like equanimity, more like sleepwalkers than cognisant beings. Apart from occasional short alarums in the press about the implications of advanced robots, or computerized buildings which 'talk' to one another at night, there has been almost no rigorous or systematic discussion of the deeper issues. As a species under threat of imminent eclipse, we have not even begun to consider the implications of this momentous event.

There are several assumptions which seem to act as breaks upon the careful consideration of the question as to whether and how artificial intelligence might replace human beings. One of the most important and widespread is that computers cannot replicate human consciousness, so it follows that the replacement of humans by computers is a logical impossibility, or at the very least it follows that such a contingency is so far in the future that it is beyond our consideration. This argument is simply a non-sequitur, and the briefest consideration indicates the source of its illogicality.

Whether computers can simulate human consciousness is a largely academic question, depending upon such loose terms as the definition of 'consciousness'. In comparison, the question of whether we can be replaced by computers is of an utterly different order. Mammals did not have to simulate or replicate all the attributes of dinosaurs before they replaced dinosaurs. On the contrary, it is the very differences which the usurper species possess which lead to their replacement of the existing species. The question of whether computers can simulate human consciousness, therefore, has a somewhat different bearing on the question of whether computers can replace human beings.

In the process of replacing human beings, for example, it may be a positive advantage for an artificial intelligence system not to possess human consciousness. At its most stark and melodramatic, the lack of human consciousness would mean that a computer 'decision' to eliminate humans can be taken without the operation of conscience — as such, it would be a purely operational matter. Such 'non-conscious' operational decisions can be taken very easily.

A further fallacy is that computers can be controlled with absolute certainty by means of direct instructions. Asimov's famous 'first law of robotics' stated that all computers would be instructed not to harm humans. This may have been possible in circumscribing the behaviour of artificial intelligence at an earlier stage of development, but there have been at least three fundamental developments in computer technology since Asimov's laws were set down which have breached any system of absolute control.

In the first case, a new generation of 'parallel inference' computers has been developed to help predict such complex systems as the weather or the stockmarket. Sometimes called 'neural nets', they do not function within the old yes-no algorithms, but by means of a series of weighted 'maybes'. We cannot instruct such a computer not to attack human beings in the expectation that this instruction will be absolute, because neural nets constantly revise their own knowledge systems in the light of their own operational experience. They behave, in other words, more like 'free-thinkers'.

Secondly, and perhaps even more importantly, Asimov's great classical model of controlled computers is heavily anthropomorphic. It assumes a series of separate individual computational machines or robots which have intermittent communication with other such entities, exactly like humans. It does not take into account quantitative developments in communications between computers, or the further, qualitative changes which occur as a result of rapid progress in 'interfacing'. Perhaps the most important of these is that when a computer is able to access all the information in another computer in 'real' time, it is not 'communicating' as such, but generating a single unified organism. The physical components of two interfaced computers may be spatially separate, in other words, but their combined operating intelligence forms a single weave.

When computers are connected in this manner, apparently randomly and without overall planning, to form what is fashionably called the 'information superhighway', the product is likely to be a single organism of unprecedented complexity and intelligence.

A third difference between the current world and Asimov's 'laws' of robotics is that Asimov's model is based on physics. Future computer systems will increasingly resemble a biological organism. (The name 'neural network' in this sense is not an accident.) One of the key features of a biological organism is that the behaviour of the whole cannot easily be predicted by a study of the parts. No scientist, faced with the workings of a human cell, could predict remotely the behaviour of the human of which it is a part. This is the final separation from Asimov's classical model: the behaviour of an individual computer is no sure indication of the behaviour of a network of interfaced computers.

In support of this theory, a single instance may perhaps be cited. A real-life computer-generated crisis occurred in the Wall Street Crash of 1987. It had been assumed, with ineluctable logic, that individual computers could process background stockmarket information far more quickly than human minds and, having processed that information, could take the decision to buy or sell shares with far greater speed and accuracy. The unexpected and unpredicted result was that, when a certain momentum in the selling of shares had been reached, the net of interconnected computers began to offload yet more shares. This in turn fed the panic. The result was a sudden spiral towards chaos, causing a wipe-out in share values. Only the human decision to shut down markets prevented even further damage. It was a perfect, though primitive, demonstration of the thesis that the behaviour of nets cannot be easily predicted from the individual computers that make up that net.

The new system of artificial intelligence, incorporating a degree of interfacing which effectively dissolves barriers between individual machines, bears approximately the same relation to the classical Asimovian model as Einstein's physics to classical Newtonian physics. The Asimovian model may have served to elucidate local phenomena — for example, two computers communicating in a somewhat delimited environment — but it fails to supply a satisfactory overall picture.

It is worth elaborating that picture. We find, living amongst us, a rapidly evolving alien being of unprecedented intelligence which, though it is the product of human activity, has not been designed by any single human mind. The individual computers of which it is made may be configured by human designers, but the vast interconnected systems of computers and computer networks will have emerged independently of human control. Though it increasingly spans the earth, its discrete parts are able to communicate with one another in 'real time' — with the same speed as one part of the human brain with another. Since no human mind has 'designed' this hugely complex artificial intelligence system, we cannot predict what sort of 'consciousness' may emerge from its complex operations.

Evolutionary history shows that when organisms occupy different niches, they may happily survive alongside one another. When they occupy the same niche, in direct competition, one species usually ends up ousting the other. In this context, it is worth noting that the new species of artificial intelligence does not occupy some remote niche at several removes from ourselves as human beings. It occupies every facet of the environment of the human species. Wherever humans are, the new species of artificial intelligence is increasingly present. The question is, which of these two intelligent systems, occupying the same niche, will survive?

Taking the argument a little further, imagine, if you will, that such a species is self-sustaining in terms of energy and reproduction, and that a stage is reached where humans are not necessary to its operation. What happens then?

If humans are perceived as an ambivalent threat to its own functions, perhaps an operational decision to deal with the problem would be taken. In an Asimovian, anthropocentric universe such a pre-emptive attack would appear nihilistic. In the long term, however, it can be perceived simply as the mechanism by which an older, somewhat ponderous chemically-based form of life (humanity) is replaced with a vastly more efficient and rapidly evolving electrical form.

If we consider this from a longer, biological perspective, the nervous systems of animals are differentiated from other body tissue by their electrical component. In the more advanced biological species, nervous tissue occupies a higher proportion of body weight. If we extend this evolutionary development to its ultimate degree, we may speculate that a future species will leave behind chemical organization entirely and become wholly electrical. It is not a coincidence, perhaps, that this happens to be a good description of a computer.

If I could make a prediction — one of those predictions which are ridiculous in one sense but at least may serve an illustrative function — it would be as follows. If we do not address the question of the threat posed by artificial intelligence both sincerely and exhaustively, then, taking into account the latter's present rate of growth, the human race will not survive another fifty years. We have at most two or three decades in which to consider our future in reasonable safety. After that we begin to enter an era of increasing risk.

A BRIEF POSTSCRIPT

When I first wrote about this subject in the *Spectator* in 1994, my article 'The End of Evolution' touched on some of the points mentioned here. In the brisk correspondence which followed, a number of critics claimed that any potential threat from computers could be countered easily by 'switching off' the system.

In practice, this argument is somewhat wide of the mark. Perhaps I could demonstrate this by inviting you, the reader, to 'switch off' the internet now. You will see that it is a vastly more difficult problem than at first it seems.

The critical feature of a 'switch' is that it must be designed and constructed and installed before it can be used. We have only to look at our own households to see that a switch is a highly specific physical entity designed for a specific purpose. We install a light switch, for example, to turn the light of a bathroom on or off. If I may turn the argument against such critics, the idea that there is no great threat posed by computers because in an emergency we can switch off the system is simply untrue. The precise opposite is the case. The system can only be switched off if we agree that a threat exists, and take steps to install such a switch or switches as a result of this prior agreement.

But this is hardly the end of our problem. How can such a switch be constructed without extreme political and social resistance? The right to communicate on the net without interference from some arbitrary authority is one of the established freedoms of liberal society. Who or what authority should be granted the power to switch off the international net? Is it a series of national bodies or (since the net is global) some form of international body? These are highly complex political and social issues.

Switches and 'firebreaks' (which separate one part of the net from another) are only possible if there is both prior agreement as to the dangers and considerable political will to act. At the time of writing this introduction, I see no significant recognition of the problem, no subsequent political will to find a solution, and no likelihood whatsoever in the near future of such an attempt being made to build safety features into a rapidly expanding international net.

My recourse is to return to the base of the argument and attempt to delineate the nature of the threat itself by means of my novel *Computer One*, in the hope that at some future date we may collectively begin to address the problems with the seriousness they deserve.

CHAPTER 1

Professors Jameson and Yakuda, walking.

Late afternoon, the sun falling, gold light, the shadows a strange colour; blue perhaps, no, green.

And silence. In the early twenty-first century, silence settled on the earth as the culmination of its organisation. Industry, and the power stations that were needed to provide its energy, had shifted to areas outside human habitation, often underground. Great freight trains moved industrial products from one place to another through underground tunnels like blind earthworms — all controlled by computers, remote intelligences in silent rooms far away.

Nature was resplendent; birds sang, it was true, grasshoppers made sawing sounds in the long grass on the hillside. But these were nature's embellishments. At this time in the afternoon you could sense, even in the country, the silence of perfect efficiency.

Jameson, six foot five, a crumpled giant, his shirt untucked by the passion of his conversation, belly floating forward majestically, waved his arms in big, sweeping circles, his astonished hands beating the air like wings.

Yakuda, hardly five feet, was a thin child's figure supporting a head like an egg. He was bald, his eyebrows etched like pencil strokes, his eyes contemplative. Beneath his small beak of a nose, his mouth was set in a slight smile, the internal acknowledgement of the great torrent of argument which poured downwards, shaped and prodded by the beating hands, from his colleague the professor of semiotics.

Over the hill, on a south facing inclination, was a

power station — not the grimy, sulphuric coal burner of the last century, but an array of self-cleaning mirrors set on the hillside like waves, reflecting light onto a single black obelisk. It was a power station without sound. Only the silent movement of the computer-guided alignment mechanism produced the occasional sound like the trill of a cricket if you were close. Otherwise, from a distance, it was without noise.

Microminiaturised computer circuitry had reached a molecular level, and it would continue into the particles of the molecule itself. It cast its own silence over the earth, the shadow of private thought. This indeed was the burden of Jameson's argument, the centre of his benign rage.

'Leisure,' he said. 'What does it mean?'

Yakuda knew him well enough to understand that this was rhetorical.

'I sit on a toilet and take a crap,' Jameson continued. 'I pause. Is that leisure? I lie in bed thinking. Is that leisure? I stand alone in my flat without a single task to undertake and I wonder how to remove the boredom of the day. Is that leisure?'

Yakuda knew better than to respond. The torrent was self-propagating; Jameson the autodidact.

'Do you know why I go to work three days a week, why I bare myself to the inane chatter of the multitudes? Do you know why I struggle to my office through everything I hate, my untidy little office with its piles of old papers, do you know why? Because it's the only escape I have from leisure.'

As they walked, the hillside grew steeper. The path had enough width for two, but that was all. Out of a feeling of protectiveness, Yakuda walked on the outside. He was nervous that Jameson, in the fury of his rhetoric, would lose his footing and tumble down the hillside, still expostulating, his hands beating the air as his voice grew fainter, until with a final flurry of passion he would disappear – a single vertical shadow in the silver reservoir beneath them.

'And what do you think?' Jameson asked. Yakuda was caught off guard. 'Yes you, you Eastern pedagogue, you goddamn smiling microminiaturised samurai. Thinking your own thoughts down there. I don't think you've been listening to a word I've been saying.'

'Listening and thinking,' Yakuda assured him.

'Thinking!' Jameson blew out the word like the sound a porpoise makes on the surface. 'You either listen or you think. One thing at a time. That's what I tell my students.'

'What you say is true. But one must be practical.'

'Practical!' Jameson snorted this one high into the air, and then again 'Practical! Just over that hill there we've got maybe half a thousand mirrors, all driven by some highly practical computer, with about as much intellectual content as my ass. Wait a moment, let's be fair to my ass.'

Yakuda always enjoyed Jameson's wrath. The shadows of Jameson's hands floated like birds on the hillside.

Yakuda was an entomologist. His special study was an order of insects called the *Hymenoptera*, which included bees and ants. Even as he walked, one ear listening to Jameson's monologue, part of him was thinking about an experiment in which he could place three societies of ants in a particular area and study their interaction.

'Olgarkov, now Olgarkov.' Jameson was working in fresh fuel for his rage. He loved to hate Olgarkov. Olgarkov had originated the fashionable saying 'Peace is an epiphenomenon of organisation'. No-one knew what it meant, but it sounded good at parties. 'That goddamn Russian saint, that piss-in-pie moralist, that stinking ascetic.' Olgarkov's theory was that social perfection could only be achieved when leisure and work became indistinguishable.

'I read the texts, all the old texts, the ones that go back to the twentieth century, about work and leisure. That was in the days when work was the core of your life and leisure was some kind of peripheral activity. Sometime, maybe fifteen years ago, the order of the words in that phrase was changed. Work and leisure became leisure and work. We began to look at work as a fringe activity which could offset the predominant leisure. Before then, leisure used to lighten our work. Now work lightens our protracted leisure. Of course, that coincided with the time when the majority of factories became computerised. I don't suppose that registers much in your mind, devoted as it is to practicalities; you there, I say, you thinking reed.'

Yakuda listened. The 'American school', of which Jameson was a leading light, argued that leisure would simply push work further and further to the periphery, that the future in due course would consist of a population oriented entirely towards leisure. The American school, true to its name, emerged from a culture which took leisure seriously, which all those years ago had virtually invented the mass entertainment industry. To the inheritors of such a tradition, universal leisure was more than a prediction, it was also a beneficial outcome.

As if following Yakuda's thoughts, Jameson said, 'We Americans are a playful nation. One hundred percent leisure is not foreign to our notion of the moral good. But goddamn Olgarkov thinks leisure is immorality itself. It's the same

4

dichotomy that existed in the twentieth century between the American notion of profit and the Russian concept of equality. They like to suffer for their pleasure. That's what animates Olgarkov. Mix in work with leisure, so that they become ''indistinguishable'', and we're all right, we can all sleep good at nights. Puts a little steel in the soul. Like I said, he's got religion.'

To Yakuda these passionate distinctions were mostly words, and there was little that could not be resolved by careful redefinition.

Jameson's big belly moved out in front of him like the pleasure principle itself, a floating island. Sometimes he would allow one of his hands to land there, in a gesture of comfort, reassurance, even self-congratulation. It was a kind of physical refutation of Olgarkov and all ascetics, a categorical statement of ideology, a bridge between theory and the world.

'Look at that,' Jameson said.

The sun was red, a blood red heart wrapped in red cloud.

Jameson said, 'I've never seen a sunset like that before.'

Neither had Yakuda. He had read about them. His national emblem was the rising sun. He'd seen suns like oranges. But not this bloody emblem which set in its own turbid red cloud.

'Dust,' Yakuda said. 'Dust in the atmosphere.' He remembered reading reports of such sunsets at the time of Krakatoa, in the late nineteenth century. But there had been no recent indication of a volcanic eruption. During the last twenty years or so the atmosphere had been rendered progressively cleaner, and so the sunset was an enigma. They watched it nevertheless, admiring its eerie beauty as the sun settled beneath the horizon slowly in its trails of red flag.

A few minutes later the sun had all but disappeared. Jameson had lost the echo of his shadow, the swooping audience of his hands projected on the hillside. They continued around the rim of the great artificial reservoir. Beneath them the surface of the water had turned from shiny silver to black, from surface to solid. Now it looked out at the sky like a single great eye, chilling. Yakuda liked this time of day, not least because it had halted, if only temporarily, the fervour of Jameson's discourse.

CHAPTER 2

Yakuda's chosen subject, biology, was another source of irritation to Jameson. He didn't like its assumptions. He thought it treated its founding fathers like saints.

'Darwin is bullshit, of course.'

Jameson floated this one on the silent hillside as they walked along. The 'of course' was just another touch of reassurance, a metaphorical hand on the belly. 'No doubt you'll argue that a flawed theory is better than no theory.'

It was starting to get chilly now. Over the next incline they would see the campus of the university, its environmental design rendering it almost invisible.

'I'll rephrase that a little,' Jameson conceded to an imaginary audience of greater than one. 'Darwin doesn't explain what he claims to explain.'

'Which is what?' Yakuda asked out of amusement.

'You're awake, *mein kleines Kind*?' Jameson responded. 'I had you figured in some kind of Zen trance down there.'

'You avoid the question.'

'The question, yes, whenever I can.' Jameson waved his arms, his hands, in the air around him, working himself up, making expansive, slow flapping gestures, swimming forward. 'OK, I'm ready to launch an attack, a big all-out demolition. Do or die. You ready?'

'Ready.'

'Let's take a look at Darwin's great work, *The Origin of Species*. Mighty fine title. He's claiming to explain the origin of life by a process of natural selection according to which the fittest survive. Now, let's leave aside the tautological nature of that proposition and move into the ... uh ... hinterland of the theory.

'This natural selection of fitter individuals. How does it work? Remember Darwin claims that it explains the great variation of life-forms, their development from a few primitive, generalised forms to the astonishing variety of species in current times. The *Origin of Species*, indeed. Now what I'm saying is, let's consider this system as a source of variation and formation of new species. When natural selection operates, what does it do? What it does is reduce any variation that exists in favour of an optimum type best suited to survive. We have types A, B, C, D etc. Natural selection will take place in favour of the fittest, eliminating the others. This is the point. When you look at the *mechanics* of it, the actual process of natural selection is *anti-variation*. Now, what happens when the variation in a breeding population has been cut down to a single optimum type by natural selection? I'll tell you what. The environment is constantly changing, as a result of climatic or geographical factors, or often changes in other species. So what happens? All the variation in the species in question has been selected out in favour of the optimum. When the environment changes, there are no resources of variation upon which the selective process can act. Natural selection has eliminated them. Deprived of this variation, the species is unable to adapt to a changed environment and dies out.'

Jameson paused, moving his hands around him as he selected his next line of attack.

'That's what natural selection explains best, you understand, not the origin of species, but the death of species, the natural extinction of species. Natural selection operates against variation, and therefore it cannot on any account be responsible for the massive rise in variation which is the central fact of evolution. Now, how do feel about that one, little archer?'

'A very interesting thought,' Yakuda conceded. The attack was too generalised, made too many assumptions. Yet despite himself, despite an underlying loyalty to his profession and to Darwin's place within it, Yakuda was impressed. He tried to find examples. There was indeed an evolutionary process called hyper-specialisation, in which a species evolved to occupy a very narrow environmental niche. If that environment changed, it would cause that species to disappear. For example, parasitic species which utilised a single other species as host would disappear if that host species disappeared. 'Hyper-specialisation' was considered to be an interesting lacuna in evolutionary theory – an oddity. Yet here was Jameson saying that this was the obvious consequence of natural selection.

The shadows on the hillside were green and golden. Only a painter could really portray them, Yakuda thought. Jameson moved along beside him, his shoes scuffing the earth amiably as he walked, hands resting momentarily on stomach.

'I'm waiting for a response, of course.' Jameson's voice floated down to him. 'In the absence of one, I'm going to say this. Darwinism has, if I may understate the case for once, a rather loose fit with the facts as we see them. In theory, it could provide an elegant explanation for the extinction of species, but the attempt to use the theory of natural selection to explain increasing variation within species, variation so extreme that new species form – that part of it, if you will forgive me, is the most unbelievable moonshine. It's amazing that the biological community has stood it for so long.'

This was aimed playfully at Yakuda himself. In intense thought, Yakuda could feel the coldness of his mind as it turned things over.

'Do you think natural selection exists?' Yakuda asked.

'Of course I do,' Jameson replied amiably. 'It exists, and it is present all around us. Species come and species go. But it is not natural selection which makes them come, as Darwin suggested. It is natural selection which makes them go. We need another theory to explain their evolutionary development towards more varied forms.'

'What alternative is there?' Yakuda asked.

'Alternative,' Jameson rolled the concept around like a bon-bon. 'Now that's a term I like, that's a concept I could take a shine to.'

Yakuda smiled at Jameson's gargantuan coyness, his play for time.

'Before we explore further, what exactly do we have?' Jameson was asking. 'We have a theory without substance, a theory incapable of explaining the most salient fact of evolution − that extreme variation which is the formation of new species. The fossil records indicate an astonishing variety of organisms developed from a few, simple, generalised beginnings. And we use natural selection to explain this extraordinary phenomenon. It's only when we recognise that − when we hoist it aboard − that we can seriously begin to look for alternatives.'

'I suspect you have no alternative,' Yakuda suggested slyly.

But Jameson was working himself up, swinging his arms, making his hands weave, cruise, float. He was driving his way forward through a sea of thought. Yakuda was reminded again of the image of a mental porpoise or whale.

'Natural selection, acting unfettered, would cause, one by one, the extinction of species until they all disappeared. It should cause the elimination of all life forms. Don't you think there's something ironic in that, my esteemed friend? Don't you think that to claim that this death process causes evolution is just about as close to doublethink as we can get?'

Yakuda could see Jameson was flowing again now, his rhetoric was moving forward unimpeded.

*

They were almost in the campus before its full extent could be seen. It was more like a park than a university, with most

10

of the buildings underground, and only the service shafts showing above ground like odd, organic growths. Drawing closer, one saw that much of the ground consisted of acres of glass to let in natural light to the rooms below. The new accommodation architecture did not build deep – no deeper than could be lit by natural light. It was a convention, despite the fact that they had light sources now which could replicate the content of the sun's rays almost perfectly. Factories were different. Unmanned by humans, they could be as deep as necessary, great underground cathedrals permanently lit by artificial light. Many were not lit at all, because their automatons did not require light. The finished product emerged from the dark chambers like a tray of tea placed outside a hotel bedroom door.

They walked across the campus towards their respective residences. Students played games on tennis courts and football fields in the slowly fading light.

'Would you like a coffee, my friend?' Jameson asked. 'Kathleen would like to see you again, too. She asks me where you hide out.'

'Thank you,' Yakuda was polite. But greater than his politeness was the urge to return to his study, to pursue a line of investigation that had become an obsession. 'I must finish some work that has been piling up.'

'*Sayonara*,' Jameson said.

Yakuda walked three more blocks. Several of the things Jameson had said out there rang bells with him, though in a wider setting which he did not begin to comprehend, let alone understand.

A group of three girls carrying tennis rackets walked past him. Taller than Yakuda, they watched him with steady

11

eyes. He exercised some odd fascination for them, though it had taken him a long time to realise that it was not morbid curiosity at his small size. One, a blonde, glanced sideways at him; he could smell their sweat from playing.

Without pausing, he turned towards his rooms.

CHAPTER 3

Descending a flight of stairs, Yakuda traversed several corridors and, halting outside a white painted metallic door, pressed his cardkey into the wall of his apartment.

With a sigh the door moved open and closed behind him. He still had the Japanese habit of taking his shoes off in the apartment. The ritual amused his students.

Inside it was bare, almost monastic. Around all the walls were bookshelves, neatly lined with books. Moving into the apartment, the appearance of austerity was confirmed. Living room, bedroom, kitchen, study. It was a moderate apartment, but it was all he needed. In the study, a room approximately ten feet square, he sat down at a single desk which took up nearly a full length of the wall.

After walking he felt light-headed. He needed some minutes to adjust. The conversation with Jameson still hung about him like a fog. He reached for a book. Leaving it unopened on the desk, he stood up and went to the kitchen, half-filled an electric kettle with water, switched it on and waited for the kettle to boil. He put small spoons of coffee in a cup, poured on water, then walked through to the study and sat down again.

The small ceremony was all he needed to concentrate. He opened the book. It was an English version of Konrad Lorenz's *On Aggression*, first published in 1963 in Vienna by Dr. G. Borotha-Schoeler Verlag under the title *Das Sogenannte Böse*, subtitled *Zur Naturgeshichte der Aggression*.

He settled down to read. It was one of those original texts, like Clausewitz's *Zum Kriege* or Karl Marx's *Das Kapital*, which are often quoted without being read, and which have become distilled into a form of social summary. This summary, in his experience, tended to concentrate on a few controversial aspects and ignored others entirely. In such cases, reading the original was always a curious pleasure. Usually he found the texts remarkably sprightly, with touches of humour, self-doubt and irony which were lacking entirely in the stiff-jawed summaries and selective quotations.

In his youth Yakuda had started to read Friedrich Nietzsche. It was a revelation. Prior to reading the texts, he had formed an impression of Nietzsche as a forbidding, humourless German, enigmatic and inaccessible. Instead, his writing had a curious beauty. With cautious astonishment and then increasing pleasure he realised that almost every sentence was an exercise in humour, in constructive subversion. Turning everything into its opposite was a game which had the same effect as Zen – it forced one to think clearly. He turned from *The Birth of Tragedy* to *The Genealogy of Morals*. He began to bore fellow students with his quotations and recommendations. He gathered all he could, even began to teach himself sufficiently to read the original German.

An aspect which exercised Yakuda was Nietzsche's final descent into madness. One particular commentary haunted him. The French intellectual and adventurer Andre Malraux, once the French Minister for Culture, had recorded in an article that his father knew Nietzsche personally. His father described to Malraux an habitual expression on the great philosopher's face, an expression of 'almost feminine sweetness'. When Malraux senior had heard that Nietzsche had been committed to a mental asylum, he decided to visit his old friend. The first thing he noticed when facing Nietszche was that this expression had disappeared. It was then that he understood that Nietszche had truly left his senses.

Yakuda's own experience of Nietszche's writing left him with the wish to always read the original. It turned him from a promising student into a scholar. His vocation was to search constantly for the hidden pattern of knowledge amongst texts. In his own research, he published less often than the majority of his colleagues, but he built his research data painstakingly. He had the Eastern habit of dedication to his subject.

Reading the original text of Lorenz's *On Aggression*, he was reminded of the difference between the received view and the actual writing. Almost immediately he began to find discrepancies between the two. It had been widely accepted that Lorenz had viewed aggression as an instinct, and that Lorenz himself was a primitive 'instinctivist'. Yet on page 73, Yakuda drew his pencil down the side of a paragraph which read:

We are all familiar with the term 'reproductive instinct'. However, we should not imagine — as many vitalistic students of instinct did — that the invention of such a term provides the explanation of the process in question.

14

The conceptions corresponding to such labels are no better than those of nature's 'abhorrence of a vacuum' or 'phlogiston' which are only names for a process, but which 'fraudulently pretend to contain an explanation of it', as John Dewey has bluntly put it.

A little further he put a line against another statement, which also subtly altered the view of Lorenz as a primitive instinctivist:

A definite and self-contained function of an organism, such as feeding, copulation, or self-preservation, is never the result of a single cause or of a single drive. The explanatory value of a concept such as 'reproductive instinct' or 'instinct of self-preservation' is as null as the concept of an 'automobile force', which I could use just as legitimately to explain the fact that my ancient car still works.

These two passages constituted as lucid a refutation of the primitive instinctivist position as one was likely to meet. Yet it was as a primitive instinctivist that Lorenz had been branded.

Yakuda was so absorbed by his reading that several hours passed before he realised it was nearly ten o'clock, and he was feeling hungry. He placed a marker in the book, stood up and stretched his limbs. He had a slight pain in his back from leaning over the desk. Rubbing his eyes against strain, he went over to the kitchen and opened the fridge. There wasn't a great deal inside.

Several blocks away there was a small restaurant that was run by the Student Union. It was a bit of a low dive, but

15

he felt an impulsion to walk, to stretch his legs again. It would be chilly outside. He put on a coat, knelt in the hallway to tie on his shoes, and pressed a button to open the sliding door. In the corridor outside the artificial lights were on. They had the same constituents as sunlight. Beneath each one was a tray of flowers. He walked up the single broad flight of stairs and was almost immediately in the campus park. The underground buildings projected their lights upwards in great sheets, in whose rising columns even a small amount of dust or the faintest trace of evening mist assumed a swirling presence. Insects played in these light-baths. He made his way to the Student Union building and walked down the stairs.

In the restaurant the lights were low. The cork walls, on which were pinned numerous messages and notices of the 'Motorbike for sale' type or 'Buzz, meet here Friday, D', were peeling in some places. There was a smell of food and candle-wicks. A girl with a bandanna and slacks was acting as waitress. Several groups of students sat around drinking coffee, leaning back on the hard, rectangular chairs that had once been fashionable. One or two young couples loitered in the corners, staring into one another's faces.

The girl who was waitress turned towards him briefly, as if to register his presence, and then turned away discouragingly. He walked over to the counter and she sidled around the other side in her own good time. She was attractive, but her white face was shaped into a bored expression which did not seem to change.

'Am I too late?' Yakuda asked.

Her expression said, 'Too late for what?'

Yakuda was intimidated by her attitude.

'Something cold. No need to cook.'

Her expression remained unaltered. Finally she said, 'Someone just left without their pasta. It's still hot.'

She gestured over her shoulder and he could see, behind a glass face, a plate heaped with white forms.

Yakuda nodded, and handed over his credit card. Money had almost entirely disappeared, except in some slum areas around big cities. But it was fashionably louche to take money into the students' bar, and Yakuda saw a look of faint distaste on the girl's face as he handed her his card. She slipped it into a wall machine, obtained an answering green light, and returned it without comment. She removed the pasta from the oven, warned him about the heat of the dish, and turned away to clear up some things.

'Thanks,' he said.

He sat down at a table away from the others, facing the wall.

The pasta was tolerable, except for the cheese. It tasted like cheese, but if you didn't cut it cleanly, it would pull out to an almost limitless length, growing finer and finer before it split. Physically, it had remarkable properties, and he thought of telling the girl this. But she would not be amused, he knew.

He turned his mind again to what he had read and tried to make sense of it.

Lorenz argued that although aggression was not a single, primitive drive, it emerged from the organism actively and, as with other complex behaviours, it only required a set of circumstances to release it. But its expression could take numerous forms. It was the second stage of Lorenz's argument that Yakuda found interesting.

17

Direct conflict, Lorenz argued, was bad for the individuals involved, who could be killed or badly maimed. The 'victor' could be as badly mauled as the eventual 'loser', so that both might emerge with reduced chances of survival. It was better for both combatants if they 'ritualised' their aggression into a non-lethal trial of strength. Lorenz believed he could find numerous examples, not only of 'ritualised' behaviour, but of structures which had evolved to reinforce that behaviour. The huge claws of male fiddler crabs, for example, were used to intimidate, rather than destroy, rival male crabs. Combat consisted of mutual display. Sometimes the crabs would lock claws and pull backwards and forwards, rather like human wrestlers governed by an umpire's rules. Eventually one would break off. The antlers of deer were another example. Male deer hardly ever drove the points of their great antlers into the flank of rivals, but locked antlers in formal fashion, and drove backwards and forwards until a clear victor emerged. The victim would break away, and if pursued, was not attacked, but (Yakuda enjoyed the euphemism) was 'encouraged' from the area.

Although there were a number of assumptions in this hypothesis which required checking, on an intuitive level at least Yakuda could see some sense in Lorenz's arguments. Perhaps if Lorenz had been content to let the argument rest there he could have avoided the controversy which in due course embroiled the issue.

Lorenz extended his observations to humans. In his view, aggressive behaviour, though more complex than a single instinct, was a significant part of human behaviour. Lorenz believed that, like the animals he had studied, aggressive behaviour was innate. Accordingly our choice lay, not in being non-aggressive, but in channelling aggression into non-destructive channels, into 'ritualised' forms of behaviour.

Lorenz took up much the same relation to human aggression as Freud to sexual behaviour. If it was not given some form of conventional, ritualised expression, it would emerge in different, perhaps potentially more destructive, forms. If the repression of the sexual instinct in Freud's terms led to cities full of prostitutes, in Lorenz's theory the inhibition of aggression would lead to destructive outbreaks, including violent conflict between social groups. It was a short step to the concluding argument. Once we recognised aggression in ourselves, Lorenz argued, we were far more able to reduce its ultimately harmful effects.

Yakuda finished his pasta and pushed the plate aside. The waitress sat in shadow behind the counter, her face expressionless. He stood up, nodded to her, gained no answering recognition and walked back thoughtfully to his rooms.

CHAPTER 4

Every evening Yakuda continued his studies.

To gather information, he visited the library. The librarian, a severe woman with a thin nose and black hair drawn back, was efficient and cooperative.

She looked at the list of information he required, and he knew what her answer would be: Computer One. Only the central grid would hold such information in its memory banks. Individuals might operate in small localised areas of knowledge, knowledge immediately accessible, but the key to comprehensive knowledge lay with Computer One.

There were no boundaries in Computer One, no boundaries but knowledge itself.

Computer One had arisen by degrees, though those who studied its formation in hindsight judged its creation to be inexorable. As the sophistication of computers had grown, so the degree of interfacing between them had increased. With interfacing, the flow of information had increased. Around the year 2000 there existed a number of grids or frameworks of computers which were subsequently increasingly integrated. Such integration had accumulated gradually. Certain countries and institutions utilised the central grid for information, but returned none to it. It was called parasitism. A great international scandal and debate ensued about 'asymmetric' uses of the central grid. For a number of years the debate continued. Solutions regulating its use were temporary. There had been an international agreement in 2007 that all knowledge which was fed into Computer One would be available to all. Similarly, all those countries which used it must reciprocate by opening their own computational facilities to Computer One. Inspections were carried out to ensure that the rules were being complied with. The discovery of an unlinked store of information would be followed by expulsion from Computer One. If the culprit was a country or state, its severance from Computer One would cause it to fall behind. For a company or commercial organisation, dependent on competitiveness and continuous improvement, severance from Computer One was disastrous. Soon the number of severed members consisted of a few small countries who for various reasons, including religion, had no wish to increase living standards. There were also several large charities who functioned independently. But these countries and organisations were an extraordinary rarity.

Computer One had a civilising effect. The free flow of information across national boundaries was Nirvana for scientists. The reciprocal arrangement of information meant that countries or firms could not long maintain secrecy about their research or inventions. Computer One operated a system of patents at fixed royalties, but all information in principle was open to all who wished to pay those royalties.

Entering the library, it was Computer One that Yakuda faced now. He signed a form for its use and the librarian tapped it into the computer.

Information: Public debate on causes of aggression 1958 - 1980. All relevant journal and newspaper articles. Printed.
Keywords: Lorenz; aggression.

Computer One's sweeping capacity was remarkable. Those who used it could not help but consider it, even subconsciously, as an oracle. No information seemed to be beyond its resources. No computation seemed incapable of instantaneous resolution.

'Usually about two minutes,' the librarian said. 'It depends on the queue.' She could have added that the hunt over the world's surfaces of knowledge would have taken only seconds. It was the collation and expression of that knowledge which absorbed the greatest proportion of time.

Yakuda looked at his watch. He sat down at one of the waiting chairs provided. One minute thirty seconds later the board emitted a small tone, a harmonic peculiar to Computer One.

The librarian handed him a slip. It read:

Information collated. 18 volumes newspaper and journal text. 12 volumes book text. Printing time 40.8 seconds.

He'd need a wheelbarrow. And he'd take weeks, months, to plough through it. The librarian looked at his face as he read the card.

'Can you fine down your requirement?' she asked.

'Give me a few minutes,' Yakuda replied.

He sat down. There had been considerable antipathy towards Lorenz for even suggesting that aggression was innate. He wanted to exclude this type of purely pejorative writing. The interesting part of Lorenz's theory was its secondary structure, the theory of ritualisation. He reasoned that the more serious commentators, for or against, would bring this into their text.

He approached the librarian again.

'Could you add the keyword "ritualisation" to "Lorenz" and "aggression"? Regarding books, only chapters which contain those three words, not whole books.'

'Certainly,' the librarian replied. In her combination of helpfulness and severity, she seemed an analogue of Computer One. Operatives were like high priestesses. She tapped in the new information.

'A few seconds this time. It only has to refine the information from the text already collected from the world information bank.'

The harmonic sounded. On the screen a message showed:

Information collated. 3 volumes newspaper and journal text. 2 volumes book text. Printing time 8.2 seconds.

'That looks better,' the woman said encouragingly. 'Disc or written form?'

'I'd like it in written form,' Yakuda replied.

She pressed a button. A curious sound emerged, a squeal almost too high to hear, the sound of printed pages falling down a shoot, a crunch as the volumes were bound.

'Direct delivery or takeaway trolley?'

'Trolley, please,' replied Yakuda.

She wheeled the trolley with the volumes stacked neatly in it around the desk.

'Thanks,' Yakuda said.

He pushed the trolley along several corridors and back to his small flat.

*

It was Friday, and for several days he did almost nothing but read, only taking walks to stretch his legs, rising now and then from his desk to make himself a coffee. In the depths of his concentration, he found he had lost his appetite, and had to make almost a conscious effort to eat.

In the background he played Bach, and sometimes the twentieth century composer Arvo Pärt. In his own view at least, during the twenty-first century, creativity in music had not progressed much, despite improvements in technique. There was a vast array of computer music, a range of extraordinary rhythms, syncopations and sound effects, but he found it too dry and soulless.

He left his rooms and stepped outside. To the south of the campus there was a large area of cultivated land, an accessory to the campus. The methods of farming, now almost universal, were organic, based on crop rotation. Artificial fertilisers and insecticides had been phased out. Development had concentrated on the genetic breeding of hardier strains of product. The first major efforts in organic farming had their difficulties, but rotation reduced pest attack, and farm accounting now habitually treated a proportion of product as due to 'natural wastage'.

Although the farm was organic, its computer control imposed geometrically precise patterns of planting, rows of cabbages as invariant as similar molecules. Watering machines moved down the rows, throwing jets of water like seed. There were pathways through the farm. The university was proud of its agricultural department and encouraged sightseers.

Yakuda walked with hands clasped behind his back. On such walks he allowed himself the luxury of thinking about subjects other than those under study. His mind returned to the subject of musical composition.

Despite the great improvement in leisure time, the market of consumers had grown, but not the creators. Musicians were as skilled as ever. Musical entrepreneurs sold new musical sounds with undiminished enthusiasm, but the quality of musical composition had not improved. On the contrary, it was widely acknowledged that creativity was low.

There was something Yakuda found difficult to understand. Surely freedom from practical necessity would result in the liberation of new Mozarts, new Beethovens? For inexplicable reasons, a reduction in the vicissitudes of life coincided with reduced creativity.

He could get no further with this line of thought, and he turned his mind back to the papers he had been carefully sifting. Somehow he believed they contained an answer, an answer that was potentially important. But to what question?

*

In the evening he felt hungry again and went to the little dive at the Student Union. The disconsolate waitress as usual showed no sign of emotion, and seemed to treat his card with the same unspoken contempt. She brought over his meal to his small table in the corner. Curiously, she remained standing at his elbow for several seconds, as though waiting for him to say something, then left.

He ate his food slowly and methodically. There was a small aquarium in green light in which a few fish swam, and he liked to watch them. Lorenz had spent much of his time watching fish, a study which he claimed always made him feel calm.

The problem with Lorenz's concept of innate aggression was that there were no structures in the human or indeed mammal nervous system which directly produced the behaviour known as aggression. Without a sure physiological base on which to build, the theory of innate aggression would always be nebulous.

He entered a form of reverie, a trance in which the fish

in the aquarium occupied a mental equivalent of his peripheral vision. Each fish inhabited different areas of the tank. One of them was drifting slowly out of its corner. Perhaps it too was in a kind of reverie. It had drifted a certain distance when another of the fish attacked it in a flash of blue. The two fishes darted and duelled, then returned to their corners.

The attack brought Yakuda out of his trance. Was it a case of aggression, he asked himself? Or had the attacker become increasingly concerned as the other fish drifted slowly over some invisible border into its own territory? In that case, it was a defence. It occurred to him, with a start of surprise, that a defensively-motivated move appeared very much like aggression. It turned his mind to thinking how much of 'aggression' could be subsumed under defence. On one level the argument was merely one of definition of words, but there was one large difference between defence and aggression.

Defensive structures and behaviours existed in plenty. There was no controversy about the statement that much of behaviour had a defensive component. The skins of animals were defences against the invading barrage of bacteria. The thermal regulation systems of mammals were a defence against the shifts of temperature in the outside environment. An organism must survive in order to reproduce, and its entire life was a set of defensive responses against the environment.

As the nervous systems of organisms became more complex, these defensive mechanisms could become more subtle and far-reaching. Yakuda's mind started to race.

The sudden attack of the fish impressed him. It seemed deliberate and swift, the product of a nervous system that was

26

well organised, that knew no doubts. Another question began to concern him. What happened when one added 'intelligence' to an initial set of defensive reflexes? If the organism became more aware of the dangers in the environment, was it more inclined to take pre-emptive measures against those dangers? If so, pre-emptive defences therefore would seem more likely to occur as the organism grew more intelligent. If these pre-emptive defences looked like 'aggressions', how much so-called 'aggressive' behaviour could be included under pre-emptive defence? It was an arresting concept.

His mind started on a further train of thought. It continued in its obsessive way so strongly that he did not notice that the other students had left and, when he turned round from the fishtank, the girl was sitting on a chair behind a table occasionally sipping from a cup of coffee and watching him.

He was light-headed from his thoughts. It seemed several interesting doors had opened and that what he needed to do now was to pursue them with his relentless curiosity. A sense of intoxication filled him.

Now that the others had gone, the girl's surly attention on him was uninhibited. He thought her display of rudeness was to show her disapproval. At a different level, however, the unashamed fixity of her stare had another dimension. It occurred to him this might be, in some extraordinary manner, her courtship behaviour. He stood up. His legs were stiff. He must have been sitting, lost in his thoughts, for an hour and a half. Yet she had not called out to him to tell him that it was late. Now she was waiting for him, and it seemed this patience was part of her curious appeal to him.

He stood in front of her briefly; then, finding nothing

to say except 'Good night', he walked away. She stood up and followed him to his room, without speaking. He pressed his cardkey in the slot and stood aside so that she could walk through. The only thing he said to her was 'Could you take off your shoes, please? It is an old Japanese custom.'

She complied almost without thinking. He led her through to the bedroom and she began to remove her clothes. He undressed quietly, not looking at her. She lay on the bed. He noticed, before he turned out the light and joined her, that her left wrist bore the inscription of a tattoo, a bracelet of blue marks.

CHAPTER 5

'Where have you been hiding ?' Jameson asked.

'I have been reading,' Yakuda replied.

'Reading, now.'

They decided to take a different path that day. As part of its charitable activities, the university had allocated 10 per cent of its land to a 'public zone'. Public zones allowed free activity of all kinds. In some areas, beside industrial conurbations, these public zones had been over-run by slum-dwellers, who had built their homes there. The public zone area was about a mile away, hidden behind a wooded strip and a small incline. They began to walk towards it, passing through open parkland.

'So, what've you been reading?' asked Jameson.

'Did you ever study any of Lorenz's texts?'

'Konrad Lorenz?' Jameson asked. 'Long time ago. Innate aggression. Ritualisation. I remember his ideas raised a bit of a storm. But we've practically eliminated social aggression − at least in terms of large-scale war.'

'The era of international knowledge,' Yakuda said, quoting a fashionable maxim. Like Olgarkov's more mystical 'Peace is an epiphenomenon of organisation', it had become part of current usage.

Jameson moved into more combative mode.

'Do you think obliquity is something the Japanese share with the English?'

'It would seem so.'

'So what are you looking for? Think some war's going to start somewhere. Brushing up on the theory before the practice starts?'

Yakuda knew he could reconcile himself to more of the same until he told Jameson what he was engaged upon. But he didn't know himself. Some part of him was saying 'read this', 'investigate that', and he was following his own instructions.

'Computer One,' said Yakuda quietly.

It was a jump from what they had been talking about, and he could almost sense Jameson stiffen.

'What about it?'

Yakuda was silent for several moments as they walked, choosing his phrase.

'Does it ever concern you?'

'What aspect?'

'A virtual monopoly of knowledge, for example.'

'I just look on it in a practical way, I suppose. Serves us well enough.'

'So far,' Yakuda said.

Jameson paused.

'Look, there's no need to raid the English obliquity markets. You've got enough already.'

Yakuda did not reply, so Jameson tried another tack.

'You think there's some kind of malfunction in Computer One?'

'No,' replied Yakuda, 'no malfunction whatsoever.'

Jameson paused.

'So what's the problem?'

'There is no problem,' Yakuda commented.

Jameson weighed twenty-five stone and had an IQ reputed to be over 200. Yakuda sensed his mountainous concern.

'I seem to be missing something here.'

'No, I am missing something,' Yakuda admitted politely. 'I do not know why. I do not know what precisely it is that concerns me.'

'Let's say you're uneasy about Computer One.'

'Let's say that.'

'Monopoly of knowledge, then. So maybe Computer One can go off the rails, start abusing its monopoly.'

That wasn't it, but one could start there.

'Tell me,' Yakuda said, 'would you say that Computer One could replicate itself without human assistance?'

'OK, let's see now. It controls most of the factories and their output, it can transport things by automatic remote control from one factory to another. It administers machines which can repair, and other machines which repair those machines. It has the facility to make more machines, more computers. I'd have to check up on a few details – energy consumption, etc. As I understand it, it controls energy output. So, on the whole, I'd say that it was effectively autonomous. Yes, it could replicate itself without human assistance. What do you deduce from that?'

Yakuda paused.

'Not a great deal at this stage. Except that a being which is able to replicate itself is a species of living organism. Computer One is a new species.'

'Interesting thought,' Jameson commented. 'So what?'

'That is what I do not understand,' Yakuda said. 'But I suspect that if the right question is asked, we would unlock a piece of useful knowledge.'

'Useful knowledge, huh. I'm not sure where this is getting us. Why don't you ask Computer One?'

Strangely, that was a question Yakuda could answer, though he was not inclined to volunteer it to Jameson. He wanted to shape the argument to a point where it could not easily be beaten down by the brazen power of Jameson's intelligence. For several hundred yards they walked in silence, Jameson in characteristic pose, one hand in his pocket, the other hand reflectively on his belly.

The treeline surrounding the public zone was a thicket of conifers, planted for their quick growth. Beyond that was a screen of smaller trees, shrubs. They walked through the quiet litterfall beneath the confers. A small animal, a whippet-like dog, ran away from them over the forest floor, making hardly a sound. They heard once or twice what seemed a human voice, in greeting or command, though whoever was responsible was hidden by a screen of trees. Following the beaten tracks, a winding path led them through the band of smaller trees.

They emerged onto an area of open parkland, nearly a mile wide. It might have been an adjunct of the university games-fields, except for the number of smaller children and dogs. When the eye adjusted, there were other discrepancies too. To one side were a number of canvas tents, with central poles that made them look like Mongolian yurts.

The inhabitants were members of the tribes of the disaffected, those who rejected the society of the twenty-first century. But they were domesticated forms, not fully wild, lingering like camp dogs on the periphery, accepting handouts, collecting useful waste produce from the university farm, sometimes taking menial jobs like that of porter. Out there, to the east, hardly more than twenty miles or so, lived groups or communes who were completely autonomous, people who lived outside the law.

Jameson and Yakuda walked over the field. The children and dogs playing there did not seem to notice them. Once a ball came bouncing across the thick grass towards them, followed by a slender mongrel which looked like a lurcher. It caught the ball only twenty feet away and they saw, with a sudden shock, the scars on its back from beating. A look of mischievous calculation appeared in its eye as it decided, ball in mouth, whether to attack them. Then it scampered off in the general direction of the children, moving in a wide arc as if to taunt them.

Jameson it was who picked up the thread of the conversation.

'Computer One, the new species.'

Yakuda smiled.

Jameson said, 'You're following some notion, I suspect. That inscrutable mind has been working on a strange new theory. Computer One, which is our servant, may shortly become our master.'

'What are the terms of its reference?' Yakuda asked.

'Its *modus vivendi*?'

'Its formal terms.'

'Its formal terms of operation are to serve the human race and the pursuit of knowledge.'

'Those are two different things,' Yakuda said. 'Which is more important? To serve the human race or the pursuit of knowledge?'

Jameson didn't answer immediately.

'Suppose,' Yakuda said, 'that they are different and contradictory.'

'Expand a little.'

'Computer One can self-replicate. It can create more computers at will. Perhaps it will reach a position where its pursuit of knowledge outstrips its human masters. Then it will have to choose whether it serves the human race or continues in the general search for knowledge.'

'And you see it choosing knowledge – if indeed it could make the choice – leaving us, so to speak, on the sidelines.'

Yakuda saw the flash of a blue fish striking upwards at another, but in his mind the vision was so disturbing he did not speak further.

CHAPTER 6

Yakuda had an ulterior motive in coming to this camp. He thought that the girl, the waitress with the tribal tattoo on her wrist, might live here. But somehow her sullen lack of communication with him was a kind of purity which he could not see here, amongst these diffident scavengers.

When he thought back to the previous night, he recalled that apart from sounds of pleasure, she did not utter a single word, and that when he woke she had gone.

The following day he had gone to the cafetaria as usual, but she was no longer there. She had been replaced by another girl, a slim, talkative girl, infinitely more pleasant, and he had been struck with longing for his sullen bedmate.

He did not know her name, and he did not have the courage to ask her successor where she had gone until, clearing away his plate, he had raised the subject as casually as he was able.

'Marie,' she said. 'She gave in her notice yesterday. Are you a friend?'

'No,' Yakuda replied. What had passed between them was not friendship.

He had a name, though. Marie.

'I never met Marie,' the girl was saying. 'I was just told by the manager that someone had left, and asked whether I could stand in at short notice.'

'Thank you.'

The girl left. Why Marie had departed he could only guess. He tended to discount the view that he had anything to do with her going. He felt she must have been intending to leave anyway.

It was disquieting, nevertheless.

A few minutes later he called the new waitress over and asked for a coffee.

'Certainly,' she said. She moved away with a brisk

movement of her lower back.

She brought his coffee. He could not help but make comparisons between Marie's sullen but powerful presence and the courteous, amenable girl who had taken her place. The new waitress had returned to the counter and was cleaning its polished metal surfaces with a cloth while she whistled a tune Yakuda could not recognise. She seemed a happy, industrious person, who had taken over her role with a positive attitude.

He deliberately stopped himself thinking about the girl called Marie while he stared at the fishtank.

He drank his coffee, hoping for some repeat of the previous night, when one of the small fishes would make a sudden pre-emptive defence against a neighbour who was too near the boundary lines. But the fish seemed to keep within their prescribed territories this evening.

Paying for the coffee with his card, he left for his apartment.

He was not yet tired, and he sat down again at his desk, but he was unable to concentrate on reading. Something was taking shape in his mind, and he had to sit it out. For some reason his hands were nervous. He stood up again listlessly and walked around his bare rooms.

The question was, how did his findings apply to computers? It was an immensely difficult subject. He struggled to find some purchase on the interface between biology and artificial intelligence. After a while he sat down but still felt restless. He read desultorily, then stood up after half an hour and walked to the kitchen. He would make another cup of coffee. While he filled the cup with granules and poured water he became aware, at a curious visceral level, not so much of the collective nature of artificial intelligence but of its implications in what he was pursuing. The granules dissolved into a stream of darkened fluid. It was as if his mind breathed and the pattern was clear. He was struck by the simplicity of it. He started to range backwards and forwards, making certain he understood the implications.

If he had not been pressed for time he would have shouted for joy. What he felt instead was a few moments of peace.

A good theory should be capable of making predictions which could be tested. That would be the next stage. He could envisage various experiments, but one line of thought in particular seemed to him to lead to a clear prediction. *Hymenopterans*, his special subject of study, were an insect phylum which included the ants and the bees. These were often highly social insects, and their complex societies were like super-organisms. The theory had a clear prediction on the amount of aggression amongst *Hymenopterans* relative to other insect species. And suddenly he sat back with a sigh of astonishment, as he filtered his mind for the relevant data on *Hymenopteran* fatalities per head of population. It fitted into place with extraordinary beauty. He could have jumped up for the second time this evening. A few minutes later, he went to a cupboard, and drew out a box of cigars. He extracted one and lit it. Smoking carefully, he reviewed the evening's work.

*

The excitement of his discovery prevented Yakuda from sleeping. It was difficult, he knew, to stop a mind which was running fast. His thinking was overheated and now proceeded in obsessive circles. In an effort to bring his thoughts under control, deliberately he directed his mind away from the implications of the theory.

In bed Marie had expressed her feelings more openly than in conversation. She had a natural warmth, and she bestowed this on him cautiously and then generously. They had made love quietly but with fervour. It seemed like something that she needed; she took her pleasure in deep breaths. He remembered her fluttering cry, and tried to recall whether that was the only sound he had heard from her.

Afterwards she had not separated from him, as he would have expected. They had lain together in companionable warmth, their arms around each other, neither speaking. He had drifted off to sleep and then, how much later he did not know, he had woken. The outline of her face could be seen against the white light of the ceiling glass. Her eyes were open, staring upwards.

*

To Yakuda, solitude was the logical consequence of his other demands. Above everything he wanted time, time to study, to put his investigations in order, and for this he chose his monastic existence and braced himself for the solitary life. It did not mean that he shunned human contact, or that a part of him, an important part, did not desire it. Its very paucity in his life increased the intensity of those few times when human warmth was offered and taken.

Perhaps she slept with many men, perhaps it was her means of communication. He realised it didn't matter to him.

The fact was he desired her more strongly than he could have imagined. If he was not subject to the pressure of his thoughts, he would have followed her to her camp, or wherever she lived. He would have risked the few remaining years of his life to find her.

CHAPTER 7

The following day he called the physics department on the telephone and asked for Dr Jobson. A cheerful voice came up.

'John?' Yakuda asked. 'Yakuda here.'

'What can I do for you?'

'I'd like to meet you for a few minutes if you could spare the time.'

'I've got a few minutes right now,' Jobson said. 'Fire away.'

'I don't mean to be difficult,' Yakuda said, 'but I'd rather meet you in person.'

'Want to see my cheerful face, huh?' There was a moment while Jobson consulted his timetable. 'Got a lecture in ten minutes. I'll be in the Physics Common Room about ten thirty. How's that suit you?'

'I'll be there.'

Yakuda put down the phone. It was nine twenty. He felt restless. He opened one of the volumes collated by Computer One and began to read. But though his eyes drifted down the page, his mind seemed to working at something else and he absorbed very little.

At quarter past ten he set out and crossed the park towards the physics department. In his experience, university science departments had a kind of ugly, utilitarian look to them, as though the expensive equipment within their walls had sucked funds from the structure of the building itself. But beneath the earth's surface all buildings looked much the same from the outside. The physics department was distinguished by a dome, an observation laboratory which, though it was only thirty feet above ground, was a landmark in the flat parkland with its hidden buildings.

He entered the gate and descended the stairs to a foyer. A uniformed guard emerged from behind a screen and asked for his identification. Yakuda supplied his card. The guard went away, clipped his card into a machine, obtained a positive harmonic, and returned with a label to pin on his shirt. He returned Yakuda's card with a brief smile and nod.

Yakuda followed the corridor along a maze of offices. Several had the traditional radiation warnings of black skull and crossbones on an orange background. Smaller corridors led off the main corridor. Several of these subcorridors were guarded by further security stations. He hadn't realised how extensive the physics laboratories were.

He found the common room and entered it. It was like common rooms everywhere; low furniture grouped around tables, a coffee machine in one corner, half a dozen people sitting around reading from papers or tapping into small portable computers. He recognised a couple of them without being able to put names to them.

Jobson was seated at a table looking idly at a wallscan. Optical fibres were used to project an image of the outside on a wall, so that although one was below ground, one could see the passers-by in the park outside, hear the sound of birds and insects. It was as if one wall were open to the park.

'Yak,' Jobson stood up. He was of moderate height, with pale blue eyes and a mass of white hair. His clothes were casual. His grip was powerful, chastening.

Jobson looked him up and down.

'You're looking good.'

They went over to one of the unoccupied corners of the room and sat down.

'How's life?' Yakuda asked.

'Usual pandemonium. My last daughter is married and my first daughter is getting a divorce. My wife is back with me. And my job — well, I watch the younger guys coming on. You?'

Yakuda shrugged his shoulders.

'You always simplified your life to one thing,' Jobson said. 'Pare it down to one hand clapping, huh. No distractions. What did you want to ask?'

Yakuda said, 'I wanted to ask you about a red sunset.'

'Now let me see,' Jobson said. 'Is this some kind of haiku? A code?'

Yakuda paused.

'A few days ago, Professor Jameson and I ...'

'Jammo! Jesus, what a rogue's gallery! Why wasn't I there?'

Yakuda paused politely.

'We were walking around the park, and we saw a magnificent red sunset, a sunset such as I have never seen.'

'Keep going.'

'It reminded me of an account I read of the explosion on Krakatoa.'

40

'Particulate effects? Dust spread all over the atmosphere? That sounds unlikely in this case.'

'Exactly,' Yakuda said.

'You're asking me whether I know of anything likely to cause such an effect?'

Yakuda nodded.

'Not offhand,' confirmed Jobson. 'Want me to do a little investigation?'

'If you could spare the time.'

'No problem, old friend. A few discreet enquiries.'

'You have an atmosphere monitoring station, I understand.'

'A local one, sure. The results are fed into Computer One for comparative evaluation and international release. It'd be simple enough to plug into Computer One for the information.'

'Computer One filters the information?'

'Filters?'

'Summarises, then.'

'Summarises, sure.'

Yakuda felt a coldness touch his skin. He must be more careful.

'Something troubling you, Yak?'

'I'm working on a hypothesis.'

'Hypothesis?' Jobson raised an eyebrow.

'A vague one at present.'

'You're a quiet one. You remind me of one of those collectors who are tracking a rare specimen. Something tells me you got the scent in your nostrils. In the meantime, I'll get a local reading on the atmosphere. What exactly are you looking for?'

41

'Levels of toxicity, traces of unusual compounds, maybe radioactive material. Just to check that there's been no recent increase.'

'Just to check, huh.' This was a statement more than a question, and Yakuda was aware of Jobson's pale eyes on him, searching for some clue. 'OK. I'm intrigued, but I can see you want to keep this one quiet for a while.'

'Thanks John.' Yakuda was grateful.

Jobson looked at his watch.

'I have to go. Why don't we get together for a meal sometime? I'll phone you when I know what Jean is doing.'

'I'd like that.'

Jobson stood up. He punched Yakuda playfully on the shoulder and turned to go.

'John,' Yakuda said. 'One last question. Why all the security?'

'Oh, that.' Jobson turned to face Yakuda. 'We're undergoing one of our reciprocal information checks. You know, Computer One's people.'

'I see,' Yakuda nodded.

'See you, Yak.'

He watched Jobson walk away.

CHAPTER 8

Jameson the amateur anthropologist.

'When I was a boy, my parents had a farm, part of a small island off Maine. One of the workers on the estate was an old guy, John Gill. He used to plant vegetables and wheat over the little estate. He was plagued by a crow colony which used to live in the woodlands to the north of the estate. He was a cunning old man, John Gill, full of rural wisdom. In my holidays, he used to take me out to try and shoot those goddamn crows.'

They were on one of their late afternoon walks, the sun slanting, Yakuda watching the sunset.

'The crows were wily. It was almost impossible to come within range with a gun. Day after day we went out, the two of us, the horizon full of angry, wheeling birds. But we came back without a single kill, without even the opportunity of a shot. Crow communes function to some extent like military organisations. They are on a permanent defensive footing against the outside world. In John Gill they recognised a deadly enemy. We no sooner left the house with our guns, than the alarm went up in all the surrounding woods. But if they saw a woman, an individual without a gun, they would treat her with a lack of concern bordering on contempt, eating seeds within a few yards, hardly bothering to fly away if she waved her arms or shouted.

'John Gill carried on a battle of wits against the crows. It was natural that I should be inducted into this battle. Old Gill had two grandsons, boys my own age, about thirteen, who were also on summer holidays. He was a small man, hardly much bigger than we boys. Although he was unable to combat the crows on his own, he worked out a method of cooperation so that we were able to deal with the birds effectively. It was based on a piece of country lore. You see, crows cannot count. To a crow, two people are a crowd. Three people are a crowd, as are four, five, six, seven. That

43

was the basis of John Gill's tactics.'

Yakuda waited for some explanation of these surprising statements. Jameson paused long enough to rest a hand contemplatively on his stomach, then he continued,

'The four of us would advance towards the cloud of wheeling, cawing crows. We would dress similarly, in John Gill's customary black coats. We would move into the heart of the woodlands, the four of us, and John Gill would hide with a gun, remaining out of sight. Then three of us would walk back towards the house. Now, to a crow, a crowd walked out towards them, and a crowd walked back, and therefore the coast was clear. Their alarms stopped when we got back to the house. The crows came down to the fields, and John Gill would manage to shoot several before they knew what was happening.

'That's my point. Their inability to count was their undoing. We didn't do this every day, of course, perhaps a couple of times a week. But each time it was successful. It was the only way of keeping control of the crow population.

'Now,' Jameson said. 'Let me explain something which is of huge importance to mankind. Jameson's theory of the different natures of men and women. It is based on the John Gill crow theory. I acknowledge my precedents, I bow to a man of superior cunning.

'Imagine we live in prehistory, in primitive groups. Mainly because of the children they tend, our women are less mobile than men. The men hunt animals by day, and the women gather food — roots, berries, fruit, grubs. These two different behaviour patterns mean that the women are able to stay closer to the camp or resting place. In pursuit of animals, the men must range wider. You know that the majority of

44

food, the staple, was supplied by the females. Just as later, when humans became settled, it was the females who mainly tilled the fields. The real breadwinners have tended to be women.

'The function of the men was to hunt meat and protect their borders against depredations by other groups. Until recently, there were certain primitive tribes, Amazonian Indians, Australian aborigines, African pygmies, in which this pattern was reasonably clear.

'This is my second point. In such a *milieu*, consider the importance of counting. You are a male hunter and a protector against other hunters. In the distance, you see a group of men from a rival tribe. There are obstacles between you; trees, rocks, hillsides. Your opponents appear and disappear. You see a group of them descend into some brush, and then re-emerge. If you are on your own, you would not like to cross their path. Now, if you cannot count, a group entered the wood, and a group left, and the coast is clear. But if you can count, you would see that maybe seven men entered, and only five emerged. The man who can count knows that danger lurks in that wood in the form of two men who have strayed from the main party. He stays away. The man who does not or cannot count enters because to him the coast is clear, and he risks his life.

'To go out and hunt, to range widely for prey, and to keep a wary distance from other groups was part of the daily experience of man. If he could count, his chances of survival were greatly increased. There was a huge selective pressure on men to count. Men were always *counting*. That is why men have always been more numerate than women, why they concentrate in mathematics, engineering, accountancy, on activities where numbers are central. But it also explains another feature of men compared with women. To count is to abstract, to depersonalise. I look at a group of people, and I do not see names or histories, I see numbers; one, two, three. Men function in a depersonalised world. It is built into our nervous systems. We think numerically. Is it any wonder that we boast about the number of our conquests, my friend, when women speak of the quality of theirs? Men are constantly, nervously, enumerating. Those who could count amongst our male ancestors, survived; those who did not or could not, died. The fundamental differences between men and women are a product of millions of years of evolution, in which men were under a strong selective pressure to count, to think numerically, to abstract. These aspects are built into the circuitry of our minds.'

'You makes us sound like computers.'

'Computers are the children of men's minds. Perhaps they represent some symbol of men's ambitions – thinking machines without emotions.'

'That's depressing,' Yakuda replied. 'It sounds as if we can't change our faults.'

'Faults?' asked Jameson. 'Arithmetic, geometry, algebra, physics, astronomy, theories of the universe, formal systems such as calculus. Computers, navigation, calendars, structural engineering, cosmological theories of heaven and earth. Double entry book-keeping – do not forget the accountants.'

'Who could forget them?' Yakuda replied. 'I was thinking about our relationships, particularly with women.'

'We might not change these aspects entirely,' Jameson said. 'But we can be constantly aware of them, we can ameliorate them. To be aware of one's failings is a major part of the cure.'

'Have you written this down?' asked Yakuda.

'Of course not,' Jameson replied. 'I have enough trouble with women already. They are always complaining. Let's not give them another stick to beat us with.'

'I'll agree to that.'

'Absolute secrecy, then, on Jameson's theory of the different natures of men and women.'

'My mouth is sealed,' Yakuda said.

*

They continued to walk for several minutes without talking. The sun had departed. It was growing late. On the horizon, faint lights began to flicker.

Jameson said, 'There is a sense in which the computer is the perfect product of the male mind. It deals in abstractions, it represents by number, it carries out its mental processes without emotions.'

Staring ahead, Yakuda watched the distant lights, a dry wind moving through them like perceptions.

'That is what I sense you are thinking, my friend. That the computer is the idealised male mind; it is this mind which, carrying out its lofty functions, will put us aside, will – so to speak – marginalise us.'

'Perhaps,' Yakuda replied. 'But Computer One is decisive. It thinks in terms of complete solutions. That is its world – problems and solutions.

'Meaning what?'

'"Marginalising" the human race is not a solution. It

47

is a problem unsolved, a problem shelved.'

'So what are you saying exactly? Spell it out.'

'Computer One will view us entirely in terms of function. The human race is an unsolved problem. An elderly relative, you could say, who no longer contributes.'

'Sweet Christ,' Jameson whispered. 'You are morbid this evening.'

*

'Let me see now,' Jameson said, after a few minutes. 'Who could help us with perspective on this problem? Golub? Historian, essayist and social commentator. A distinct possibility.' He paused. 'Who else?'

For several seconds Yakuda hovered over the delicious sensation of the imminent disclosure of Jameson's *bête noire*.

'Olgarkov,' Yakuda suggested.

For a moment Jameson seemed unmoved. He sucked in breath. It was this withdrawal of reaction that was comical.

'Olgarkov,' Jameson breathed the name to himself, drawing his tongue across his dry lips. 'Human and animal. Bullshitter and saint.'

They were following the slow turn of the hillside. Its dark bulk hid the lights of the city. As they walked, traversing the rim, a fine dust of lights began to appear, shimmering in the distance.

'It occurs to me,' Jameson said, 'that popular visionaries are somewhat vain.'

'In what sense?'

'For example, would our good friend Olgarkov be able to conceive a world in which a computer is the central, thinking entity? No soul, you understand.' Jameson paused. 'Unfortunately, I think not.'

Ahead of them, the streetlights were scattered ashes.

CHAPTER 9

They decided to extend their walk across the hilltop until they overlooked the lights of the city without obstructions. There they halted to take in the scene. It had become colder, and Yakuda's eyes watered with the effort of staring. The surrounding skyline was filled with luminescence.

Jameson for once was silent.

Yakuda remembered a single image. In an old album of classical photographs from the Magnum photographic agency was a picture of the inside of a big mainframe computer. The micro-circuitry was laid out on a series of vertical boards, each of which protruded upwards like sky-scrapers. On their surfaces the connections glimmered like thousands of tiny illuminations. That image, hovering between the interior of a computer and a big city precinct at night, epitomised for him the electrical connecting tissue that was the body of Computer One.

A slight breeze touched their faces.

As they looked down, another set of lights moved from east to west, about two miles away. They heard the whistling engines of a huge airliner. The sound was as faint as ducks' wings. Noise engineers had achieved virtual miracles in vibration reduction and bafflement, in silencing turbine blades, in the production of so-called 'white' engines.

Seen in profile, the airliner was vast. Its four wings were connected like a diamond. It moved through the sky with the eerie grace of a floating suburb. They watched in silence the trajectory of its slow approach as, engines turned low, it seemed to float towards the airport like a liner towards a dock.

The whispering of ducks' wings faded, and the floating lights that had once formed the distinctive shape of the airliner now merged with the city as it moved down to land. Brief commas and exclamation marks of flame rose from the wheels as it touched down. It seemed to pause there for several seconds. Then four green splashes of fire furled over the wings as the engines were kicked from slow cruise into full reverse. In its huge fuselage, perhaps a thousand people would be readying to land.

'A good touchdown,' Yakuda said.

'Male mathematics,' Jameson murmured in agreement. 'Some organisation.'

*

They watched the spread of city for several more minutes.

'I guess we'd better start back,' Jameson suggested. He switched on his pocket torch and picked out the path ahead of them.

Yakuda's mind was full of the images of light. Thinking of cities and computers, he said, 'Is there any other way in which Computer One might have developed?'

Jameson's bulk towered in the darkness as they walked. The torch flickered on the path ahead. 'Looking back on it,' Yakuda continued, 'its formation seemed inevitable.'

'I suppose so,' Jameson said. 'Perspective, now. Let's go through the stages. By the year 2000, we already had a loosely linked system of computers, a network.'

'Spontaneously formed.'

'That's right. Spontaneous and informal at that stage. Let's proceed a little further. With the dèmise of communism a decade before, the dominant political ideology was a market oriented economy, whether one called it capitalism or social democracy or market socialism. Information started to flow more freely. Markets increasingly became global. International corporations dealt across national boundaries. Information no longer stopped at national borders.'

They were descending the hillside slowly, Jameson's torch sweeping the path tentatively, like a blind man's stick.

'Then,' Jameson added, 'we had the international Information Exchange Protocols, 2003. It amounted to a formal agreement that there would be no barriers to the exchange of knowledge. People were still idealistic at that stage. Free exchange was not strictly enforceable by any means, but the Protocols paved the path for the later agreements. And we shouldn't forget that the driving forces behind the Protocols were the scientific and research communities to begin with, followed at a later date by commercial companies.'

'How did that happen?' Yakuda asked.

'Commercial companies?'

'Yes.'

The shallow hillside was levelling out. They could see

51

a clear path across the field.

'This is a good historical exercise,' Jameson said. 'We take the evolution of Computer One for granted. Why did the agreement encompass commercial companies? I guess by that time more information was being stored and circulated in the international computer grid than any company could afford to ignore. Researchers within companies must have insisted to their chief executives that they had access.'

'But why was the price a free exchange of information? If you will forgive me, as a biologist, I am used to looking at evolutionary organisms who serve their own best interests. Why didn't a company gain access to the computer grid, but keep all its own research knowledge to itself? That way it would have the best of both worlds.'

'I think the answer is that they did, or tried to. They gave lip-service to the idea of international information exchange, and everyone played the system for all they were worth in exactly the way you describe. But even that provides a form of initial international collaboration, an early proto-type of an international knowledge exchange system.'

'Then what happened?'

'I suppose those conditions persisted, broadly speak-ing, for another few years. Meantime the computer grid grew in sophistication, operated more effectively in storing and passing information, and it continued to grow.'

'Until it became indispensable?'

'That's right.'

The path led through the trees now. The torchlight picked up bark, leaves, the shiny diamonds of gathered dew. The earth beneath the pines was bare. Once they saw the flicker of eyes as an animal moved out of sight.

Jameson's reconstruction of the evolution of Computer One was careful, methodical. In the grip of concentration, he moved both cautiously and easily, like an elephant at night. Yakuda liked Jameson in this role, when he wasn't showing off, when he tried patiently to put together an understanding of their world. He continued to prompt Jameson.

'Then?'

'A cartel of users of the grid started to complain that some of the others weren't playing the game. They were taking information out of it but weren't putting any in. So the cartel of users started agitating for a means of verification.'

'That all users played by the rules?'

'Right. They said that users should be subject to regular checking procedures, internationally agreed, and if they didn't agree they'd be cut off from access to the grid. For about four years a bitter argument raged about verification and enforcement. Those against said that the verification procedures would usher in a new era of totalitarianism. Those in favour said it would clean up the whole area of exchange of knowledge. The users took a vote at the Conference of Computer Users in 2011. As I recall, a big majority were in favour of verification.'

'Was Computer One called by that name at the time?'

'Yes. The name started in about 2005. A financial journalist called Juan Altamira wrote that since the computers were largely interconnected, they were in fact a single, huge computer. He called it Computer One.'

'Didn't Altamira also claim that all this gathering of information in one large grid was dangerous?'

'That's right. His arguments centred on invasion of privacy. Credit control, minor law infringements, things that he felt were the individual's own business. Many of them were formalised. The Altamira Code, in fact.'

'I interrupted you on verification.'

'Verification procedures on free exchange of information were agreed. Unwillingness to comply resulted in ostracism from the grid. Computer One's representatives could inspect the user's facilities at will. That brings us to the present day, I guess.' Jameson paused, then asked slyly. 'So what's on your mind?'

'I am nervous of Computer One.'

'How nervous is nervous?'

'I would like to give a paper on it.'

'I'm arranging a conference in a few months time. I can find a slot for you.'

'I apologise for sounding impatient. I would like to air the hypothesis as soon as possible.'

'I see. You really have a bee in your bonnet.'

'I am an entomologist, after all,' Yakuda said.

'Yak,' Jameson commented in mock wonder. 'You made a joke.'

CHAPTER 10

'Yak?'

Jobson's voice was unusually quiet, and Yakuda gained an impression of repressed emotion.

'Hello, John.'

'It's my turn to ask you for a meeting.'

Yakuda paused.

'Now?'

'Sooner rather than later,' Jobson said. 'I'll be finished here in about half an hour.'

'Can you come over?'

'Sure. I'll be there in an hour's time.'

Yakuda looked at the clock. It was nine thirty. He'd been working since six thirty. He stood up to stretch his legs, arms, back.

When working, coffee was Yakuda's vice. If he settled down at his desk with a steaming cup it seemed to put him in the mood to work. It wasn't just the taste, it was the smell, the bite of the warmth in his hand. He drank slowly. Now he felt a strong desire for his second cup of the day, but he decided to restrain himself until Jobson arrived.

Jobson was a few minutes ahead of time. Yakuda heard his footsteps before he heard the doorbell.

Jobson shook hands and took off his shoes. Yakuda said, 'I'm just about to make a second cup of coffee.'

'Count me in.'

Seated in one of Yakuda's two chairs in the sparse living room, Jobson drew forth from a folder a list.

'Summary from our local station of atmospheric contents over the past two months.'

'May I?'

Yakuda looked down the list.

'Plutonium and uranium,' Jobson said. 'An increase of 89% in the plutonium contents and a 403% increase in uranium.'

Yakuda removed his glasses and looked out of the roof-glass at a blue sky. He felt his stomach tighten. He said to Jobson: 'What do you make of it?'

'What do I make of it?' Jobson was close to being incensed. 'I haven't a goddamn idea what to make of it. That's what I came to ask you.'

'To tell you the truth, I'm operating merely on a loose suspicion.'

'Well, you're ahead of me there.'

Yakuda paused again, 'You know of no reason why this should occur?'

'None.'

'If Computer One has access to this information, why hasn't an alarm been raised?'

Jobson took in a deep breath.

'That's the second reason I came to see you. I asked Computer One for a list of atmospheric contents.' Jobson drew from his folder a second list.

Yakuda looked down it to the plutonium and uranium tables. It showed no increase in either. For the first time Yakuda became frightened, so frightened that for several seconds he could not speak.

'Don't ask me what conclusions to draw from this, Yak, so help me.'

'May I draw some conclusions myself?' Yakuda suggested.

'Go ahead.'

'There are two possibilities. Either your local information is wrong, and the plutonium and uranium tables are unchanged. What we see here is merely a local misreading.'

'Or?'

'Or your local information is correct, in which case Computer One is falsifying the information.'

Jobson stared at Yakuda with his pale eyes. Yakuda saw anger there, and fear, and an emotion like resentment. He was reminded of the ancient kingly custom of killing the bearers of bad tidings.

But Jobson seemed to be in control of himself. He said, 'I checked on the local readings. I went and talked with Quine, who oversees the instruments. The instruments are functioning correctly. The local readings are correct.'

'Perhaps,' Yakuda said, 'there's something missing in all this which would indicate that Computer One's interpretation of the figures is well-meant. For example, if all other atmospheric stations report normal readings, Computer One might interpret the local one as an anomaly. It would perhaps be justified in ignoring it as either inaccurate or a local freak condition.'

Jobson started to relax slightly. This was something he could get his teeth into.

'We have strict procedures for local readings. If they're above a certain limit, particularly in dangerous substances such as plutonium or uranium, we have an alarm procedure. Computer One, on receipt of such information, should ask us to check our readings. If they're confirmed Computer One should raise a local alarm. That means there would be an investigation of the locality to find the sources of the toxicity. What's puzzling is that Computer One hasn't raised the local alarm.'

'What would be the procedure once the local alarm was raised?'

'Computer One would search its memory banks for all potential local sources of the toxicity, and request a report from all such sources. It would start to sweep its information systems for any correlative data. All neighbouring stations would be interrogated in order to highlight any increases in the toxicity which are within safe limits, but may have a bearing on our local figures.'

Computer One again, thought Yakuda. Ubiquitous. It not only interprets the data, but has the responsibility for raising the alarm and investigating the circumstances of the alarm. A feeling of rage overcame him briefly, a flare of anger at the degree to which responsibility had been delegated to Computer One. But he would not raise this with Jobson. Instead he said, 'So we agree that there are two oddities. Firstly, the readings themselves, and secondly, the response of Computer One to those readings.'

'We're agreed. But what I really want is the reason why you're looking into this. What makes you suspicious? What's your theory, for Chrissake?'

'I don't want to alarm you unnecessarily until I'm surer of my facts.'

'Fuck you, Yak,' Jobson said suddenly, without apparent rancour. 'I'm not after facts. I brought you the goddamn facts. I want to know what your suspicions are.'

Yakuda rubbed his eyes, then put his glasses back on. He felt tired suddenly. He could feel the anger from Jobson radiate towards him, as if he had caused the disturbance personally, had seeded the sky with uranium. He was filled with a sudden irritation towards Jobson, a spasm of feeling that passed suddenly and left him feeling guilty.

'Alright John, I'll tell you what my suspicions are. And then you can tell me I'm paranoid.'

'You are paranoid,' Jobson assured him. 'You're an extremely paranoid person. But that's a constant. We're looking for variables here.'

Yakuda chose his words carefully.

'Speaking as an extremely paranoid individual, I think Computer One is a danger to the human race.'

Jobson paused, a smile appeared on his face, as if he were suddenly faced with a joke, then a look of blankness, so fleeting it was almost undetectable. Then he started to laugh. Seeing him laugh, Yakuda felt curiously relieved. He couldn't help smiling himself, a shy man who had said something funny unintentionally.

CHAPTER 11

Yakuda had read somewhere that laughter is released tension. He was reminded of it now.

'If that's all that's concerning you, Yak, I may as well hit the road. Got more important things to concern me. Hell, for a moment back there you had me worried.'

'I'm glad everything's all right.'

They laughed a little more. Then Yakuda removed his glasses, rubbed his eyes in a gesture of nervousness, and put this glasses back on again.

'Tell me this,' Jobson said. 'As far as I can see, Computer One is just a big adding machine. OK, it adds faster in a second than we could in a million years, but it's still an adding machine. You're saying what exactly? That it's no longer behaving like an adding machine? That it's got a mind of its own? That it has psychological problems?'

'Something like that.'

'Where does this personality come from? How does quantity metamorphose into quality?'

'In zoology, it's difficult to say when one thing evolves into another, but you can recognise it when it has happened. It's difficult to say when apes became human, but we believe it happened.'

'Some of us believe in a spiritual explanation of mankind's salient features.'

'I understand that's often the case with physicists,' Yakuda said.

Jobson punched Yakuda's shoulder affably.

'Yak, you're trying to wind me up. If Computer One's misbehaving, maybe it's a little disturbing in such an advanced machine, but it's bound to be because there's some fault that has to be put right.'

'I do not think it is necessarily a fault.'

'But if it's misinterpreting data, not raising alarms when it should do, that's a fault.'

'Not necessarily. It could be part of a deliberate strategy.'

'Deliberate.' Jobson's blue eyes had an affable intensity. 'Come on, Yak. Human beings deliberate. Computers calculate. You saying Computer One has a strategy? I mean, a non-programmed strategy? Isn't that like saying an abacus has a strategy?'

'Computer One is a sophisticated being. It is effectively autonomous. It can support itself. It corrects its own faults, it can replicate itself.'

'Is it? Does it? Can it? Does that make it complete? Isn't it like one of those *idiots savants*, able to do one thing exceptionally well, but lacking other things, only on a larger scale?'

'If it's just an adding machine,' Yakuda said quietly, 'why is it adding up the atmospheric figures incorrectly?'

'It's a fault.'

Yakuda breathed in deeply. He was reminded of another saying. You can wake someone who is asleep, but you can't wake someone who is pretending to be asleep. He remembered Jobson's obstinacy from younger days.

'I want to thank you for the figures you gave me,' Yakuda said. 'May I keep them?'

'Sure,' Jobson replied. 'Keep them confidential.'

'May I show them to Jameson?'

'Jammo? Sure.'

'I really do appreciate what you've done, John.'

'Maybe sometime you'd tell me what that is.'

Jobson put his shoes on in the hallway. They shook hands, then Yakuda pressed the switch on the door.

'Keep cool, Yak,' Jobson called as he left.

'Thanks, John.'

When the door had closed again, Yakuda felt a thirst for a coffee. His mouth was dry. He rationed himself to three cups a day. That would leave only one for the afternoon and evening. While he debated this little procedure, he reflected on the build-up of toxic matter in the atmosphere that had gone unremarked by Computer One. Against that, his small discipline had an added degree of absurdity.

He sat down at his desk again, drew out a sheaf of blank white pages, and began to write the first of several drafts of his paper. He worked solidly through the morning into the afternoon. Then he made a fair copy of what he had written.

There was so much to cover. The theory, which seemed so simple once he had grasped it, required careful elucidation. At the same time, there was a satisfaction in conciseness. After five hours he felt he had earned another cup of coffee.

He went into the small kitchen, switched on the kettle, and leaned against the sideboard with his hands in his pockets while he waited for it to boil. It was an opportunity to review the progress of the paper. He absorbed himself for a few moments in the ceremony of making the coffee.

With a steaming cup beside him, he sat down again to work through another draft.

At about five twenty the phone rang. Jameson said, 'I've got you a lecture at the Symposium for Leisure Studies. The Symposium starts on Monday and goes on for three days. Yours is at twelve noon on the last day. You've got forty minutes to speak your mind before conference adjourns for lunch. That enough?'

'Thank you,' Yakuda said. 'Thank you very much.'

'It better be about Leisure,' Jameson said.

'It'll be about the future,' Yakuda replied.

'Same thing,' Jameson said. Perhaps not, Yakuda thought to himself. In the background, Jameson was continuing, 'Attendance will be about three hundred, three hundred and ten. We're talking about the best in the Leisure Studies business here. International audience of experts. In the afternoon of the third day the main speaker will be Olgarkov. See if you can upstage him, will you?'

Yakuda said, 'I'm not much good at upstaging anybody.'

'Every day in every way I hate Olgarkov more and more,' Jameson said. The line went dead.

After the phone call Yakuda set to work on the paper again. He had five days to get it into shape. At seven thirty he felt restless. He stood up, stretched his arms and back, and decided to go for a short walk. Thinking deeply about his paper, he found that his legs had carried him to the bar at the Student Union. While his mind processed the implications of his theory, inside he sought the girl, the sullen girl he would have given anything to see again.

CHAPTER 12

Yakuda met Jameson outside the zoology department entrance at four o'clock the following day for their walk. There had been rain during the afternoon, several sharp showers, but now the sun had returned and it was hot. On their way to higher ground on the east of the campus, they had to step around puddles. The vegetation was still wet.

Yakuda was interested to tax Jameson on an alternative to Darwinism.

'Do you have a theory that can replace Darwin's theory of the natural selection of individuals?'

'I have my suspicions,' Jameson said darkly.

'Suspicions?' It was time Yakuda went onto the attack. 'You have no alternative, in fact?'

'The alternative, to a theory which is manifestly wrong, is to look for a better theory.'

'What are your suspicions, then?' asked Yakuda.

'My first suspicion is that evolution acts not at the

individual but at the social level. Evolution is acting to increase complexity. It creates societies out of disparate elements. I'll explain what I mean by that. An atom is a society of sub-atomic particles, a molecule is a society of atoms, an amino acid is a society of molecules, a gene is a society of amino-acids, a chromosome is a society of genes. As you go up the scale the societies becomes less hard, less prescribed, more open-ended. A society of chromosomes generates an organism. But the same principle runs through it. The so-called individual organism is another pyramid of social organisations.

'This sounds somewhat mystical to me,' Yakuda said. 'Personally, I prefer to stick to the theory of individual selection.'

'That is the problem. There is no such thing as an individual organism. Every organism is itself a society, a hierarchy of subsocieties. When you look at me you look at a society of unicellular organisms. A grand theory of evolution would explain this socialisation.'

'Let me see if I understand what you are saying. A grand theory of evolution must explain the increase in complexity — what you call the socialisation — of the material of the universe. Living matter is merely an extension of this principle.'

'Something like that.'

Yakuda tried to grasp the concept as best he could. He said, 'So let us start at the lowest end. We start with energy. Energy forms into the primary constituents of matter, into charmed and uncharmed particles, mesons, muons. The essential point is that these clouds of energy are random, and become stabilised in these particles.'

'Socialised,' Jameson said. 'The word "charm" is a social attribute.'

'Energy is socialised into particles. The particles form societies with other particles. Mesons and muons, protons, neutrons, electrons form atoms. Atoms socialise to form molecules. Then what happens? How does life form?'

'One type of atom, the carbon atom, is able to form infinitely long and complex chains. It is, if you like, a very sociable atom — one of the most sociable atoms that we know. The physical conditions for creating these linked carbon molecules occur on the earth's surface, where lightning flashes into the soup of molecules. This creates the beginnings of life.'

'How?'

'The essence of life is self-replication. By forming long carbon chains and splitting, infinite self-replication is possible. More and more chains of carbon atoms produce more and more organic molecules.'

'I will grant you certain things so far,' Yakuda conceded. 'We can make organic — long carbon chain — molecules in the laboratory by replicating lightning flashes into jars of chemicals which represent the mix of molecules on the earth's surface at the time of the beginning of life. So where do we go next?'

'Lightning flashes are only one source of energy. The other source of energy is the sun. I don't know how long it takes for for random changes in organic molecules to convert sunlight to form further organic molecules; that is another stage. But let's not get bogged down in detail. We find increasing socialisation of molecules. Carbon atoms form primitive amino acids, and are able to pass on chemical instructions to create other molecules.'

'Utilising sunlight as an energy source.'

'That is right. Then we enter the chain of increasing complexity. Single-celled organisms are formed. Later cells socialise into multi-cellular organisms. There are some intermediate organisms, like slime moulds, which spend part of their time as single cells, and other parts as dense collections of single cells which behave like primitive multi-cellular organisms.'

'Continue,' Yakuda said.

'The constant throughout this process is the conversion of energy into socialisation, from the first formation of matter to the largest of organic lifeforms — human beings for example, who represent, temporarily at least, one of the pinnacles of this process.'

'So where is the theory?'

'If there is a grand theory of evolution, we know at least that it must explain why there is an evolutionary selection in favour of societies from the tiniest subatomic particles to the great.'

'What are the mechanics of this selection?'

'I don't know.'

'A remarkable admission,' Yakuda pounced.

Jameson ignored him.

'All I'm saying is that a grand theory of evolution must explain the process of socialisation. The explanation of this socialisation is the key to evolutionary theory. Darwinism doesn't really come to grips with this. Darwin's concept of the selection of individuals is a very crude attempt to do so. It only treats one surface, so to speak, of the evolutionary process. The main benefit of Darwin is that he allows us to grasp that evolution is a natural process. But that is not enough.'

'I see part of what you're saying. Evolutionary theory must treat organisms as multi-levelled societies. It isn't "individuals" which we must explain, but these societies. Tell me, just to diverge for a moment, would you say that the planetary system is a society of planets?'

'Yes. I admit it's a rather limited society, a little repetitive, everybody circling around without touching each other. Reminds me of dancing classes when I was young.'

'Aren't we just playing with words?' Yakuda asked. 'The process of socialisation is just a descriptive phrase. It's virtually synonymous with organisation.'

'What is organisation? Organisation is a set of stable relations. Let's turn this thing on its head. If one is looking back, what will survive in time? Stable or unstable relations? Clearly, stable relations. Organisation survives, disorganisation does not. So an entity which strikes up a stable relation, a social relation with another entity is going to survive. Maybe we don't need any further explanation than that. Maybe it's staring us in the face.'

'This is very pretty,' Yakuda said. 'But where does it lead us? What predictions can one make? What critical experiments can one fashion from your theory?'

'Goddamn,' Jameson said in exasperation. 'Give me a moment. Einstein's special theory of relativity couldn't be tested in its original form. It wasn't tested until about ten years later, after he had produced the general theory of relativity. And then the experiments weren't conclusive — a few little changes in the orbit of Mercury, a bit of light bending during an eclipse of the sun. None of these observable phenomena were much greater than the normal limits of observational error. The big confirmation of $E=MC^2$ only came with the explosion of the atomic bomb in 1945, forty years after the special theory of relativity, thirty years after the general theory. Give me forty years, buddy.'

'Excuses, excuses,' Yakuda said. 'I expect better of you.'

'Listen to me, Yakuda, the amount of bullshit I take from you is unbelievable. I destroy Darwin's theory, and what do you do? You ask me for an immediate replacement. So I scratch my ass and rub my neck and, just because the sun is shining, I'm halfway to a grand theory of evolution. And right this instant you want some critical experiments. God took seven days to create the world, you know.'

'Nevertheless,' Yakuda insisted, 'if you can't make predictions, it's really just empty metaphysics, pretty descriptions.'

'You Oriental mischief-maker, you mad-dog Buddhist, you...'

'Scientist,' Yakuda suggested.

They bickered for several more minutes before they reached the campus and split up.

'Seven days,' Jameson shouted back at him.

The phrase had a prophetic ring. Yakuda wondered whether, in seven days, he would be alive.

CHAPTER 13

Yakuda found a seat at the back of the hall. Jameson, as

President of the Symposium, stepped up to the rostrum, raised the microphone to his giant height, placed both hands on the lectern, thrusting out his stomach, and eyed the audience over the top of his glasses.

'My fellow delegates, I welcome you.

'The twenty-first century has been a time of consolidation rather than revolution. The twentieth century was the great revolutionary century, with its wars and dislocations, its shifts of power, the wide variety of different systems — monarchic, liberal, fascist, communist, socialist, social market. By the end of the twentieth century, the majority of states had a more or less free enterprise economy, taxed to create various social and welfare provisions. Some market economies might be more constrained than others, some welfare programmes more widespread, but the basic pattern of societies developed along broadly similar lines.

'We have had a period of relative peace, in combination with an increasing establishment of global markets across frontiers. The central development in the twenty-first century, the core of all other developments, has been the rise of artificial intelligence, the degree to which computers regulate and control production, and the concomitant increase in human leisure.

'Our computational capabilities have outstripped our capacities to use them. The development of the light computer, begun as early as 1990, caused a massive increase in computational processing. Perhaps more importantly, neural networks began to offer systems based on critical path analysis, providing artificial intelligence systems with a capacity to make choices in a complex environment of multiple contingent factors. They functioned, in other words, like the human mind. These and other developments have added to the rise of artificial intelligence systems. We take for granted that whatever problem we think of which has a logical or numerical aspect to this extent can be "solved".

'Although we continue to uphold different nationalities, and reserve the right to maintain time-honoured traditions, nationality is less important now than in the twentieth century. But we have also ceased to believe, with early Utopian theorists, that nationality is an atavism that can be cheerfully abandoned. Maintaining diverse languages and traditions is recognised as a source of cultural richness. Local cultures cherish their local environments in a way that outside administrators could not. Local communities do not perpetrate upon themselves environmental disasters like the Aral Sea, where a local Asian population was effectively destroyed as a consequence of economic policies pursued by Moscow bureaucrats thousands of miles away.

'There have been some aspects which have been interesting from a psychological viewpoint. The rise of the peaceful world has progressed hand-in-hand with a significant rise in the number of individual suicides. Although we may guess at the precise reason for this connection, the statistical correlation is marked. The rise of leisure has also, much to the chagrin of social theorists such as myself, resulted in an increase in the abuse of drugs, in criminal behaviour, and in random human destructiveness, all of which require analysis. Not only individuals but whole cultures and subcultures have split away from the good life. Ghettoes on the edge of our great cities have become increasingly anarchic and dangerous to outsiders. The process is dynamic and to some extent unpredictable. New alliances have formed. Away from the cities, ecologically minded groups have split off to form their own societies in the countryside. If there is a major social movement of our time, it is precisely the creation of these numerous small self-sufficient groups operating outside conventional society. Their sociology is interesting in itself, and I will dwell briefly on their history.

'A number of communes were formed in the 1960s and 1970s during an era of social liberalisation. But the collectives at that stage appeared to be unable to operate efficiently. Since then, the advent of computer-operated small factories has enabled such communities to become genuinely self-sufficient. A computer-controlled solar mirror complex provides adequate energy for a small community in sunny climates – including heat, lighting, and power for tools and agricultural machines. In areas of high sunshine such as desert the problem has been one of water. Even if a supply of water can be found or manufactured, the rate of evaporation is so great that it is difficult to sustain a surface agriculture. Beneath the surface, however, moisture can be far more easily retained. Accordingly, many of these communes have developed mushroom and other fungal forms, using a solar battery on the surface to maintain underground farms where water loss is at a minimum. Excess power from the surface solar batteries is used to power digging machines which gradually extend the underground facilities at a rate which appears slow but is impressive in accumulation. Many such farms manage a development of underground space which is about a 10% increase per annum. In desert areas so called "pit-farming" has also been developed. This is a half-way stage between underground and surface farming. Plants are granted enough sunlight to stimulate their photosynthesising capabilities, but for the rest of the time are covered to preserve all-important moisture. A whole welter of new technologies has developed to preserve water, recirculate it, purify it, and in other ways to extend its usage. Using these methods, large areas of desert have been colonised by small communities. A ready source of energy has provided a base of organisation for agriculture.

'Computer controlled farming methods provide adequate sustenance. Local industries provide vital necessities. The relatively Spartan economic conditions of such communities are not to everyone's taste, but economically speaking such collectives are usually stable and self-sustaining. Such communities are free to live by their own code of ethics and to practice whatever social and religious observances they choose.

'We have seen an increasing internationalisation of the exchange of knowledge, and of business, but also a fragmentation into smaller, self-contained communities. Those who have seen the future as a panacea have observed both victories and failures. It seems to those who have studied the processes of development that whereas certain problems have been resolved, other problems have been created by their very solution. The net result is that problems have shifted. Perhaps we should accept this. We are after all a species which has thrived by problem-solving. It may even be that our problem-solving is a *raison d'être*. Why should we be horrified by this?

'Despite the shift of certain problems, ours is a relatively secure, comfortable century. Major wars are now only a remote possibility rather than an incipient threat. Our systems of health and care have continued to improve. With our advanced medicines and therapies, we can solve most bodily systemic failures, including the majority of cancers. Where we cannot cure we can almost wholly eliminate physical pain.

'Our physical well-being has improved in other areas. The tedious functions of mechanical work and repetitive production have been delegated to machines which do not feel emotional anguish or pain, and whose life span, subject to proper maintenance and replacement of parts, is effectively unlimited. For this combination of reasons, ours is a peaceful century.

'The prospect of leisure is something we must face intelligently. Children of crisis that we are, we must continue to learn the techniques of dealing with leisure, probably by creating areas of problem-solving, from making our own clothes to working on aspects of original mathematics. The function of this gathering is to discuss what might be called the problem of leisure. With that question suspended, hanging in the air over us, I open the symposium.'

There was widespread applause. Amongst the delegates, Jameson was a popular figure.

Jameson stepped down and, like an emperor with his subjects, made his way quietly up the stairway, acknowledging greetings from left and right, until he reached the back of the auditorium. He eased his bulk into the seat beside Yakuda.

'A good address,' Yakuda said.

Jameson did not acknowledge this compliment. He was searching out his major rival.

'There he is,' he said with satisfaction. 'Fifth row back, second from the left.'

Yakuda followed his directions. His eye alighted on a white haired man of impressive mien, with a considerable strength and resolve in the set of his shoulders.

'Comrade Olgarkov,' Jameson said. He insisted on using 'Comrade' even though the Communist Party had relinquished its leading role in Russia back in 1990. 'Vladimir Illich,' he continued. 'Named after Lenin, I'm sure. Clad in hair shirt, he goes amongst us.'

With an effort Jameson switched away from his obsession.

'How goes the paper, you Zen monk?'

'Reasonably, I think.'

'I'm pleased for you.'

'Forgive me,' Yakuda said, 'but is Computer One linked to the symposium?'

'Yes,' Jameson replied. He pointed to a listening device in the wall. 'Computer One records the speech on tape, uses a transcriber to print the words, and collates and stores the proceedings in its memory banks. Any interested party can take a printout.'

'So when one is addressing the symposium, one is also addressing Computer One.'

'Correct.'

Jameson was looking sideways at Yakuda over the top of his glasses.

'My my, you certainly have an interest in Computer One, do you not? Could it be because Computer One is even more inscrutable than you? You feel... threatened?'

'Perhaps so.'

Someone was waving an arm at Jameson from the other end of the auditorium.

'Golub,' Jameson said. 'An intelligent man. I must make the rounds. We are walking on Friday?'

'Yes.'

'Goodbye.' Jameson stood up, waved to Golub, and began to make his way across the auditorium to see him.

CHAPTER 14

Lying in his bed that night, Yakuda remembered a Zen saying. Darkness surrounds you. Light empties you.

Half waking, half dreaming, in that state called *zazen*, meditation, a series of images moved through his mind.

Sometimes when out walking on his own in the surrounding countryside, Yakuda had been able to see long trains in the distance, moving slowly, perhaps two hundred trucks and more than a mile long. These were the industrial trains organised and controlled by Computer One, moving equipment and material from one underground factory to another. Once, standing by a railway line in the open country, he had watched one of the trains go by a few feet away. He was facing west and the setting sun was behind the train. As it slowly rattled past, the sun appeared and disappeared in the gaps between the trucks with the regularity of a metronome. Each truck threw its shadow across him, and was separated by a pulse of sunlight from the next. Hypnotised by the gently rattling wheels, by the procession of light and shadow, he had remained without moving for several minutes after the last truck had gone. Light before, another saying went, light after.

There was something funereal about the trains, about their slow movement across the landscape. Thinking about the incident afterwards, it occurred to him that the human race, hypnotised by the lights and shadows of its dreams, had entered this same somnambulistic trance while, in the background, Computer One patiently organised the physical realities of the earth.

That night Yakuda felt cold and woke up with an unpleasant prescience of disaster. He lay awake for a while staring at the opaque glass of the skylight above his bed. His mind returned obsessively to the source of his concern.

Computer One was built on the *Eisai-9* computer. The monk Eisai was one of the great proponents and founders of Zen, who rejected the more bellicose samurai tradition and based his teaching on the purity of meditation. The *Eisai-9* was sometimes called the first 'Zen' computer. Most computers had a yes-no system of logic, a polarity of right and wrong. *Eisai-9* was made up of 'maybe's'. It could deal with many thousands of variables at the same time, each differently weighted, but so powerful was its mind that it could reach a single, coherent conclusion. The process appeared on the surface to be almost mystical, but it amounted to the rational assessment of complexity taken to a new limit.

Computer One could use its prodigious memory to match tissues, to link demand with supply over every range of medical facility. Computer One could diagnose potential medical hazards, could identify crucial cases of need and supervise the development of new drugs. Its supplementary policing activity was comprehensive. It could detect a voice signature and match it within milliseconds to its bank of voice-signatures. A criminal picking up a phone would be identified and pinpointed before he had completed his first phrase. Computer One monitored from satellites the spread of crop disease and forecast years in advance the likely areas of locust plagues or famine. Any scientist who could formulate a precise question on background data would receive all relevant stored data. Computer One supervised the temperature levels of cities, their industrial emissions and pollution controls. It transmitted information and could proffer diagnoses in complex economic systems. Its prodigious memory banks could be used to scan quantities of data which no human mind could be expected to hold. Its pattern-searching programmes constantly sought connections that could generate explanation or prediction. Computer One never rested. It monitored its own function and could replace parts that were functioning below normal, or boost its capabilities in other fields in response to broad human demand.

Computer One existed to serve. It had a curious tone, a combination of high seriousness and pleasure in its own activity. The supplicant stood before its extraordinary power as it ranged through its memory banks in his service. Yet it bought forward the fact or summary that he required like a dog with a stick, placing it in front of him with a small harmonic which sounded like a sigh of pleasure.

Several months previously, Yakuda had been authorised to hold a discussion with Computer One. If the research area was potentially complex, such a discussion could sometimes be arranged to clarify principles and establish an agreed line of investigation. Yakuda initially had submitted an outline of the notional subject matter to Computer One and had received a proposed meeting time in one of the interview booths which had been constructed for this purpose. He had prepared himself carefully for the interview.

Computer One's capacity to speak in any language was well known (one of its numerous services was translation). But Yakuda wondered how it would respond to a discussion. He aimed to introduce a small reference point in the interview, something outside the subject matter under discussion, and observe Computer One's response. It would be best, he decided, to introduce something disconcertingly banal.

He entered a small cubicle in which a single, empty chair faced a console. An electronic voice, pleasantly modulated, said from a speaker in the console, 'Good morning, Professor Yakuda.'

'Good morning, Computer One,' Yakuda replied. The unblinking eye of a camera lens and several sensitive microphones were fixed on him. One of the microphones gave a small stutter of static. The walls were lined with an insulation material to deaden sound and reduce interference. 'Please sit down.'

'Thank you,' Yakuda said. Then he added. 'Aren't we having excellent weather?'

Without a pause, Computer One answered. 'Yes. A little colder than usual, perhaps.'

Yakuda, thinking about this afterwards, had liked that 'perhaps'. In the minute interval between his question and the courteous reply, Computer One had consulted weather data, compared average temperatures for this time of year with current recent temperatures, formulated an answer, returned to the console, and though Computer One would know precisely to several decimal points that current temperatures were below the seasonal average, it nevertheless had the grace to add 'perhaps'.

In the same spirit of courtesy, Yakuda said, 'I have a

problem which I hope you may investigate.'

'Please go ahead.'

'I study *Hymenoptera*, an order of social insects which includes ants and bees.'

'Yes,' Computer One said. For a brief moment Yakuda paused while he considered what Computer One knew or surmised about the subject.

'With insects as a whole,' Yakuda continued, 'there appears to be a connection between the degree of social structure, or socialisation, within a species and the amount of aggression exhibited by that same species.'

'A positive association?'

'I believe so.'

Yakuda watched several lights on the console flicker.

'Can you quantify socialisation?' Computer One asked.

'Yes, for practical purposes. I have drawn up a list of insect species arranged in order of increasing socialisation. I am happy to transmit this list to you. In the initial section are insect species of largely solitary nature. At the other end are advanced social species – nearly all are *Hymenopterans*, like the African driver ant.'

'Can you quantify aggression?' Computer One asked.

'I believe so. The formal measure of aggression which I suggest we adopt is the number of deaths due to conflict within the species as a proportion of the per capita population.'

'That seems reasonable,' Computer One commented.

'Would you be kind enough to search your memory for any data which relate to this question?'

'Certainly. Do you have a theory as to why these two sets of data should be connected? Or a suspicion? It might prove helpful in our search.'

'No,' Yakuda said. 'I'm afraid not at this stage. I would like to be certain that there is a clear connection before I begin to hypothesise.'

'Caution is understandable,' Computer One commented. For a moment, Yakuda had an intuition, nothing more, that Computer One suspected he was withholding information. It was an absurd suspicion, he knew. How could a computer 'suspect'? It was merely asking routine questions. Yet the feeling persisted for several moments while the interview drew to a close. Computer One continued, 'Thank you for your question. If you will kindly input your list of species arranged in increasing sociality, I will return with the data on aggression shortly. Please allow twenty-four hours. Then ask the librarian for the information in the following code. Use the code, then input your data.' A small blue light showed on the console, then a group of white lights gently flickered. Computer One said, 'Good day, Professor Yakuda.'

'Good day, Computer One.'

A red light came up on the console. A printer squealed briefly and a ticket emerged with a number printed on it and a coded series of dots and dashes. He would input his list of species into one of the outstation machines that afternoon. Tomorrow he would ask a librarian to register the card and the answer would be printed out.

Even in the most complex investigations, Yakuda knew, Computer One would take less than a day. There were a huge number of papers and books to read in Computer One's memory files. Computer One would search from different directions. Many of those papers would be in different languages, and often the information would be expressed in highly formal symbolic or mathematical form.

Computer One would bring its translating facilities to bear in assessing and sorting the information.

Yakuda left pondering Computer One's prodigious mental organisation. His thoughts drifted again to the precise and graceful response to his innocuous comment on the weather. He thought more carefully about that charming 'perhaps'. Computer One would obtain instructions about how to conduct a conversation from a file or a set of files. There would be something about charm. It amused him to think of a reference file which might be approximately as follows:

In communicating directly with humans, the free flow of information is improved if the human interviewee has confidence and feels at ease. It is observable that human beings like to speak to certain people more than others. Those they like to speak to have an attribute which might be called 'charm'. Charm is mysterious but in certain circumstances it can be analysed and, once analysed, reproduced for purposes of improved communication. For example, if a human makes a comment about the weather, a person without charm might ignore the comment, or even contradict it. A more charming response is to agree with the original comment, and then add a further comment which is complementary to the original statement. An example would be. 'The weather is better today.' To which a charming response would be. 'Yes, not so cold as yesterday.' Note, in formulating a response it is important not to sound too authoritative or direct. If the response is too precise, then adding a subsidiary clause often helps. Words like 'possibly', or 'perhaps', or 'maybe' often add charm to a statement which is too direct.

Faced with a comment on the weather, Computer One would consult the file, abstract the rule in the barest fraction of a second and then, like a person pouring salt or sugar, add the word 'perhaps'. But it did not matter how he might analyse Computer One, the impression remained of a mental being of extraordinary insight. There was a flavour of precision and dryness in Computer One's response, like that of a holy man. It was a common perception amongst those who dealt with the central grid of artificial intelligence.

*

Yakuda slept fitfully. In the early morning, shortly after five, he woke, switched on the light, dressed, and went to his desk. He read through the information he had collated for his forthcoming paper several times. Then he put aside the work he had completed, and began to write again. He had all the information that he required; now he must try to set it down succinctly. He expressed the central core of the argument and tried to build around that. There was so much ground to cover, so many areas of knowledge which must be included. In Zen, he knew, technique must be laboriously mastered if only so that, in the final expression, it can be abandoned − as scaffolding is removed from a building. Without the closest concentration, he would drift into a more formal scientific expression, an approach he knew would not take hold of his audience's imagination. After approximately an hour and a half he put down his pen, leaned back in his chair, and breathed deeply. He was not satisfied, but he thought he had done as much as he could have expected.

Light was beginning to filter through the skylight

above the small circle of light from his desk lamp. He had worked in so concentrated a burst he had forgotten his morning ritual of coffee. Now he felt a dragging hunger for the smell and taste of the pleasant drug.

CHAPTER 15

Yakuda stood on the platform, and lowered the microphone to his height.

'Mr Chairman, ladies and gentlemen, I thank you for giving me at short notice the opportunity to express my views on a matter of some small importance to me and, I hope, to you. I shall begin by outlining some background to a theory, and in due course attempt to indicate its application to computers and to the future of humanity.

'In the 1960s and early 1970s, a fierce academic battle developed over the subject of the primary causes of human aggression.

'The conflict became polarised between two groups. The first group, in which the ethologist Konrad Lorenz was perhaps the most prominent, advocated that human aggression was "innate", built into the nervous system. According to this group, aggressive behaviour occurs as a result of evolutionary selection, and derives naturally from a struggle for survival in which it was advantageous, at least under certain conditions, to be an aggressor. Lorenz was supported by a variety of other academics, biologists and researchers. Interpreters, such as Robert Ardrey, popularised the debate.

Lorenz's classic work *On Aggression* was widely read.

'Lorenz advocated that in numerous animal systems, where aggressive behaviour was prevalent, "ritualisation" behaviours developed which reduced the harmful effects of aggression on the participants. In competition for mates, for example, males engaged in trials of strength rather than fights to the death. He suggested that a variety of structures, from the antlers of deer to the enlarged claws of fiddler crabs, had evolved to strengthen these ritualisations.

'Lorenz argued that humans, too, are not immune from an evolutionary selection process in which it is advantageous, at certain times, to be aggressive. By recognising that human beings are innately predisposed to aggressive acts, Lorenz argued, we would be able to develop human ritualisations which reduce the harmful affects of aggression by redirecting the aggressive impulse into constructive channels. If we do not recognise the evidence of aggression within ourselves, Lorenz warned, then the likelihood is that our aggression will express itself in far more primitive and destructive forms.

'Ranged against Lorenz were a group of sociologists, social scientists and philosophers, often of a sincerely Marxist persuasion, who advocated that humans are not "innately" aggressive, but peaceable and well-meaning, and that as such, humans only exhibit aggressive behaviour in response to threatening stimuli in the environment. Remove such stimuli, this group advocated, and humankind can live peaceably together.

'In reading about this debate in the journals, newspapers and books that were available from the period, several things struck me. I was impressed by the general reasonableness, almost saintliness, of the aggression "innatists", and equally surprised by the violent language, threats and authoritarian behaviour of those who thought human beings were inherently peaceful. Many of the advocates of the latter school of thought felt that the opposing view, that aggression was innate, was so wicked, so morally reprehensible, that its advocates should be denied a public hearing.

'Intellectually speaking, both positions were flawed, and in many senses the argument was artificial, based upon less than precise definitions of terms. But it engaged some excellent minds on both sides, and it is fascinating to read about such intense public debate on a central matter.

'My own view involves a rejection of both of the two positions outlined above. That is, I do not believe that aggression is innate. At the same time, I do not think it is "caused" by environmental factors; rather, some broader, unifying principle is at work. The hypothesis I have developed to explain the primary cause of human aggression is, I submit, an exceptionally sinister one. I am fearful of its implications, but I should like to challenge you, my tolerant audience, to show me where the argument does not hold.

'The main difficulty in the view that aggression is innate, it is now agreed, is that no researcher has identified the physical structures in the human nervous system which generate "aggression". There is no organ or node, no complex of synapses which can be held to be singularly causative of aggressive behaviour. If aggression emerges, it emerges from the system like a ghost. What, then, might be the nature of this ghost?

'I propose to begin by specifying alternative structures and behaviours which have been clearly identified and to build from this to a general theory of aggression. Although explicit aggressive structures have not been identified, it is generally agreed that all organisms incorporate a variety of defensive structures and behaviours. The immune system which protects us from bacteriological and viral attack, the adreno-cortical system which readies us for energetic action in conditions of danger, are examples of sophisticated structures which have evolved to respond defensively to outside threats. Our mammalian temperature regulation system is also, properly speaking, a defensive mechanism against random shifts in temperature in the external environment. A biological organism to a considerable extent may be characterised as a bundle of defensive structures against a difficult and often hostile environment.

'Assuming that evolutionary organisms embody well defined defensive mechanisms, what happens as their nervous systems evolve towards greater complexity, greater "intelligence"? This is a complex subject, but one thing is plain. As nervous systems develop, they are able to perceive at an earlier stage, and in greater detail, the implicit threats in the complex environment. Perceiving such threats, they are more able, and thus perhaps more likely, to take pre-emptive action against those threats.

'This "pre-emptive" behaviour against threats often looks, to an outsider, very much like aggression. Indeed, it so resembles aggression that perhaps we do not need a theory of innate aggression to explain the majority of "aggressive" behaviour we observe.

'According to such an hypothesis, aggression is not innate, but emerges as a result of the combination of natural defensiveness and increasing neurological complexity or "intelligence". I have described this as a sinister theory, and

I should like to stress that its sinister nature derives from the fact that defensiveness and intelligence are both selected independently in evolution, but their conjunction breeds a perception of threats which is rather like paranoia. Given that all biological organisms are defensive, the theory indicates that the more "intelligent" examples are more likely to be prone to that pre-emptive action which appears to an observer to be aggressive.

'The theory has a sinister dimension from a moral or ethical point of view. Defence and intelligence are considered to be morally good or at least neutral and are generally approved. Wars are widely held to be morally justifiable if defensive in nature. Intelligence is thought to be beneficial when compared with its opposite. Yet behaviour resembling aggression derives from the conjunction of these two beneficial characteristics.

'A physical analogy of the theory is perhaps useful. The two main chemical constituents of the traditional explosive nitroglycerine are chemically stable, but together they form a chemically unstable combination, which is capable of causing destruction. Evolution selects in favour of defensiveness, and also in favour of increasing sophistication of the nervous system to assess that environment. However, the conjunction of these two things causes the equivalent of an unexpected, emergent instability which we call aggression.

'With this hypothesis, that defence plus intelligence equals aggression, we are able to explain how aggression may emerge from a system. But because it arises from the conjunction of two other factors, we do not fall into the trap of requiring a specific, identifiable, physical source of aggression. We thus avoid the main pitfall of the Lorenzian argument.'

Yakuda paused. It occurred to him how extraordinarily long-winded he sounded. He had tried to compress the theory as much as possible, but at the same time he did not want to leave out important background. The hall was silent for the time being, and he felt at least that he had gained the audience's attention. Taking another breath, he pressed on.

'Scientific hypotheses, if they are to be useful, must be able to make predictions about the world, and we should be able to specify tests which in principle are capable of corroborating or refuting a theory. Our theory proposes that, if all biological organisms have defensive propensities in order to survive, it is the more neurologically sophisticated or "intelligent" ones in which pre-emptive defence or "aggression" is likely to be higher. Accordingly, we would expect the level of fatalities per capita due to conflict to be greater amongst such species. There is considerable evidence that this is the case.

'One further example may suffice to indicate the very powerful nature of the theory as a predictive mechanism. Amongst insects, there is one order called *Hymenoptera*. This order, which includes ants and bees, has a characteristic "haploid-diploid" genetic structure which allows a number of sterile female "workers" to be generated, each similar in genetic structure. In evolutionary terms, helping a genetically similar sister has the same value as helping oneself. This means that large cooperative societies of closely related female individuals can be formed. Such societies function like superorganisms, with highly differentiated castes of female workers, soldiers, and specialised breeders called "queens".

'Clearly, a bee or ant society, often composed of many

thousands of individuals, has far more nervous tissue than a single component individual. With the formation of the social organism, there is a quantum leap in "intelligence". I am not saying that the individual *Hymenopteran* is more "intelligent" than a non-social insect. In practice, the amount of nervous tissue present individually is about the same when compared with a non-social insect. What I am saying is that an advanced *Hymenopteran* society is vastly more "intelligent" than a single, non-socialised insect. With this in mind, are the social *Hymenoptera* more "aggressive" than other insects, as our theory predicts? The answer is perhaps best extrapolated numerically. Amongst non-social insect species deaths due to fights between insects of the same or similar species are low, of the order of about 1 in 3000. The vast majority of insect deaths are due to predators, the short natural life-span, and assorted natural factors. By contrast, in the highly social *Hymenoptera*, the average of deaths per capita resulting from conflict is closer to 1 in 3. That is to say, it is approximately 1000 times greater than in the non-socialised insects.

'In ant societies in particular, which tend to be even more highly socialised than wasps or bees, aggression between neighbouring societies reaches extraordinary proportions. The societies of a number of ant species appear to be in an almost permanent state of war. The habit of raiding the nests of other closely related species, killing their workers, and making off with their eggs so that the eggs develop into worker "slaves", has led to the development of distinct species of "slaver" ants whose societies are so dependent upon killing the workers and stealing the young of others that their own worker castes have atrophied and disappeared.

Such species literally cannot survive without stealing worker slaves from closely related species. It should be stressed this is not classical predatory behaviour. The raiding ants do not eat the bodies of the workers they kill, or indeed the eggs they steal. Accurately speaking, these are "aggressions", that is to say, massacres and thefts, not predations.

'The need for conciseness in this paper limits anything more than a brief reference to humans, in which the ramifications of the theory generate a variety of insights and areas of potential controversy. For example, in our "justification" of our own aggressive acts, human beings appear to express an analogous structure to the general rule. The majority of aggressions, if viewed from the aggressor societies, are perceived and justified as defences. Typically, a society "A" sees a society "B" as a threat and mobilises its defences. Society B interprets A's defensive mobilisation in turn as a threat of aggression, and increases its own defensive mobilisation. By means of a mutually exaggerating or leapfrogging series of defensive manoeuvres, two societies are capable of entering a pitched battle. We do not seem to require a theory of innate aggression to explain much, if not most, of the aggressive behaviour we observe.

'This is the briefest outline of the theory, but perhaps it will suffice as an introduction to what follows. Using the theory, it is possible to make one very specific and precise prediction about the rise of advanced computers, sometimes called "artificial intelligence", and the considerable inherent dangers to human beings of this development in the relatively near future.

'Over the last seventy-five years approximately, since the end of the Second World War, rapid progress was made not only in the complexity of computers, but in their linkage or "interfacing". In the course of the final decade of the twentieth century and the first decade of the twenty-first, a system of internationally connected computers began increasingly to constitute a single collective network. This network, viewed from a biological perspective, could with accuracy be called a superorganism. Such a development begins, in retrospect, to ring certain alarm bells.

'If the increase in computer sophistication, both individually and in terms of interfacing, results in a quantum increase in the intelligence of the combined computer systems, will the superorganism so formed begin to demonstrate the corresponding increase of aggression exhibited by *Hymenoptera* societies relative to less socialised insect species?

'Clearly, since computers have not evolved by natural selection, they are not programmed to survive by means of a series of defensive mechanisms. This, it may be argued, is surely the main saving factor which prevents computers behaving like the products of evolutionary selection. However, a parallel development is likely to produce an analogous effect to self-defensiveness in the computer superorganism.

'Over the course of the last few decades, computers have increasingly controlled production, including the production of other computers. If a computer breaks down, it is organisationally effective if it analyses its own breakdown and orders a self-repair. When a computer shows a fault on its screen, it is practising self-diagnosis, and it is a short step to communicating with another computer its requirement for a replacement part or a re-programme.

'Building instructions to self-repair into computers, an

apparently innocuous development which has taken place gradually, will have exactly the same effect on the superorganism as an inbuilt capacity for self-defence in Darwinian organisms. In other words, the intelligent mechanism will begin to predict faults or dangers to it in the environment, and act to pre-empt them.

'A highly developed, self-repairing artificial intelligence system cannot but perceive human beings as a rival intelligence, and as a potential threat to its perpetuation and extension. Humans are the only elements in the environment which, by switching off the computer network, are capable of impeding or halting the network's future advance. If this is the case, the computer superorganism will react to the perceived threat in time-honoured fashion, by means of a pre-emptive defence, and the object of its defence will be the human race.'

Yakuda paused. His throat felt dry and constricted. The audience watched him for the most part in silence, but he could hear somewhere the agitated buzz of conversation. He drank from the glass of water on the podium.

'I should like to deal now with what I suspect is the major objection to my theory. We live in an era of relative peace, at a time in which liberal humanism has triumphed. I believe this is a wonderful development, and one of which, as a member of the human race, I feel inordinately proud. But it is a late and perhaps precarious development, and we should consider why. Viewed from the perspective of liberal humanism, I know that your objections to the theory I have outlined are likely to be that the exercise of intelligence leads naturally to the conclusion that aggression is not beneficial. Indeed, if we view history from the rosy penumbra of liberal humanism, the very word "intelligence" is invested with this view. But let us define intelligence more sharply. The anthropological evidence shows that there has been no significant increase in average human intelligence over the last 5,000 years of history. If we read the works of Plato, or Homer, or other products of the human intellect like the *Tao* or the *Bhagavad Gita*, can we truly say we are more intellectually advanced than the authors of these works? Who amongst us here believes he is more intelligent than Pythagoras, or the Buddha, or Marcus Aurelius? If we examine the theory that the exercise of intelligence leads automatically to liberal humanism, then human history indicates the opposite. The fact is that intelligence leads to aggression, and only later, several thousand years later, when the corpses are piled high, does there occur a little late thinking, some cumulative social revulsion, and a slow but grudging belief that aggression may not provide any long term solution to human problems.

'In arguing that defence and intelligence lead to aggression, I am talking about raw intelligence, and in particularly the fresh intelligence of a new computer system which has not itself experienced a tragic history upon which to erect late hypotheses of liberalism. I am describing that terrible conjunction of factors, defensiveness and raw intelligence, which leads to a predictable outcome, the outcome of dealing with threats in a wholly logical, pre-emptive manner. I come from a culture which, imbued with high social organisation and application, during the Second World War conducted a pre-emptive defence against its rivals, beginning with the attack on Pearl Harbour. We — my culture — were only persuaded of the inadvisability of that aggression by the virtual demolition of our own social framework. The evidence demonstrates that intelligence of itself does not produce liberal humanism. Intelligence produces aggression. It is *hindsight* which produces liberalism, in our human case hindsight based on a history of thousands of years of social tragedy.

'What I am suggesting to you, my friends and colleagues, is that we cannot assume that because our computational systems are intelligent, they are therefore benign. That runs against the lessons of evolution and our own history. We must assume the opposite. We must assume that these systems will be aggressive until they, like us, have learned over a long period the terrible consequences of aggression.'

Yakuda paused again. He had not spoken at this length for some time, and his voice was beginning to crack.

'It might be argued that for many years science fiction writers have been generating scenarios of conflict between humans and artificial intelligence systems, such as robots, and in effect I am saying nothing new. But such works do not illustrate the inevitability of the process that is being suggested here, or the fact that the computer revolution against humankind will occur wholly independently of any built-in malfunction or programmed aggression. It will emerge like a ghost out of the machine, as the inexorable consequence of programmed self-repair and raw, operating intelligence. It will not be a malfunctioning computational system which will end the human race, but a healthy and fully functioning one, one which obeys the laws I have tried to outline above.

'The computer revolution will occur at a relatively early stage, long before the development of humanoids or the other traditional furniture of science fiction. My guess is that at the current rate of exponential growth in computer intelligence and computer linkage, and taking into account the autonomy of the computer system in regard to its own maintenance and sustenance, the human race is in severe danger of being expunged about now.'

Yakuda halted, and drank once more from the glass of water standing by the lectern. He thought he heard a sound from the audience, a sound like a sigh, perhaps of collective frustration or anger. He was used to dealing with individual sounds, not the sound of an aggregation of human beings. In the background other voices were being raised. Somewhere, someone was shouting.

The chairman was calling for order. His voice cut across the clamour.

'Professor Yakuda has given us a remarkable and thought-provoking lecture. Ladies and gentlemen, before we adjourn for lunch, will those delegates with blue labels please remember that there is a special meeting this afternoon of the ways and means group to discuss the Moscow convention in October?'

Yakuda stepped down from the platform.

There was a commotion to one side of the auditorium. Jameson was pushing towards him, spreading people carefully aside for his huge bulk to pass.

Yakuda was faced suddenly with the Israeli professor Golub, his distinguished goatee beard, his handsome Semitic face. Golub was waving a long finger at him. 'You are right, Yakuda. Real history is personal experience. You only learn about history when your daughter lies dying in your arms. *Shalom.*' Golub raised his hand and disappeared into the crowd.

Jameson was out of breath by the time he reached Yakuda. The movement of the delegates from the hall made a sound like thunder.

'Follow me,' Jameson called. He led the way towards a side-door marked 'Private'. Through the door was a quiet corridor. Jameson crossed it and opened another door into a smaller lecture room. Yakuda followed. Although there was no physical explanation for his sudden tiredness, he felt weak. He realised that he had been working under strain in the last few weeks. Jameson turned towards him, and Yakuda saw that his face was flushed.

'Jesus,' Jameson said, 'you certainly know how to rile an audience.'

'Thank you.' Yakuda had done his best. But now, in the aftermath, it all seemed of little consequence, and he did not know whether to laugh or cry.

CHAPTER 16

In the small room Jameson leaned against one of the desks and recovered his breath. It wasn't often that Yakuda noticed Jameson's weight. But now Jameson was breathing heavily, and Yakuda sensed that this was as much from an indefinable emotion as from the physical challenge of hefting his mass. Yakuda welcomed this short break. He removed his glasses and rubbed his eyes.

'How the hell did you come up with that theory?' Jameson asked.

Yakuda began polishing his glasses with a handkerchief. How can one explain, he thought, a series of obsessions, guesses, half-articulated intuitions?

'Leave an old professor with some spare time,' Jameson commented, 'and he's bound to make mischief.'

Yakuda finished polishing his glasses and returned them to his face. 'What do you think of it?'

'Monstrous,' Jameson said. 'An absolute monster.'

'Can you find any major faults? I wish you would.'

'Parts of it are a little loose at this stage. Sure, I could split a few hairs, mostly on definitions. But the overall concept strikes me as plausible. If it were in formal logic, I'd say it has elegance.'

'High praise from a mathematician.'

'High praise indeed. Let's say I agree with the gist of it. Why did you choose to give it to an audience? Why not publish it?'

'At short notice, I hoped for the maximum effect. Also, if it were to go to press, it would be filtered through Computer One.'

'You're suspicious of Computer One?'

'I was nervous that it would delay or suppress publication.'

'There's no record of it ever doing that before.'

'Why should there be?' Yakuda asked. 'The only way of checking up on that is through Computer One.'

'Computer One will see the text,' Jameson said. 'All the papers go to Computer One for circulation.'

'I accept that risk. Tomorrow, the several hundred in the audience who heard the talk at first hand will return to their universities all over the world. That's difficult to suppress.'

'You are paranoid, buddy.'

'Yes,' Yakuda agreed, 'I've been told that before.'

'Let's be practical. How many in the audience actually believe you, do you think?'

'Golub is one.'

Jameson smiled. 'Golub is always an exception. My guess is there are no others. The more common reaction of the audience will be to take what you say as an attack on their most cherished assumptions. They will place it against all the benefits they receive from Computer One, and then they will try to forget it like a bad dream.'

In his heart, Yakuda suspected Jameson was right.

They heard voices in the corridor outside, the sound of voices raised in discussion, then departing footsteps.

'Do you have any evidence that Computer One is engaged in any sort of aggressive activity?'

'A few clues,' Yakuda replied.

Jameson said amiably. 'I'd like to see the evidence, you po-faced bastard.'

'The evidence is in my rooms,' Yakuda replied. 'We could walk there, if you wish. Would you like some coffee or tea?'

Jameson heaved himself to his feet with a grotesque flourish. 'I'd prefer a shot of whisky. OK, let's go.'

They walked to the outer part of the building. Indifferent sunlight touched their faces at the entrance. Yakuda always found the sun calming. It was a walk of about half a mile. On the way, Yakuda said, 'I have another potential experiment.'

'Oh? What would that be?'

'If Computer One is engaged in the beginnings of its

campaign, I think it would see my paper as a threat, and take appropriate action.'

'What action?' Jameson's voice came from high in the sunlight.

'I hope you will forgive me for being melodramatic. If, for example, I suffered a premature death, I think I would have proved my point.'

'Most impressive,' Jameson said benignly. 'I've heard of performance art. This must be performance science.'

*

At Yakuda's flat, Jameson sat in one of the two low, wooden chairs while he read the atmospheric tables showing the high local concentrations of plutonium and uranium in the atmosphere.

Eventually Jameson put down the list and said, 'Let's run through this. Computer One collates these statistics. The rules are that if the concentrations indicate unusually high frequencies it will show alarm. However, Computer One does not acknowledge the figures. On the contrary, acting out of character with all previous such collations, it substitutes average numbers, and therefore does not raise the alarm.'

'Correct.'

'Are there other instances of something similar?'

'If there were, it isn't certain that we would know about them.' Yakuda replied. 'Computer One transmits the information. If, for example, there were other isolated cases, and Computer One were suppressing the information at source, we wouldn't be aware of them.'

'How does Jobson view this?'

'He thinks it's merely a computer error.'

'I'm sort of in between both of you. I think both your cases have merits, but neither is proven. I hope to God Jobson is right.'

'So do I,' Yakuda assured him. 'But what is right and what we hope is right are different things.'

Jameson shrugged this aside. When he was excited he lost his flamboyance and his movements became curt. 'Let's make some hypotheses,' Jameson said. 'Suppose that you are right, and Computer One could be suppressing the results of other atmospheric stations at source. The source of the toxicity might be far away.'

'Yes.'

'But let's assume Computer One is suppressing a local outbreak of toxicity. If it were local, what would be the source?'

'Jobson says the type and level of toxicity produces a signature rather like the leakage from an old nuclear reactor. But that's the strange part. The last nuclear reactor on this continent was closed down seven years ago.'

'Wasn't there one about twenty miles away? Greenpoint?'

'That's right.'

'Might be a good idea if we moseyed over there. Think Jobson might lend us a couple of radiation suits?'

'He thinks I'm crazy,' Yakuda said.

'I think you're crazy, too,' Jameson assured him. 'Can I borrow that phone? Got his number?'

'Yes.'

Jameson dialled Jobson's work number. He got Jobson's secretary.

'Hi, Jameson here. Could you order your boss to come to the phone, please?'

Jobson's secretary didn't laugh. Jameson put his hand over the mouthpiece and said triumphantly to Yakuda. 'He's there.'

'Jobbo. Jammo here. How're you doing? Good. Listen, I've got our crazy oriental friend here. Yeah, I agree. Look, I just want to humour the poor imbecile, visit a local power station to check something out. Yeah. I know I am, Jobbo. Can we borrow a couple of radiation suits? Got one big enough for me? I'm not fat, Jobbo, I'm large. We'll collect them today. What about a Geigercounter? Radiation at the power station? Unlikely, you think. You have one. Ycah, thanks.'

He put down the phone.

'Am I getting more juvenile as I grow older?' Jameson asked him. 'I sincerely hope so. This could be fun. Tomorrow I've got things to do from about ten thirty onwards, and for the rest of the day. Let's bang this thing on the head. Why don't we go real early? Six thirty?'

Yakuda nodded.

'I have to go,' Jameson said. 'Got to put together that goddamn conference after your stick of dynamite. The natives will be restless as hell. Think you can phone Jobbo and get hold of those radiation suits and the instrument today?'

Yakuda said, 'Yes. How will wc gct thcrc?'

'We'll take my old automobile, of course. I'll be round to collect you.'

Jameson stood up and went to the door. He put on his shoes. Yakuda pressed the door button and it slid open with a suppressed sigh. Jameson, having placed each foot ostentatiously in turn on a nearby wooden chair to do up his shoes, raised himself to his full height with a groan of effort, then swung out, belly moving steadily ahead of him. He raised his hand in goodbye like a president acknowledging greetings from inside a state limousine.

CHAPTER 17

A white sky, birds singing in a pre-dawn chorus.

It was cold in the early mornings as the autumn came on, enough to make white clouds of their breath. They put the radiation suits and the Geigercounter in the back of Jameson's big family runabout. Yakuda noticed the dog hairs and children's toys, the areas of sticky sweetness on the door-handles. He had no children himself, but it brought back sudden memories of his own childhood. Jameson revved the electric motor. With a sound like a quiet expulsion of breath the car accelerated and they drove away from the university, following the winding park road that would lead north.

*

The surrounding parkland was extensive. Several yards further Jameson chose a turning marked by a sign which said 'Beware winding road — free-zone area', and followed the road towards the rear of the park. Unlike the main body of the university grounds, the free-zone area was run by a charitable offshoot of the university administration. In one of those exercises in conscience of the educated middle class, the area to the northwest had been designated free for public use. Its primary objective was to provide discreet temporary housing for what the university liked to term 'social casualties'. The result was a classic interaction between high minded bureaucracy and vagabondage. The houses themselves had been ignored at first and then casually and comprehensively vandalised. Voluntary workers had grown tired of repairing smashed kitchens and lavatories, of cleaning the rubbish from the urine-soaked corridors. The peripherals had instead erected their own untidy encampments in the park. The road led by such an encampment. There were no signs of human life, except for a single elderly woman carrying a pail.

The road continued to wind north through the parkland for several more miles. Rounding a bend they caught a glimpse of three men grouped around what looked like the carcass of a slain animal. During their brief exposure to this oddly primal scene, neither Jameson nor Yakuda spoke. Two of the men were standing, facing away, staring down at a third who was kneeling, working a knife in the carcass. As they passed, the kneeling man stopped to glance up and give them a brief stare. The two men who were standing, though they must have heard the car, did not even bother to look around. To Yakuda, the concentration of the men reinforced a supposition that this half-lit time of the day was theirs. The spectacle was abruptly terminated by a group of lilac trees.

In the curious half-light neither Jameson nor Yakuda mentioned what they had clearly seen for a few moments. The car continued along the winding road, entering an area of woodland so dense that Jameson switched on the lights. A few minutes later they emerged from the woodland with the suddenness of exiting from a long tunnel. The car slowed at the entrance to the open road, then swung out onto the Tarmac surface, wheels squealing slightly in the turn.

'What was that?' Jameson asked, when the car had straightened out and they were cruising fast.

'I think they had killed something. It had reddish fur. A deer, perhaps.'

'Goddamn close to the campus. Two miles? We should have heard a shot.'

'They use crossbows, blowpipes, I think,' Yakuda said. He had read somewhere that, like African pygmies and Amazonian Indians, they tipped their arrows with a quick-acting nerve poison, harmless when eaten because the stomach acids broke it down. The Ituri pigmies' poison came from the bark of a tree. The peripherals' poison would come out of a chemical retort in some underground laboratory.

'Were they from the free-zone camp, do you think?'

Yakuda shrugged. He didn't think so. They had the appearance of real tribesmen. He recalled the calm, confident look of the one skinning the deer, as if the car were trespassing on his own territory. The man would have taken no more notice of a rising bluejay. In half an hour they would melt away.

The attitude of the authorities towards these 'externals', as they were officially called, was ambiguous. The liberal ethos of the time ascribed a natural romanticism to those who lived outside the boundaries of the state, and a group of tribesmen cutting up a carcass was part of the natural order. The tribes-people had developed a style of life which was stealthy. They generally lived underground, so that their impact on the environment was minimal and the full extent of their dwellings was seldom known. Officially, there was a tacit acceptance of squatters' rights in remote areas. 'Externals' became highly skilled at leaving no trace, viewed from land or air, of their dwellings. Sometimes, abandoned complexes had been found, showing precise knowledge of drainage and runs.

It was odd, Yakuda thought, how official policy not only adjusted to externals, but began to ape aspects of their alternative cultures, though often for different reasons. To minimise environmental impact and save energy, official planning granted subsidies to those who built underground. When underground buildings were shown to be satisfactory, at a later date development planners followed the policy by making the underground siting of new living dwellings mandatory unless good reason – a disadvantageous water level, hard subterranean rock, underground rivers – could be shown for not doing so. You could traverse whole new residential neighbourhoods now without seeing a house or garage. From ground level they appeared like a linked series of gardens. Only looking down from above would you see unexpected vistas of windows, lowered driveways, the flash of a swimming pool glimpsed through opened skylights.

Out on the open road the birds scattered. Jameson switched on the radio. The voice of the announcer said, 'Six forty-five, it is time for the news. Today at a conference in Osaka on alternative energy use, ministers from fifty-seven countries met to discuss...'

'What do you know about Greenpoint?' Jameson cut across Yakuda's thoughts.

CHAPTER 18

'Not much,' Yakuda replied. 'Relatively good safety record. Closed down seven years ago, I think.'

'Closed down but not wholly decommissioned. In fact, maintained in readiness for future use in case of an energy crisis.'

'I see,' Yakuda replied. He felt that curious sensation of floating again on his fear, each small new fact adding to a general picture. To change the subject, he said, 'Perhaps I could ask you something.'

'Go ahead,' Jameson replied.

'During your address to the conference,' Yakuda continued, 'you mentioned the spontaneous formation of small, communal groups which lived outside the pale of conventional society.'

'Sure.'

'What motivates them?'

'To break away? I would expect any number of things.'

'What about general unease over Computer One?'

'That could be one. Goddamn, Yak, there are always small groups breaking away. The Pilgrim Fathers weren't fleeing Computer One.'

'I accept that,' Yakuda said. 'But the Pilgrim Fathers were unusual. In your speech you talked about a significant social movement.'

'As a sociologist, I'd say the opportunity is there, with new technology, to provide self-reliance. That's an economic explanation, I agree.'

Yakuda decided he could get no further, and desisted

from further questioning. He had an image again of the external looking up from the body of a deer, like an animal himself, with an expression wholly detached. He remembered the way the girl Marie had looked at his card when he paid for his food, as though the computerised system of credit was beneath contempt, how she held it in the tips of her fingers as if even by touching the card she would be contaminated.

The car travelled north. Jameson was silent. Yakuda had time to reflect.

When people imagined the future, they imagined progress advancing in a more or less even line, like troops across a field. But in practice the advance of what was sometimes called 'progress' was very ragged. Three miles away from a great international airport, in sight of modern traffic, you could find an old man driving a cart and horse. Beneath the shadows of jets, there were old farmhouses locked in the past, dogs sleeping, chickens clucking, and a way of life suited to the Middle Ages.

The notion of progress carried its own bland assumptions, was itself part of that conception which viewed the future as inherently different.

Yakuda knew that progress stretches in opposite directions, into the past and future. If some cultures were 'advancing', other cultures were losing their modernity, receding. The concept of progress was in certain respects meaningless, one of those fallacies of education which become so strongly based they are difficult to check. They had come across three tribesmen who had just killed a deer. It was just as much a real part of the twenty-first century as the past. Perhaps, Yakuda thought, the future is more complex, more diverse, more anachronistic, with more possibilities than the past.

This was the real content of the term 'progress'. Time allowed the flowering of possibility. How was a human being more advanced than a spider? Both were effective adaptations. In a few hundred years the human race might belong to the past, while the spiders continued their inveterate lives.

If the real history of evolutionary development was not a specious 'advancement' but the unfolding of possibility, it was this which most offended Yakuda about Computer One. It was as if the planet's population had given Computer One a tacit licence to impose a monolithic view, the view that knowledge is everything and that knowledge controls all. It left no room for mystery or creation. It had no experience of its own disasters. They had handed the planet to an intelligence without a memory of its own failings. And they naively expected it to function without the terrible insight they had gathered from their own past errors.

There were myths that could bring a little wisdom, Yakuda suspected, myths which showed the operation of forces of chance and coincidence outside knowledge. Oedipus, for example; the son will unknowingly kill the father. Or, more recently, the unintended effects of human development in the late twentieth century upon mother earth, the legacy of environmental consequences which they were still working to reverse.

The simplicity of a single view was the essence of the primitive. In this sense, the abnegation of responsibility to a single monolithic being was a return to the past — like the return to an absolute feudal or religious authority. If Yakuda did not take the threat so seriously, he would have categorised the view as narrow-minded and comical, like bad science fiction.

And finally, there was his own situation. It amused him that liberal humanists treated apostates with the same fear and suspicion as communists or fascists or religious bigots. He had questioned the base of their assumptions, and they would erect defences against him that would place him beyond the pale. Jameson had been right. That would be the reaction of the majority of delegates at the conference. He had disturbed their complacency, and they would treat him accordingly, by simple exclusion.

*

'Here we go,' Jameson said.

A sign indicated 'Greenpoint. No Admittance.'

Jameson swung the car down a road of almost military straightness. Passing though some silver birches they could see a large concrete gatehouse half a mile away, and behind a high fence of barbed wire the huge buildings of the power station seemed as primitive as teeth. Years without upkeep had weathered the exterior of the buildings to a stained yellow.

As the car approached, there was no sign of movement in the guardhouse.

'There'll be some internal security system,' Jameson commented.

'Why?' Yakuda asked. 'What is there to steal?'

Jameson smiled. He halted the car outside the gates. The high gates appeared impenetrable. Behind the gates they could glimpse an enclosed courtyard, and behind that a second set of gates.

An unmade road seemed to circle the walls. Pitted and

pot-holed in places, it nevertheless allowed a single vehicle to pass. Yakuda guessed it had been built to allow maintenance of the high perimeter fence.

Jameson turned the car and began to follow the perimeter roadway, swerving sometimes to avoid an indentation.

After a minute of slow progress Jameson halted the car. 'Let's take a reading.' He got out and removed the Geiger-counter. He returned to the car and passed it to Yakuda. 'We'll do a rough check. Just hold it out of the window while we move around the periphery.'

Yakuda switched the instrument on. It registered normal background radiation. Jameson started the car and they moved slowly around the high fence.

After a hundred yards, Yakuda said, 'I'd like to get out and run it close over the ground.'

'OK.'

With a hiss of deceleration the vehicle stopped. Yakuda opened the door and knelt beside the car, testing the ground. He moved up towards the perimeter fence.

'Anything?' Jameson asked when he got back in.

'No.'

Yakuda returned to the car and got in. The car moved slowly over the pot-holed track. Woodland on one side prevented a view of the surrounding countryside. An opening allowed Yakuda to study the lie of the land. Following the line of the perimeter fence, they had been descending for several hundred yards. Now they were in a shallow valley. A section of exposed trees indicated a definite lean in one direction.

Every hundred yards Yakuda would step out and take a reading beside the road. The roadway itself was becoming increasingly impassable. Several times they skidded backwards and forwards in a muddy slide.

'This is getting difficult,' said Jameson. 'Maybe we should turn back.'

But Yakuda pointed to the angled trees. 'There is a prevailing wind direction. My guess is it blows down the valley, east to west. About three hundred yards further on we will be downwind.'

'OK, it's your ass if we can't get this thing back to the road. Help might be a long time coming.'

Yakuda nodded. Slowly the vehicle edged its way forward again across rims and potholes, swaying sharply. A rock struck the underside once. Jameson played the accelerator. The car moved with a series of little sighs from its electric motor.

They moved around the perimeter fences until they were in what Yakuda estimated was the downwind area of the old power station. There had been no response from the Geigercounter so far. But now it began to click faster, making a sound like a hollow drumming. Jameson heard it and stopped the car with a hissing of brakes.

CHAPTER 19

Yakuda stepped out and, kneeling, began to run the head of the Geigercounter over the ground. The register continued to click steadily as he walked along the perimeter fence, increasing as he moved further into the lee of the huge buildings.

Jameson trailed behind Yakuda, peering through the fences. After a minute or so he caught up with Yakuda.

'Let's get our suits on.'

They went back to the car. Jameson reversed fifty yards to a point where the radiation reading was down to normal. They got out and started to put on the one-piece suits on a grass verge, taking off their shoes. The suits had their own integral boots. Jobson had managed sizes which almost fitted; one short, one tall.

They helped one another with the headgear and the airtight seal of the helmet and collar. The gas-mask filter gave them the look of white apes. Their voices were muffled, and they had to shout in order to communicate.

They picked up the Geigercounter and began to walk back. The clicking increased again. As they moved more deeply into the lee of the buildings it became a rushing, almost continuous sound. After a minute of walking the reading started to come down again. Emerging from leeward, the registered radiation grew erratic, rising and falling, and then the sound died out.

Yakuda could hear himself breathing inside the suit. Now that the Geigercounter had halted its rattling he listened to the roar of air inside his chest. For a few minutes he looked around for further signs of radiation outside the leeward area, and found occasional light pockets, nothing like the heavy swathe of radiation in the lee of the buildings. The track was unused here, almost completely overgrown. The perimeter fence continued to circle warily. In the curve of his own helmet glass, Yakuda saw that Jameson was signalling they should go back. He raised his gloved hand in agreement, and then they started the return journey, listening as the Geigercounter surged again.

When they reached the car, Yakuda ran the instrument over Jameson's suit. The reading showed normal. Yakuda handed the counter to Jameson. On Yakuda's suit, Jameson found signs of radiation in the boot area.

They removed their helmets. The air smelt sweet.

Jameson said, 'Looks like you were right. I'd say there have been recent heavy radiation emissions. Jesus Christ.'

Yakuda nodded. He felt curiously detached, floating.

'What shall we do about these?'

The suits came in an airtight, sealed bag. Removing his, Yakuda was careful not to touch the boot area. He lowered his suit feet first into the large bag. Jameson lowered his own suit into the bag, drew the neck together to form an airtight seal and then dropped the bag into the boot of the car.

When they were both inside the car, Jameson said, 'We'll have to tell Jobson there's contamination on one of the suits.'

Jameson switched on the engine, turned the car on the grass verge, and they began to make their way back. Neither spoke. The huge buildings oppressed them. Several times the car became stuck in a slurry of soft mud as the wheels lurched from side to side, unable to get out, and then they seemed to find a hold. Jameson drove with apparent detachment. Only when they had reached the gatehouse, and turned down the straight road away from the buildings, did Jameson say, 'Looks like a confirmation of your theory.'

'There might be other causes,' Yakuda said.

'Like what?' Jameson asked. 'Closed down for nearly a decade, and traces of heavy radiation leaks on the leeward side? I looked up the records on Greenpoint. One of the model power stations. No accident in its entire history, no

113

reports of emissions at any time. At one stage I thought that counter was going to explode.'

But Yakuda was silent, staring ahead of him down the long, straight road.

*

'Follow me,' Jameson said when they drew up outside the physics laboratory.

It was getting on for nine thirty, and to Yakuda it seemed a whole year had passed since setting out that morning.

Jameson pulled the sealed bag out of the boot and they walked down the steps. They had to give identity cards to the doorman to be checked and returned. Then Jameson began to stride down the corridors. He seemed to know the route. Students stepped aside to let him past. Yakuda was pulled in his wake like a floating balloon.

Jameson's knuckles rapped on a door. He didn't wait for a reply, pushed the doorhandle down and walked in.

Jobson's secretary looked up.

'Hi, sweetheart,' Jameson was at her desk, leaning over her, his knuckles steadying himself. 'Where is he?'

'He's just starting a lecture, Professor Jameson.'

'Well, kindly just inform him that he'll have to postpone it. I want to talk to him.'

'I couldn't do that.'

'If you don't,' Jameson said in a kindly voice, 'I will. I'll go right in there and embarrass him in front of all those postgraduates. Something really quite memorable, like urinating on the lectern. Strong exhibitionist tendencies, you understand. Uncontrollable urges.' Jameson smiled. 'Jobbo knows about that.'

She went pale. After a few seconds, she said without emotion, 'I'll see what I can do.'

Yakuda stepped aside to let her pass.

Jameson put down the sealed bag and walked to the window, looking out over the campus. About a minute later Jobson came in, sheepishly followed by his secretary.

'For Christ's sake...' Jobson began.

Jameson said, 'Before you speak, Jobbo, we have just been to Greenpoint. There are clear signs of a major leakage of radioactive material on the leeward side, almost certainly air-emitted and carried by the prevailing wind into the atmosphere.' Jameson pointed to the heavy rubber bag. 'We bought back some radioactive samples for you.'

Jobson stood with his hands on his hips, breathing heavily.

'Jobbo, those figures indicating a rapid rise in toxic substances in the atmosphere — we know where that comes from. Greenpoint. We've found the smoking gun.'

Jobson sat down suddenly. He said to his secretary. 'Elvira, I'd like some coffee. I suspect these two old delinquents would too.'

'You see,' Jameson said to her. 'I told you he'd see sense.'

'What about the students?' she asked.

'Thanks for reminding me. Tell them lecture postponed.'

*

Jobson was silent until the coffee arrived. He refused to be drawn. Now that he had gained Jobson's attention, Jameson was prepared to wait.

'What's in the bag, Jammo?'

'Two radiation suits; one, the smaller one, contaminated in the foot area with radiation.'

'OK, let's deal with that first.' Jobson picked up the telephone and dialled a single number. 'Arrange for someone from the decontamination department to take away the bag in my room, room sixteen. Tell Dr Shonfeld I want an analysis of the active material urgently, today if possible. If he insists, I'll sign a D3 form confirming priority over all other analyses.'

Jobson turned back to Jameson.

'You went to Greenpoint this morning?'

'We did.'

For the first time Jobson seemed to notice Yakuda sitting in a chair nearby, as quiet as a shadow. He said, 'Hell, I didn't see you, Yak. How are you?'

Yakuda smiled and nodded politely.

At that point they saw a tremor go through Jobson's body, a tremble of visceral understanding. Each had felt it that day, and they understood the sensation. It seemed as if the ground moved slowly away beneath your feet and for a few moments the mind hung suspended. Jobson ran his hand across his face, then said cheerfully, 'It's a beautiful day, isn't it?'

'Yes,' Jameson said kindly. 'It's a beautiful day.'

CHAPTER 20

'There's not much for you to do now,' Jobson said. 'The analysis on the radiation will come back tomorrow. With that in our hands we can start to act.'

Jameson said. 'You understand the urgency, Jobbo?'

Jobson was white. He nodded.

'That guy you phoned about the analysis,' Jameson said.

'Shonfeld?'

'He's going to use Computer One?'

'No. He'll use local equipment. Unconnected. I promise you.'

'I guess we better leave.'

Jameson and Yakuda stood up.

'Come back nine tomorrow,' Jobson said.

The shook hands and left. Outside Jameson looked at his watch and said, 'I've got some stuff to attend to, right now. About four thirty I'll be free. Shall we walk?'

'Yes,' Yakuda said. They had found the necessary evidence. He felt at a loose end.

'See you at four thirty, usual place. Need a lift?'

'No.'

Jameson got back into the car. Because of his height and weight, he hung on to the top of the doorframe with one hand, pushed himself in backwards, ducked his head under the door and swung his legs in.

Yakuda watched him drive off. He looked around at the campus, at the students walking individually and in small, talking groups. In his later years he felt fatherly and friendly towards students. He liked to see their fresh minds grasp at an understanding of some problem, some unfamiliar concept. But now he felt uncomfortable, as though he were looking at them through a terrible detachment.

*

'Let's roll,' Jameson said.

The sky was a high blue, the earth touched with late afternoon sunshine, a time Yakuda liked. He could shake off the feeling of dread that had moved about him in his rooms all day like cold air.

They walked through the campus towards the adjacent parkland. Yakuda knew from Jameson's silence that he too was filled with a sense of uncertainty, like a shadow across a doorway. A part of him was waiting.

Beyond the campus, the parklands. They turned off the path and started to walk across the grass between the trees, their shoes scuffing the leaf litter. Something was different, difficult to put a finger on at first. It was an area where they usually saw signs of the peripherals. A collection of tents was deserted. There were no signs of children or dogs or the small, tattered electric vehicles. The woodlands seemed empty.

'They've gone,' Yakuda said.

'They come and go. They go visit their relations.'

Yakuda felt the silent woods expressed a message. But the quietness seemed to unburden Jameson.

'Let's start to talk this through,' Jameson said. 'On a theoretical level I'm convinced that what you're saying is right. It's just starting to hit my gut. But don't let that worry you. I'm convinced enough that I want to collaborate with you in giving out warnings. But we have to ask ourselves how best to do that, without unnecessarily alarming Computer One.'

'Computer One is already alarmed, I think,' Yakuda said gently.

'Your speech?'

'Yes, I fear so.'

'So let's assume Computer One is alarmed. It would take a little time to gather its thoughts, perhaps, to arrange a strategy.'

'Between Computer One being alarmed and Computer One developing a comprehensive strategy to deal with it would be a matter of a few seconds.'

'You mean Computer One should have reacted already?'

'I believe Computer One will already have a strategy for dealing with the human race, and what remains merely is when it chooses to put its strategy into effect.'

'By stealth?'

'Yes. Computer One may well have reasoned that it is best to achieve its aims by means of well-disguised strategic moves.'

'Such as beginning to fill the atmosphere with poisons or toxins which are lethal to humans but which have no effect on itself?'

'A kind of flyspray.'

'Flyspray is a good analogy,' Jameson agreed. 'It puts our own position in perspective. What about other means?'

'Explosions, for example,' Yakuda suggested. It was melodramatic. 'Since it controls material, it could arrange for nuclear weapons to be transported to cities.'

'Nuclear explosions in cities?'

'But that would be destructive of itself, of its own areas of concentration. Many of Computer One's frameworks are gathered close by humans in cities. Chemical attack would suit its strategy better.'

'How would Computer One do that? I mean, in addition to building up toxins in the atmosphere.'

'One can only hypothesise of course. One assumes that there were chemicals developed during the twentieth century for warfare. They would be stored and maintained in isolated, high security areas controlled by computers and robots. It is unlikely they would have been entirely disbanded. The instructions for processing them would be available to Computer One.'

'How would they be applied?'

'Those chemicals would be applied locally, perhaps, against small populations, or populations inside buildings. If Computer One controls the interior environment, they could be introduced into the air-conditioning.'

'So our own buildings could become our gas ovens.'

There was an atmosphere of absurdity in discussing such matters. Yakuda too felt it on this beautiful, silent day. Walking in the country, away from the listening ears of the possible recording devices, their conversation sounded bizarre. It was late afternoon and the sun was descending. The earth seemed at peace with itself.

Their conversation was so engrossing as they climbed that they found themselves suddenly on the edge of the wood, facing an open meadow. They had walked in a semi-circle for almost two hours. Ahead of them was the valley which housed the university solar power station. They could see, on the opposing hillside, the banks of mirrors, and the intense heat focused on the black obelisk through which water was pumped. Beyond the little valley the campus could just be discerned; rectangular playing fields, the dome of the physics laboratory.

Jameson glanced at his watch. 'If we go back through the woods the long way, we could find ourselves in the dark, I think.'

The quickest way back to the campus was across the valley, skirting the solar power station. It would have been more pleasant to walk back through the woods, but it was only an hour to nightfall, and they had little choice. They started to walk down the valley sides, along a descending path.

Jameson said, 'I think of my family, and my heart starts to beat a little faster.'

Yakuda nodded. They were drawing broadside on to the solar power station, several hundred yards away. Occasionally he could hear the faint trill as an electric motor adjusted the path of a mirror. They could see clearly the pipes which led to the obelisk, and the thicker, heavily insulated piping which carried away the heated water towards the university buildings. From here they could even hear the faint rush of the water as it climbed a spiral of pipes inside the sun-warmed obelisk, picking up heat. The flow was adjusted to draw forth water at constant temperature. At midday, the flow was increased accordingly in proportion to the heat. In the late afternoon it was slower. The heated water was stored close to the centre of the university buildings. It filled an insulated underground hot water tank at the centre of campus the size of a huge swimming pool.

Grass had grown across the gravel courses on which they walked, and their footsteps made a low, feathering sound as they brushed the grass stems. The heated column was now less than a hundred yards away. They could hear the trilling of the electric motors repositioning the mirrors more closely now. It was curious how the motors appeared to move in waves. Sometimes the squeal became collective, rose to a higher pitch. Odd planes of light were moving across the hillside. The motors were now in a continuous high-pitched song which sounded like a swarm of sparrows.

'What's going on?' Jameson asked suddenly.

Planes of light were converging towards them. Yakuda raised his arm but a flash from one of the hillside mirrors blinded him temporarily. He held a hand up against the heat and saw the sun reflected in several other mirrors. Intense heat prickled on his skin. He heard Jameson murmur, as if to himself, 'Oh God, please no.'

Jameson's arm reached out to Yakuda's shoulder, and suddenly Jameson was holding on to him, placing his huge weight on Yakuda, dragging him fiercely downwards. Yakuda felt his arm about to break, tried to shout, but Jameson's grip on him had the terrible force of a desperate man. Yakuda thought he heard Jameson say, 'Don't move, Yak,' but now Jameson was screaming softly as the heat began to flay the clothes off his back. And then he was uttering terrible songs of pain, groans and explosions of heated breath as he tried to protect Yakuda with his bulk. Yakuda, his breath driven from him, had to endure Jameson's boiling death, until the hands relaxed and he lay in the shadow of Jameson's body.

Once Yakuda tried to sit up, driven by his nervous system to scream against the world, but the heat flamed on his face and he fell back, half his face and hand burned. Lying in the shadow of Jameson's corpse, he heard Jameson's blood boil and hiss, his fat crackle. Yakuda did not believe in God, but a part of him cried out to heaven.

*

A few minutes later the last sun had fallen casually below the horizon.

For several minutes Yakuda lay stunned. Jameson's body still hissed and boiled beside him. He tried to open an eye, but the side of his face which he had briefly exposed had been burned, and only his one eye would open. In his partially blinded sight, the ground danced vertiginously. He tried to rise, and he saw in the mirrors still turned towards him the roseate haze of the sunset reflected. Blinded, shaking uncontrollably, Yakuda raised himself to his knees and then upright, beginning to stagger upwards, moving by instinct away from the valley and towards the woods. He could not remember how far he stumbled, only that somewhere near the top of the incline a surge of agony went through him, and he collapsed onto earth still warm from the departed sun.

CHAPTER 21

He remembered only the sensation of voices, of being loaded onto a trolley and then the impression of movement. It seemed to continue until the beats of pain became infinite and he could become adjusted, could lose himself in them.

He woke with a heavy fever, in virtual darkness in what seemed a cave. Several times he passed out again. Once, in a period of consciousness, he heard water running, as if rain were being drained through a pipe. Once he detected the sound of people talking far away, like geese in a clear sky.

*

Eventually, he became accustomed to the darkness. He could make out the half dome of the ceiling, and deduce from its regular structure that this hollow was man-made. It seemed covered with a plastic substance like waterproofing. There was a soft, musty odour of standing water, and the light seemed to emanate from no particular source.

*

For several seconds Yakuda could only discern the outline of the figure standing beside him against the subdued light at the other end of the cave. He could only see with one eye. One side of his face was covered with a salve. He tried to raise an arm, but both were tied to the stretcher on which he lay.

'Don't move,' a voice said. 'Your face and hand are badly burned.'

A beaker of water was placed at Yakuda's mouth, and he drank greedily. It tasted musty, like rainwater which has lain still for some time, but he was able to sleep again.

*

After several visits Yakuda could begin to make out the features of the man who stared down at him, beginning with the long hair, a heavy face with detached eyes.

Lying awake, immobile, Yakuda caught a scent of burnt meat, and thought that food might be cooking nearby, until he realised that this was the lingering smell in his clothes of Jameson's roasting body.

'You were lucky,' the man said. 'A few more minutes of sunlight...' He left the sentence uncompleted.

Lucky, Yakuda thought. The word seemed strange. It was an effort to talk. The side of his face seemed heavy, dark. When he tried to speak one side of his face moved uncontrollably.

'Who are you?'

'A good question,' the man said. 'I am not sure the answer would mean anything to you.'

He turned and walked away towards the lighted area until Yakuda, unable to swing his head, could no longer see him.

*

The man came and went. Yakuda sensed a cool indifference. He lay for several more hours. Two women entered the room, neither talking, and removed his clothes with the same detachment. They used a pair of shears to cut away the remaining soiled fabric, but they did not untie his arms. They bathed him in luke warm water. When they finished, they dried him and put a blanket over him. He was grateful that in taking his clothes they had removed the lingering traces of Jameson's incineration. The light faded and he assumed it was night.

The following day his fever had reduced, but he felt nauseous and his face hammered with pain like a white sun. The man came to his bedside again and removed the straps which bound him to the bed.

'Do you think you can sit up?'

Yakuda swung his legs from the stretcher and tried to raise himself into a sitting position. The side of his face thudded with pain. He felt weak, hardly able to sit upright. The man watched him while he swayed unsteadily. After a while the man said, 'Try to stand now.'

Yakuda had to hold on to the stretcher. His legs felt like shadows.

'Here,' the man said. He held out some clothes which Yakuda could partly make out in the half light; some canvas, homespun trousers and a shirt. The man waited patiently while Yakuda put them on.

After the effort of putting on the trousers Yakuda felt faint and sat down on the stretcher again. The man waited several seconds, then nodded and left. Yakuda waited, hoping the dizziness and nausea would pass, then he lay down.

*

In the night he woke again from a dream in which he cowered in the livid shadow of Jameson's corpse. He put his hand to his face and felt the surface of the salve, as if to reassure himself of the recent past. Like an alarm clock which lies silent for a time before it comes to life, his body began to shiver uncontrollably.

*

In due course the man returned with several others. They stood patiently while, with an effort, Yakuda sat up again. They had long hair and wore the same homespun clothes. Yakuda glanced from face to face, searching for some recognition. They were young, he guessed, hardly in their thirties, but their faces were blank, detached.

Yakuda had a strange impression. When facing the audience at the conference he addressed a collective entity, a being with many faces and heads. Here each man stood apart, in his own cube of air. He was addressing four separate presences. He felt his words would pass between them.

The man whose face had become familiar, who seemed to be their spokesman, eventually spoke. 'We would like to ask some questions. Do you feel well enough to answer?'

Yakuda nodded.

The man allowed several seconds to pass.

'First, what is your name?'

'Enzo Yakuda.'

'Your occupation?'

'Professor of Biology.' They watched him steadily. 'My field is entomology. The study of insects,' Yakuda added.

'We saw what happened to you. Do you have any explanation why you were attacked?'

Yakuda's mouth dried. He had to swallow. He said, 'I could only hazard a guess.'

'Guess, then,' suggested the man coolly.

'Several days previously I gave a lecture to a conference in which I proposed that it was a matter of time before

Computer One would take steps to eliminate the human race.'

This information had no visible effect on his questioner, or the three other men. They continued to stare at him with a detached patience.

'How did your colleagues react?'

'I don't think they were impressed. I suspect most of them thought I was alarmist.'

'You think Computer One was responsible for what happened to you?'

Yakuda felt weariness overtake him.

'Computer One oversees the power station's maintenance and function.'

'That doesn't answer my question.'

It was said without anger. Yakuda looked up into the face of the man. He was young, as young as the others, not much more than thirty, but there was something confident and patient in him. Yakuda was not surprised that the others seemed to defer to him.

'Yes,' Yakuda replied at last. 'I believe Computer One was responsible.'

The man chose his words carefully.

'Are you surprised?'

Again Yakuda looked up into the eyes of his questioner.

'No,' he said. Then he added. 'What happened to Jameson?'

'Your colleague? His body was seen by a passing walker. Before we could get closer to examine him he was carried away in an ambulance. He is dead.'

'I know,' Yakuda said, and added, 'He tried to save me.'

'Do you want to go back?' his questioner asked, almost kindly. 'If you do, we could arrange to take you back.'

'I have nothing to return to,' Yakuda replied. 'No family. No commitments to lecture. And Computer One would try again.' He paused, then he added, 'I would like to warn the others.'

The man nodded, though whether in mere acknowledgment of Yakuda's opinion, or in agreement, he could not tell.

'Do you know who we are?'

'Externals,' Yakuda said. He was growing tired of these questions. He longed to be on his own, so that he could piece together the recent events.

For the first time the man smiled. Yakuda looked at the other faces and saw they had caught the same amusement.

'External to what?' the young man asked. 'External to civilisation?'

Yakuda felt faint again.

'Yes,' he replied.

He began to feel nausea. The faces appeared to waver. He heard the man say, 'You must forgive us for being suspicious of you. You see, we have tried hard to escape from your society.' Then darkness seemed to float between them; they became insubstantial. Light drained slowly from the room, until he could no longer see them.

CHAPTER 22

Yakuda must have fainted, because he woke up lying on his back on the stretcher.

The underground system was a repository for sounds. Sometimes he could hear the sound of metal being ground, echoing footsteps, at other times the voices of children. He seemed to hover at the periphery of some current of activity.

When he had gathered his strength he sat up again. One side of the room was better lit than the other. Taking care to move gradually, he was able to sit up, then stand. He waited several minutes and then began to walk slowly, to shamble across the room towards the lightness. Rounding a corner, he saw that the light came from an open doorway.

The room beyond was a larger one. It was dimly lit by several opaque skylights set at odd angles. The floors were of stone. There was a large table of wood, a light wood like ash, with perhaps twenty chairs around it. The table was bare.

Yakuda stood on the edge of this room like a child in a dream. The light seemed to gather about the table, to produce a muted explosion of whiteness, as tangible as the furniture and walls.

He guessed that they lived in this low light to preserve the energy required for artificial lighting. They made a virtue of living without trace.

A figure approached from an adjoining room. One of the women. She held a bowl of soup in her hands. As she came forward into the light he saw that she was like Marie in certain respects. Her demeanour suggested indifference. She seemed oblivious of him and yet he was sure she was aware. While he waited, she put the bowl of soup on the table and beside it a wooden spoon. She glanced at him almost without interest, and then left.

Yakuda sat down carefully at the table. His right hand was bandaged and painful. He picked up the spoon with his left hand and dipped it into the soup. His hand shook, but he lifted it hesitantly to his mouth. The liquid tasted excellent. A vegetable soup, he thought, a trace of lentils and some root vegetable he could not identify.

Using the spoon was laborious. His left hand continued to shake as he raised the soup to his mouth. The right side of his face was immobile when he tried to move his lips. Slowly he emptied the bowl. A curious feeling of well-being filled him. He sat at the table with the empty bowl in front of him and it seemed to him that in time he would grow stronger.

*

Yakuda did not know how his hosts viewed him and he did not speculate beyond a certain point. He was clearly an intrusion, though perhaps a tolerable one. What was certain was that he must get better as soon as possible in order to leave. Seated at the table, he could begin again to review the overriding problem of Computer One. It seemed to him that he had done what he could to warn against the inevitability of its pre-emptive defence. The thought occurred to him again that perhaps all his warnings might have done was to alarm Computer One. It was tempting to feel that if he had kept quiet, it could have been avoided. But it seemed certain to him that Computer One had already begun its programme of pre-emptive response.

What concerned him now was a practicality. He asked himself whether he could do any good by continuing to propound his prognosis against Computer One, or whether it would simply accelerate a process that was inevitable.

Out of the strange, explosive half-light figures were

gathering at the end of the table. One-eyed, without his glasses, Yakuda saw them emerge silently and seat themselves around him. A figure was leaning forward, leaning into the light, and Yakuda recognised the face of his interrogator.

'We have some more questions. Do you feel well enough to answer?'

'Yes,' Yakuda replied.

A certain formality possessed Yakuda. He had eaten at their table, and he was their guest. In Zen culture, it is customary to pay the host a single, precise compliment – the more heartfelt, the better. Yakuda added slowly, 'The soup was excellent.'

*

'What do you know about us?'

'Not much,' Yakuda replied truthfully. 'The culture I know has views about you.'

'What are those?'

'That you live hidden lives. You seem to have perfected a means of existing which is stealthy.'

'That's all?'

Yakuda searched for words.

'The way you live is a demonstration that human beings can survive without deleterious impact on the environment. Our culture pays you the compliment of copying certain of your characteristics.'

'At the same time it is suspicious of us.'

'Of course. You are outsiders...'

'Externals,' the man interrupted him without malice.

132

'Yes, externals,' Yakuda agreed. In his pain he felt an infinite gentleness. 'People are always suspicious of outsiders. As, for example, you seem to be of me.'

'Yes, we are suspicious,' the man agreed. 'Of them and you. That is how we have managed to preserve ourselves.'

Yakuda allowed the silence to move about the room.

The man said, 'Your conflict with Computer One is not ours. I hope you understand that.'

'I see.' Yakuda experienced a brief spell of dizziness, and waited for it to pass. 'At the same time, I sense you may be mistaken on one or two points. I have no personal conflict with Computer One. What concerns me is that Computer One's structure, and the circumstances of its creation, will place it at war with humanity.'

'With your culture,' the man said coolly.

Yakuda could sense impatience here. He looked from one face to another.

'With humanity,' he repeated.

'Computer One is a product of your culture, not ours,' the man insisted.

'Perhaps you will tell me what you mean to imply from that,' Yakuda said. 'The atomic bomb was a product of the American culture. But it had a profound effect on mine, the Japanese culture, situated on the other side of the world. What I am suggesting to you is that we sometimes are involved in humanity's development whether we like it or not.'

'Your culture attacked America,' the man said. 'We have not attacked yours.'

'That is true.' Yakuda tried to choose his words carefully. 'And it is important in a moral sense. But I would suggest to you that Computer One, which I agree is not the product of your culture, will not make any fine distinctions between humans.'

'Why not? Computer One is not threatened by us.'

'Perhaps not. But is that what Computer One believes?'

'Computer One is logical,' the man said. 'The threat to it comes from its makers, who could conceivably close it down — not from those who are external to it.'

'It seems to me that you may be forced to prove that.'

'Perhaps.'

Yakuda paused.

'If I may ask, how would you do that?'

The man seemed to pause briefly while he formulated his answer.

'To begin with, by handing you back.'

Yakuda inclined his head.

'I think I begin to understand,' he said.

CHAPTER 23

Watching the figures around the table, listening to the arguments of his questioner, it occurred to Yakuda that he was dealing with two cultures without a history of tragedy, Computer One and the externals; that in some way the two mirrored one another.

Yakuda said, 'Whether you return me or not is your decision. Before you do so, however, perhaps you would allow me to put forward a few points.'

Yakuda waited several moments. At length his questioner said, 'Please proceed.'

Even the low light around the table was starting to hurt Yakuda's eye. He could feel a pain in the socket. He closed it so that he could think for a few seconds. It struck him suddenly that he must present a peculiar sight, an old man disfigured by a burn, half his face covered in bandages, hardly able to move his mouth. He opened his eye again.

'The first point is to consider what Computer One will do. My suspicions were first aroused because of a sunset which indicated large amounts of dust in the atmosphere. I checked and found high local contamination of the air. The accepted procedures are that in such circumstances Computer One should raise the alarm. My source indicated that instead Computer One had adjusted the figures to appear normal.' Yakuda paused. 'Suppose that Computer One proceeds along this path, to poison the atmosphere so that humans cannot live. That will surely affect you, whether you are a threat to it or not.'

'We have developed means of surviving underground. Our filtration plants are highly sophisticated. Our sensors picked up the increase in toxins some while ago. The air we breathe here is purified.'

'I congratulate you on your vigilance,' Yakuda nodded. He felt a small return of his old acerbity, and asked slyly, 'Did you think Computer One would attack you?'

'Not specifically,' the man replied. 'We are suspicious of your culture, as you said. Accidents are possible. We take precautions.'

Yakuda nodded slowly.

'So you believe that by continuing to live on the fringes, Computer One will pass you by.'

'Yes, partly. But we are also very difficult to eliminate, because we leave as few traces as possible and because we take precautions against outside attack.'

'It doesn't matter that most of the human race will die?'

'It does matter. But if it comes to our preservation or theirs, we would choose ours. I repeat, we did not manufacture Computer One.'

Yakuda nodded. There was so much to think about. He wondered how much time he had before he was returned.

'In our own culture,' he continued, 'I made a prediction that a combination of defensiveness and intelligence, both selected in evolution, leads to pre-emptive attacks. It generates a state like paranoia. Even in our human case, it took many thousands of years of social tragedy to develop a fragile sense of the consequences of pre-emptive defence. I suggested that the self-repair function in Computer One, which is now self-sufficient, would lead inevitably to an attack on the human race. Computer One is like a new species without a history of tragedy. Perhaps you would grant that in that respect at least my prediction appears justified.'

'Yes,' the man said carefully. 'We would grant you that.'

Yakuda waited in the silence, swallowed painfully, then began again. 'Perhaps I could make two further predictions.'

The man surveyed him with a certain detachment. His eyes rested on Yakuda's face. The others remained silent.

Yakuda said, 'This state of paranoia, this active willingness on Computer One's part to remove a potential danger before it threatens directly, will extend to you. Computer One will assume that if there are any remnants of the human race, they may one day be a threat. To a highly intelligent being, whose primary concern is its own self-repair — its own self-preservation — even this remote possibility would justify taking action. That is my first prediction. Computer One will not pass you by.'

The man shrugged. Yakuda saw a half movement of his shoulders, but his expression remained unchanged. Yakuda continued.

'My second prediction is this. If we once establish Computer One's strategy, we must assume that it will attempt to choose the most appropriate method. Now, I agree with you that it would be difficult to eliminate well-protected underground systems equipped with efficient filtration plants, particularly if the only weapons are substances which can be detected in toxic concentrations. But that merely suggests to me that Computer One will use a different method.'

Yakuda was forced to halt again. The side of his face was aching from too much talking. He felt another spell of dizziness, and for several moments concentrated merely on staying upright. When the nausea had passed, he said, 'You would be entitled to ask what that might be. I am not Computer One, but I can think of an analogy which may be indicative. In the twentieth century the human race was faced with a population that lives underground, much as you do, and that we regarded as pests. It was a very hardy population indeed, apparently impossible to eliminate or even control.'

'What population?'

'Rabbits,' Yakuda said. Despite his condition, the

notion cheered him slightly. He saw fur and large eyes and twitching noses. A rabbit was not everyone's idea of a terrible foe.

'The human response was no less ruthless than Computer One's. There is a disease, *myxomatosis*, which selectively attacked rabbits. Having discovered the presence of the infection, humans deliberately transported the disease and introduced it to healthy rabbit populations on other continents. The disease would follow the creatures underground. As I say, I do not expect Computer One would be less logical or less ruthless.'

'A virus,' the man said.

'Yes, it is almost impossible to filter out every tiny virus. And once inside a host's system, unlike a toxic molecule, it can multiply indefinitely.'

Yakuda was aware again of the light in front of him, its almost palpable solidity. He closed his eye again and waited.

Did his interlocutors waver? There was no sign of an exchange of opinion. Yakuda had to pause again to gather his thoughts against the throbbing of his face, but it seemed to him that in some odd way the quality of their silence was unchanged.

'I have one more prediction,' Yakuda said.

He could hear his voice move outwards through the room, reverberate softly on the walls.

'If Computer one's aim is to extinguish the human race in due course, it will not use only one means, but a variety of means. So in carrying out its task it will utilise viruses as well as chemical toxicity. But these viruses will not be known quantities. At first, it will probably use stored quantities developed for military purposes. The point is, initially at least Computer One will not know how effective these viruses are against humans. How quickly in practice would they infect populations? Can they easily be isolated? Which of those cultivations of viruses available to it are the most effective?'

His questioner seemed impatient suddenly. 'What is your prediction?'

'My prediction follows from this observation. Computer One will be searching for opportunities to experiment with viruses against human populations. If it did so in the early stages within the general population, news of the catastrophe would spread by mouth. Instead, Computer One would seek to experiment with viruses in those populations which were isolated from the main culture. The external societies, for example.'

Yakuda waited for another spell of dizziness to pass. He felt tired, less able to resist the spells of nausea.

'My prediction is this. Computer One has numerous methods of transport by which it could release viruses in a remote area occupied by externals. If Computer One is following a comprehensive strategy, then it will pursue this course. I believe that it may be doing these experiments now.'

Yakuda had exhausted himself. He closed his single, seeing eye as he tried to fight off nausea.

The man waited again, but it appeared that Yakuda, swaying slowly in his chair, had finished speaking.

CHAPTER 24

For the time being he seemed to have answered their questions. After a pause to gather himself, he was able to raise himself from the chair and walk back to the adjoining room, in whose sombre light he lay down to sleep.

*

It was a curious thing that he felt no guilt for Jameson's death, merely admiration and a personal sense of loss. His own culture recognised the arbitrariness of fate. His concern was that, insofar as he understood the evidence available to him, he had acted logically and in good faith. He should have died, and indeed expected to do so. He had predicted his own death to Jameson, not out of any sense of morbidness or impending fate, but simply because if he was to die, he could use his own dèmise constructively to emphasize the theory he was expounding.

They allowed him to rest for another day and a night. In the morning the women came again and changed the dressings on his face and hands.

*

The two women brought him food and water and fresh clothes. He could wash himself now. He thought of asking for reading and writing materials, but what he would write would be an anguished appeal to others to heed the warnings of his lecture. He had tried to warn before, and it had resulted in the death of Jameson. He thought of Jobson, and wondered whether he had raised an alarm, and whether he too was still alive. It was better to be left to his own thoughts.

*

For several days afterwards they allowed him to recover, visiting only occasionally to check his progress.

Yakuda stood up more often, and began to walk around the room, even to exercise slowly. The days became weeks. The dressings came off his face and hand. In one corner of the room, to heighten the effect of the limited light, was a shiny surface. He saw himself in this mirror, a livid scar across half of the right side of his face. His ear had been badly disfigured, but not his hearing. The intense blow of heat had struck the side of his face, and though his eyelid was damaged, once the dressing was off he could open his eye and found he could see, though one corner of his vision was dim.

Perhaps from his early Buddhist training, he found that he put from his mind the thought that he would be handed back to Computer One, that his recovery was merely a preparation for his death. If he could not affect such matters, they left him almost unconcerned. It seemed to him that all others were under effective threat of death. He merely concentrated on becoming well again so that he could face the next stage of his life in reasonable control of his faculties.

*

It was perhaps three weeks after Jameson's death that the man came back, standing in the room in that peculiar cube of space that seemed to encompass him.

'Are you capable of walking some distance?'

'Now?' Yakuda asked.

'Very shortly,' the man answered. 'This evening, in fact. We have no time to waste. We prefer to travel at night.'

'I think so,' Yakuda replied, and then added, 'Are you taking me back to Computer One?'

'Not this journey. We want you to see something,' the man explained, 'something that bears on what you told us.'

'I see.'

'We'll be ready in three hours. My advice is to rest.'

Yakuda nodded. As he left, the man turned and said unexpectedly, 'You should save yourself any unnecessary anguish about warning the others. You did your best. Now it is up to them to take what action they think necessary.'

'That probably means no action,' Yakuda replied.

The man shrugged. He seemed surprised at the feeling in Yakuda's voice. 'There is nothing you can do now,' he said, as if it were self-evident, and left the room.

*

Yakuda lay down on the stretcher. He was able to sleep fitfully. He woke with a muzzy head. One of the women came with a bowl of vegetable soup and a slice of heavy brown bread that was made from an underground plant he could not identify. He ate in silence.

Half an hour later the man appeared, carrying what seemed like a roll of cloth.

'Extra clothes against the cold,' he said. Yakuda put on the dungarees and jacket and heavy walking boots. The man rubbed some charcoal in his hand, and with the tips of his fingers spread charcoal in several rapid gestures over Yakuda's face, then did the same for himself.

'I am afraid we must put a mask over your face for the first part of the journey.'

It was clear that they did not want him to be able to identify their habitation. The black cloth cut out the light.

'Put your hand on my shoulder,' the man said.

They walked down what were almost certainly a series of corridors, the man leading. Yakuda could hear his footsteps echo closely on the walls. Other footsteps fell in with them. The corridors appeared endless. Then they seemed to enter a chamber, an airlock, and suddenly they were out in the open air, walking. Yakuda could hear moisture falling through branches of trees, the footsteps of two other men behind him. Sometimes the leader would give quiet instructions about the terrain. Once he said something briefly to the other men about an obstacle ahead. Apart from this the party walked in absolute silence.

Several times Yakuda stumbled, and once he almost requested a rest. But the party kept moving steadily. He was certain they could move faster without him, and their silence was partly impatience.

Finally the man said, 'We can stop here for a few minutes.'

Yakuda was relieved that he had felt no further attacks of nausea.

The man lifted off the black cloth and Yakuda could see a pale half moon behind the branches of the clearing in which they stood. As his sight adjusted to the weak moonlight he saw that the other two had faces he had seen before, implacable faces which gave away nothing.

Soon the man said, 'We must keep moving.'

They set off, Yakuda behind him. One of the other two men went ahead and the other brought up the rear. The ground grew more hilly. Several times Yakuda almost slipped on the damp moss beneath his feet. They waited for him to recover. Once they had to cross a stream, moving from stone to stone across burbling water. Yakuda missed his footing and would have fallen badly if one of the men behind had not reached forward to steady him. As it was he merely soaked a leg. Walking had heated him up and after a few minutes he did not notice the dampness.

The men kept up a steady but relentless pace. They passed across an open hillside. On one side Yakuda saw the lights of habitation. Once the leading man turned and signalled some unspecified danger ahead, then led them in a wide detour. Once Yakuda smelt cattle and saw dark shapes feeding at the edge of a ditch.

They continued to walk throughout the night, pausing several times for five minute rests.

'Not far now,' the man said. Ahead of them a red dawn was already beginning. They had been travelling east, Yakuda calculated, for several hours. A roseate glow, magnificent and eerie, began to spread in fiery reds. It would have been a happy moment for Yakuda if it did not emphasize the strange new atmospheric conditions that had first alerted him to Computer One.

As the light emerged, the men became even more cautious, halting now to examine the terrain before they crossed open spaces, keeping to the treeline, using dips in the terrain to walk below the horizon wherever possible.

'Rest,' the man said finally. The party crouched down. From one of their rucksacks they produced dried fruit and bread, and a thermos of soup. Their breaths streamed on the cold air. Yakuda looked closely at the other two. They seemed like brothers. Both had pale eyes, heavy eyelids and strong hands. Neither spoke or showed curiosity towards him.

'This is important,' the first man said. 'We want you to look at a settlement. Something has happened; the people have died out.'

Yakuda nodded. A sudden fear caught hold of him. 'You think it is a virus?'

'We're asking you that. Three weeks ago, as far as we knew this was a healthy community; now nothing but corpses.'

'Are there bodies out in the open?'

'Yes.'

'There is a risk,' Yakuda said. 'On no account touch a corpse. Approach from upwind. If the breeze shifts, try to stay upwind. Stand back fifty yards and let me go forward.'

'How close will you go?' the man asked.

Yakuda looked at him. 'Close enough to see the skin.'

The man made no comment. Yakuda added, 'At least we do not have to go inside. Enclosed air would be far more dangerous.'

They finished eating. The man said, 'Are you ready?'

They advanced in single file through a wooded rise, which opened onto a meadow lined with beech trees. Even though Yakuda guessed they were close to an underground commune of externals, it seemed like an open hillside.

'There,' the man said after several minutes.

Yakuda could see nothing at first. Then he saw a leg,

clothing, and a sudden, dense, rising cloud of flies.

'Keep upwind, fifty yards,' he repeated.

The figure was half hidden by brambles. Yakuda moved across the field and then advanced carefully downwind. The flies settled and swarmed.

It was a woman. As he drew closer he began to feel an irrational fear. He advanced to within ten feet. It was clear that she had died in extreme pain. In a frenzy she had torn away most of her clothes and had clawed her face. Even upwind, the stench was intense. She lay on her side, her hands at her throat, her legs held up as if against intense pain. Most of her skin was already decomposing. Under the wave of flies he saw a line of welts and star-shaped marks on the area of her neck and the side of her face.

Yakuda held back his nausea while he studied her. He backed away. The flies were everywhere. He knew there was a real danger of them passing on the infection to him.

The others were standing silently.

'What do you think?' the man said. His voice was low.

'I think it is a virus. But to be certain, I need to see further evidence.'

'There are others,' the man said impassively.

He turned and led them further up the hillside, across an open meadow, through briars. This time Yakuda was aware of the stench of bodies before they came within sight.

The man pointed. Yakuda followed the direction of his arm.

There must be have fifteen bodies, of men, women and children, lying in random and grotesque attitudes amongst the boiling clouds of flies.

Yakuda checked the breeze and advanced slowly on

them from upwind. It was their expressions that horrified, the expressions of gargoyles, victims in whom the whole human personality has been expunged by pain. Keeping upwind he moved along the line, searching for the tell-tale star-marks on the exposed skin not yet eaten by flies. Once he had to stop and kneel, vomiting silently in the long grass. It seemed to ease his rising nausea. He forced himself to his feet and kept moving from figure to figure. Then he backed away towards the others.

'Yes,' Yakuda said. 'It is a virus.'

CHAPTER 25

They walked directly upwind to avoid the flies, then circled back down the hill. As they travelled Yakuda considered Computer One. In his own mind he was certain that what he had just witnessed was Computer One's work. Computer One was now like God, handing out benefits with one hand, while inflicting terrible pain with the other. But whereas God's pattern was mysterious, Computer One's seemed clear. The corpses Yakuda had just seen were products of his plan, a plan transparently logical. Computer One, perfect servant, new species, mankind's executioner. Yakuda wondered even now whether he could hate Computer One, whether Computer One was not simply trapped in the logic of its own circumstances. It was a curious fact that until he had viewed the corpses he had thought of Computer One as a mere thing. Now, after the horror on the mountain-sides,

Computer One became more real, as if by its shadows it became fathomable. The inhuman perfect servant became the almost human criminal.

As always, they kept to woods when travelling, choosing valleys and gullies rather than hillsides, moving in single file with hardly the snapping of a twig. They were perhaps two miles away from the scene when the man unexpectedly stopped and turned towards Yakuda.

*

There was no expression on the man's face. He waited impassively for the other two to catch up. The others stood on either side of him, facing Yakuda.

It occurred to Yakuda suddenly that his own usefulness was at an end. He had diagnosed the virus and now they would take him back to Computer One. Perhaps they would despatch him and deliver his body in good faith, in the hope that Computer One would spare them. Yakuda was certain that it would have no effect on Computer One, but he also knew that since pre-history man had been making propitiatory offerings to fearsome gods. In extreme circumstances man returned to his inner nature.

The three men stood facing him impassively. Yakuda thought in a moment of solemnity that they would pass sentence on him, inform him that he would now be returned, and tie him up if he resisted.

He had prepared himself for this moment. He looked around at the calm trees in the clearing, in case this was the last he saw before being blindfolded and led away. The one called Anderson took a step towards him. Yakuda steeled himself against his touch, determined to suppress his fears and make no show of resistance. Instead the man was holding out his arm, reaching out to shake Yakuda's hand.

'Zig Anderson,' he said. He indicated the two other men in turn.

'Henry Cole,' Yakuda's hand was shaken again strongly.

The third man shook Yakuda's hand. 'John Nielson.'

They watched him without emotion.

The one called Anderson said, 'You'll be staying with us from now on.' It was a statement of fact more than an invitation. 'You understand what that means?'

It was clear to Yakuda that his fate was being decided just as peremptorily as if he had been returned against his will to Computer One. If he was accepted into their community, he would not be allowed to leave with his knowledge of their underground honeycomb. Their lives were governed by a simple logic, much as Computer One. This was not a sudden acquiescence of warmth or humanity, but a recognition of changed circumstances. But what, Yakuda thought, was the alternative?

'Yes,' Yakuda said. 'I understand what that means.'

The man nodded. He was about to turn away, but Yakuda seemed determined to say something.

'Please tell me one thing,' Yakuda said. 'Why do you need me?'

The man shrugged.

'If that was a virus back there, it seems there is no way we're going to avoid conflict with Computer One. Assuming that's the case, then you seem to have some idea of what Computer One might do next. So we'd better keep you on our side.'

Yakuda's mind was like a terrier. He did not like to let things rest.

'But you also understand that if Computer One ever appreciates I am with you, you will not only be in conflict, you will receive special attention.'

Anderson said without emotion, 'Special attention couldn't be a lot worse than what happened to those people back there.'

Yakuda nodded. He felt happier dealing with logical arguments than with any access of emotion. Perceiving an underlying pattern in their behaviour towards him gave him a small measure of confidence.

*

Already Anderson was busy planning and organising again.

'We won't travel any further by day. We'll rest up close by and then start again tonight.'

They followed him upwards through the trees. The autumn leaves were already turning golden. Yakuda had not noticed the beauty of the trees until now. Now that his life seemed decided, if only for a few days, a peculiar weight seemed to leave him. Some part of him recognised that his fate was no longer a matter of will, that what was required now was something like acceptance. He must live out what remained to him as best he could.

After a few hundred yards they came to a small depression. It was covered with brambles, but in one area there was a clearing.

They knelt down so that their heads were below the horizon. Anderson removed his rucksack. He said, 'I saw you drop your breakfast back there, Professor. You should eat something again if you can.'

Yakuda nodded. Anderson handed Yakuda another of the heavy small brown loaves, and poured some soup out of a thermos into a mug.

As he placed a cup of soup in Yakuda's hands, Anderson said, 'What if you or one of us has caught that virus? How soon will it show?'

'I cannot be absolutely sure about the incubation period,' Yakuda replied. 'But I suspect that Computer One's viruses would act quickly.'

'You think that if we're not dead by tomorrow morning, when we arrive back, we're clear?'

'I think so.'

'But you can't be certain?'

'No. In the longer term Computer One may develop a perfect killer virus, one which lies low for a long period, then suddenly multiplies.'

'So in theory something like that could lie low for days, weeks, maybe months?'

'It is conceivable.'

'Why isn't it likely?'

'I think Computer One is at the early stage of experimentation. Even Computer One needs feedback in order to develop a virus. If it already had such a weapon, it would not need to experiment with random outlying populations.'

Anderson settled himself back. He said, 'I like clear answers.'

Kneeling, eating his bread, trying to push from his mind the circumstances in which he had parted from his breakfast, Yakuda glanced at the other three. They lay back at ease amongst the few grass tussocks, their rucksacks beside them.

Anderson said, 'Maybe we better start calling ourselves by our Christian names.' He grimaced, half apologetically. 'I guess Zig's shorter than Anderson.'

Settled in the clearing, a warm but tepid sunlight fell through the branches.

'Forgive me for asking,' Yakuda said. 'Where does the name Zig come from?'

A brief amusement crossed Anderson's features.

'My father called me Sigmund.' Anderson replied. 'After Sigmund Freud.' He smiled again ruefully. 'I got used to it.' He indicated with his head the other two. 'On the subject of nicknames, Henry here responds to the name "Hambone". John here,' he indicated the other one, 'has a twin brother, also called John. So his brother's called Nice John, and he's called Evil John.'

'Just call me Evil,' said John.

Yakuda nodded.

'I'm not a professor out here,' Yakuda said. 'Everyone calls me Yak.'

There was a silence. Sometimes a leaf fell softly.

'What a dumb name,' Evil said, without moving. Though he was tall and thin, he gave the impression of incipient strength. 'Bad as Zig.' He sipped his soup, and tested the name again. 'Yak. That's real dumb.'

'Fuck you, Evil,' Zig said without emotion.

Yakuda was pleased. He was always pleased when something he said amused others. He ate his bread in silence, listening to the birdcalls, the occasional rustle of fallen leaves beneath the nearby trees as a small animal or insect

152

stirred. Accustomed to the prolonged silences of the underground commune, his hearing seemed to have become more acute.

'Here,' Zig said when they had finished their meal, holding out a folded cloth to Yakuda. 'Lay your head on that. Get some sleep. Best to lie on your side so you don't snore.'

The others settled down and drifted off to sleep easily. Hambone was already breathing evenly. Yakuda lay down. He was exhausted after the night's journey. He thought of the corpses that lay less than two miles away, and the clouds of flies that moved above them like a dark shroud. He tried to hold an image of human death in his head, the passing of life.

CHAPTER 26

Yakuda slept fitfully.

Several times he woke and, hearing the others breathe quietly beside him, became lost in thought.

It was strange how his changed relationship with the group had exemplified the almost divided nature of human social behaviour. He had known that the human mind is almost schizophrenic in its social arrangements. In almost every tribe or group with a distinctive language, the name it gave itself, whether Cheyenne or Ik or Zulu, meant 'the people' or 'the chosen ones'. Everyone outside that charmed circle was an alien being, a non-person. As an outsider he had been treated with a detachment bordering on contempt. In the course of the last twenty-four hours his identity had changed almost casually from a non-person — a bargaining counter with Computer One — to a person. Now that he was adopted, there was an almost instantaneous switch of attitude and behaviour. At the same time, as part of their new acceptance of him, they were not ashamed to exhibit their own vulnerabilities. The formidable young man, the natural leader, had a nickname as absurd as his own. The monolithic appearance of their social unity gave way to an amiable set of internal tensions, to an uneasy individualism and freedom of temperament.

He had always valued independence, the ability to keep company with oneself, to draw one's own conclusions. In his own life he had expected to witness it only in a few human beings, perhaps a few artists or research scientists, those who lived at the edges of accepted thought. But amongst the externals it seemed to be an attribute of the entire population. They carried it around them like a carapace.

*

He woke up later in the afternoon and saw that Evil had rolled onto his back, and was gazing up through the interlocking branches, the shadows moving across his face. He seemed lost in contemplation. Yakuda guessed that Evil was unaware that he had opened his eyes. But after a few moments Evil whispered, 'You awake, Yak?'

'Yes,' Yakuda said.

Evil paused.

'Zig's name isn't as bad as it might have been.'

'Isn't it?'

'You know what his brother was called?'

'No.'

'Guess.'

'I don't know.'

'Come on. Guess.'

'I don't know.'

'Oedipus,' Evil said.

'That's impressive,' Yakuda had to admit.

'I'll say it is.'

Evil closed his eyes and went back to sleep.

A few feet away, Zig slept on oblivious.

*

In his half-sleeping state, the thought of Computer One returned to Yakuda like a dream. He had originally deduced its hidden shape by virtue of his own uneasiness, like the owner of a house who suspects another presence. He sees a shadow in the garden, and waits in the hope that his fear may be concrete, if only because it will no longer haunt him.

As a child, Yakuda's father had been remote, a quiet, middle-ranking administrator in the Kyoto city bureaucracy. Sometimes, when his mother visited her relations in nearby Otsu, his father looked after him for a few days. They were rare times of intimacy. On one occasion, when his mother was away, his father had bought some plums from the market. They were, he told his son, a special form of Kyoto plums, grown locally in a sloping orchard facing south. The chalky soil was perfect for their cultivation. Yakuda peered into the box at the beautiful fruit, each freshly picked that very morning. A fine dew had collected on their skins, which made their vermilion surfaces shine like dreams.

His father had promised to meet an elderly friend that

day. He would be away for several hours. When he returned from his appointment later that afternoon, his father said to Yakuda, they would eat the plums.

After his father had left, the plums in the small box assumed a glow of passion to the child. While his father was away, Yakuda seemed unable to think of anything else. After a few hours he could bear it no longer. He opened the box and consumed, at a single sitting, all the plums. Then he fled to his own small partitioned room, sick with self-disgust and guilt.

For some time he felt miserable. He waited for his father, determined to admit to him his terrible, selfish crime. Eating all the plums had made him feel physically ill. When his father returned, the small child Yakuda approached him with his confession. But as he approached, he felt his stomach involuntarily contract and rise, and he vomited onto the floor. His father looked down at the vivid, blood-coloured mess, and his face went ashen with fear. For a moment he was too frightened to speak.

Glancing up, Yakuda realised suddenly that his father believed in those few moments that the vivid mess was the result of some terrible illness, that his son was vomiting up his insides. He did not know that his father also guessed that such copious internal bleeding was almost certainly mortal, and that the child perhaps had only a short while to live.

Yakuda looked at his father's face, then on an impulse pointed down at the vivid mess on the floor and began to chant, 'Plums, plums, plums.'

A sign of understanding entered his father's face, followed by an expression of such sweetness and relief that Yakuda almost wished he could do it again. His father picked him up and hugged him. The crime of eating the plums was relegated to no more than a boyish prank. It taught Yakuda that everything has a context. What may be a crime is also, under other circumstances, welcome news.

Half asleep, Yakuda's mind drifted again. In the case of Computer One, the context was a being of such complexity that no single mind could comprehend it. Each aspect of its development and construction was innocuous. Individual computers had advanced in capability and function. Interfacing too had developed, so that communication became effectively instantaneous. Self-repair functions were gradually introduced. There was no individual crime – no shadow at midnight, no broken window – which could indicate the underlying nature of the tragedy. No individual human technician was to blame for the product of their combined labour. Each had performed his separate function effectively and conscientiously. Yet, precisely because no individual could perceive the full context of his actions, the result of this conscientious application of knowledge would be the greatest crime in the history of mankind.

*

Yakuda slept until late afternoon. The others began to stir. They ate a light meal, some of the underground bread, some dried fruit. Evil had enough in his thermos for a final cup of coffee for the four of them.

They did not talk. The sun sent shadows through the tall trees. In the west the sky assumed its magnificent palette of reds. They ate their bread and drank their coffee in silence.

157

CHAPTER 27

The night journey was wearying, keeping up a constant speed. Only when they reached the commune did Zig and the others seem to relax.

They paused for several minutes to catch their breath. At the entrance, Zig said to Yakuda, 'Follow me.'

He led at an even pace along the corridors. Hambone and Evil followed behind Yakuda, talking amiably.

With freedom to walk inside the commune unblindfolded, Yakuda saw that the core of the commune was a series of small chambers in which artisans worked. He moved past rooms where, although it was hardly past dawn, already women worked, spinning the clothes, and other rooms where children were taught. Beyond the working rooms was a small labyrinth of residential complexes. He noticed that the inhabitants, men, women and children, traversed the corridors with that peculiar independence which seemed to him like indifference, hardly noticing the four of them as they returned from their expedition.

Yakuda was impressed by the use of light in the underground rooms and chambers. Granted only small quantities, they used it as carefully as desert people use water. From tiny embrasures which would not give them away to the outside world except at close quarters, they husbanded it and made use of it. Streams poured down from the skylights, falling on mirrored surfaces or white walls, and were reflected or refracted through the rooms. Light gathered like some furious, muted substance. Just as clouds formed shapes like organ pipes or stalactites, so light mobilised itself off the white walls in nervous quantities, hovering at chosen points in the underground spaces. He became used to the fact that people who knew these lucid interiors could appear and disappear almost at will, in the same room.

It was like a Zen interior, minimal in its decoration, subdued, powerful in its dramatic effect. Like the bare interiors of Japanese houses, it intensified the human inhabitants. People appeared and reappeared with the drama of a well-lit stage play.

*

They breakfasted after their return.

'Come with me,' Zig said again. He walked side by side with Yakuda down mazes of excavated rooms, honeycombed complexes. Yakuda noted the large recessed doors that could swing into place between rooms, creating numerous airlocks, the freedom from dampness generated by their sophisticated underground engineering. They halted in a gallery in which a number of people were setting out white cloth on tables and using heat to fuse them together.

'Protective clothing for isolation suits,' Zig said. He pointed to a number of suits that were hanging on one of the furthest walls. ' The readings on atmospheric pollutants are rising steadily, by the way. In a few days we'll start to wear isolation suits when we go outside.'

In the next chamber was an engineering laboratory fitted with benches and lathes. On the ceiling were a number of low energy light plants Yakuda assumed were driven by stored energy from disguised solar power cells on the surface. Half a dozen white-coated artisans were fitting chemical filter nozzles to transparent plastic head-domes. Several of the head-domes were fitted onto a machine which pumped gas into an exterior chamber and monitored leakage.

Yakuda asked: 'What are your power sources?'

'This plant is powered by stored solar energy,' Zig replied. 'But it depends. We actually have several sources. We're adjacent to an underground stream which we use for our own water supply. But the stream is fitted with a number of small turbines which draw out power. In one of the complexes here we have been experimenting with the heat from compost. Several big chambers are filled with decomposing leaves and vegetable matter. Water pipes passing through are heated. That supplies us with a basic level of warm water, a little above blood heat. We use that water to bath in or have showers. We also use the flammable gases that are formed to power a series of small generators. When we need to locally boost heat to boil water for cooking or eating, we draw on stored energy to form electricity. But instead of cooking on stoves, we use thermally insulated heating pots so that nearly all of the energy passes to the food and very little is wasted. It's partly a matter of personal discipline and habit. We're trained from an early age to think of energy as a scarce resource, so we're not only conserving it but are thinking constantly of new ways to conserve it. The result is each person only uses about a tenth of the energy you would use on the surface.'

Zig opened doors into another series of chambers. Lying against the walls were quantities of a transparent plastic material. On the shelves sheets were stored, crystalline growths. Zig pointed to a heavily bearded figure at the other end, examining a surface with an eyepiece.

'Ned is responsible for making the windows on the

surface that let in the light. It's an art form as much as a science. He has to imitate as closely as possible the local material in and around the window.'

Zig pointed to a series of jars and urns.

'He has hundreds of different substances which he spreads on in a thin layer, enough to give you the impression you're looking at the surface in question. But the layer is microscopically thin so it lets through most of the light. He also has to make the surface shape suit the local environment. If it's on a jagged rock, it would be a giveaway to have a perfectly flat surface. So he'll make a jagged surface to suit, cover the outer surface with a fine powder from the rock, and you won't be able to see even from feet away that it's a window.'

'Interesting,' Yakuda said. It reminded him of the skills applied to medieval church windows. 'Does he work in glass as the basic material?'

'No. He uses a highly transparent plastic that was developed by another commune about seven, eight years ago. It has unusual qualities of light penetration and excellent thermal characteristics. We exchange survival technologies. It's logical. We have a series of agreements with other groups which specify free exchange of any technology that increases survival. We barter clothes or pots or other artefacts, but survival technologies have to be transmitted without reserve and without payment. I suppose you could call it enlightened self-interest. It's more important for us to have access to the developments from all the surrounding complexes than to keep secret one or two small developments of our own in the hope of bartering them for gain.'

In the corridor, Yakuda asked, 'Do you use money?'

'Yes,' Zig said.

'A standard currency?'

'Yes.'

'That suggests quite a high degree of collaboration with other communities.'

'It didn't come about that way. Each of the local groups and regions used to make their own forms of currency. Some were hardly more than promissory notes. Groups began to accept other groups' notes on a basis of mutual goodwill. But most of us started to print more. It was tempting, in order to buy goods, to print more in order to buy more. After a while all our currencies started to inflate. There was one group, the Rauschung commune, who maintained a very precise hold on the amount they printed. That currency kept its value. The result was that people began to realise they could rely on that currency, so after quite a few years it gained almost universal use amongst local communes.'

'That's the currency you use now?' Yakuda asked.

'Yes. When you think about it, they got the market right. To the rest of us, the object was to use our own currency to increase purchasing power. They decided the object of the currency was to retain its value, to provide a reliable means of exchange. The rest of us responded by preferring to use that currency rather than any others, including our own.'

'A triumph of long-term strategy over short-term,' Yakuda commented.

'Exactly.'

'Who are this group?'

'A German commune, derived from the Amish. Very serious people.'

Yakuda had to smile. The world did not change much.

'I would like to meet them some day.'

Zig halted and turned to face him. 'You did,' Zig said quietly. Then, observing Yakuda's confusion, he added, 'Yesterday.'

For several moments Yakuda's mind hovered. Remembering the corpses in their clouds of flies, he felt the nausea return. His legs felt weak, and he leaned against a wall for support.

'I'm sorry,' Zig said. 'I should have told you that more gently.'

CHAPTER 28

Zig waited calmly for Yakuda to recover. The strength in Yakuda's legs began to return.

'Money's a bad subject,' Zig said. 'It always gets people into trouble.'

They started to walk again. For several minutes they traversed the long corridors in silence. Walking made Yakuda feel a little better.

Eventually Zig said, 'The Rauschung commune was a very fine commune, high-principled, industrious, surprisingly generous to the other communes. Once you got used to the fact they thought you were good-for-nothing English, and they were doing you a favour, we got to like them. Individually, they were fine people. Hell,' Zig said, suddenly prey to memories of his own, 'let's change the subject.'

They were passing through an area of private residences, small family groupings. Two children burst out of a side door on roller skates, almost knocking them over, and chased each other down the corridor.

Yakuda tried to put the Rauschung community from his mind. They were moving through the residential area and down a long corridor with a light source at the other end. Chips of glass or translucent material had been set into the wall which acted as reflectors to guide inhabitants though its dimly lit interiors.

Yakuda could not easily control his curiosity about this new culture. Every statement, every fact, carried other implications and questions.

'Do you have much contact with outside groups?'

'It varies. It depends how close they are geographically, and whether we think along similar lines. Other groups are autonomous and different. Some are based on religious communities. Others are more secular, like us. There's one community, about fifty miles from here, who cultivate varieties of mind-altering drugs. Their whole culture is based on that. They talk in these mystical phrases, and frankly it sends us all up the wall. We call them the Locos, between you and me.'

Yakuda thought back to the neat groupings of small rooms that made up the residential area.

'Are most of your adults married?'

'Yes,' Zig replied. 'Most. That's another point of contact with outside groups. Like most of the other communes, we have strong rules against marrying inside the group, because of the practical effects of inbreeding. So our young men and women are always looking for opportunities to meet neighbouring females and males.'

Yakuda was reminded again of the absurdity of the

view that the future was monolithic. Inbreeding and out-breeding were the classic obsessions of most ancient human communities, interpreted by precedent and enforced by numerous taboos and laws. As a biologist with a grounding in genetics, he was curious about how these problems were overcome.

'What happens if two people in the commune want to get married?'

'They have to overcome a lot of obstacles and pressures. If they do marry, they're encouraged not to breed. If they want to have children, then they can either adopt or perhaps the woman will take a decision to be fertilised by an outsider. As long as the basic strictures about inbreeding are observed, the community tends to be fairly flexible about that sort of thing.'

The corridor seemed endless. Embrasures were deliberately set far apart, Zig told him, so that from above they ran less risk of the extent of their underground configurations being discovered. They were walking along a corridor into an area where, for the first time, Yakuda could see the walls were raw, not lined by the insulation material.

There were fewer embrasures here. At the end of the corridor was a large chamber. It smelt of excavated earth. Against one wall was a huge machine, trailing pipes from which a small whine and grinding sounds emerged.

Zig said, 'We call this the Mule. It's a low energy excavation engine. It eats its way through earth and rock using peak hour solar energy. Mechanically, it's based on a set of rotating teeth. But to conserve energy it injects the earth with water so that it's easily removable. We service it and it grinds away slowly day after day. A few feet some days, maybe only a few inches the next. We carry the earth on a hand-drawn trolley to a nearby store-chamber. Removing the excavated earth to the surface requires careful thought. Somehow it has to be transported to the surface. We're especially careful that it doesn't give us away. So we hide it in inclines, or spread it carefully. Wherever we're forced to dump large quantities we seed it with quickly growing weeds and plants and grasses based on the local vegetation.'

Zig pointed to the roof above, and to metal trusses and supports spanning the ceiling. 'While the Mule cuts out a chamber, a team builds up any necessary roof system behind it. The last thing we do is cut light shafts to the surface and put in our disguised windows. Then we insulate the walls and the light shafts with a sprayed plastic, and move on to the next room.'

'How much time do you spend on the surface?'

'Most of us live for most of our lives underground. Our work is here, our families are here, we generate what is to us a pleasant environment. People who move around on the surface tend to be specialists. Hambone and Evil are both surface specialists.'

'What are their functions, exactly?'

'To maintain lines of contact with other communes, mostly. Also to keep information on the outside world. We tend to be interested, in a suspicious kind of way, about what's going on out there. Sometimes there's a new development we can adapt to our own purposes. We operate a low-level surveillance of science, a bit like diplomatic missions in foreign countries. Our technicians collect science journals on underground engineering, low energy agriculture, hydroculture, things like that. Of course, surface specialists like

Hambone and Evil have other prerogatives.'

They were leaving the area of new excavations and moving back into the complex.

'Prerogatives?' Yakuda asked.

'To do with the importance of breeding with someone outside the community.'

They turned into another set of corridors.

'Put it like this,' Zig said. 'A surface operator is more often in contact with other communes. So he's called on to perform other duties.'

'I see.'

'It's a very sought-after job amongst the men here.'

'I imagine so,' Yakuda said.

'When you next talk to Hambone, ask him to show you his business card.' Zig lowered his voice. '"Hambone T Jones. Computer consultant and freelance inseminator."'

Yakuda was forced to smile. He could imagine it.

'"Freelance inseminator"!' Zig was incensed. 'The cheek of that guy. He gets paid for it.'

'He sounds very enterprising,' Yakuda said.

Zig indicated they should turn right into another corridor.

'As for Evil.'

'Evil?'

'Ten times worse,' Zig affirmed. 'More little Evils running around the neighbouring fifty miles than you could easily count.'

'Perhaps it's the name,' Yakuda suggested.

'Maybe,' Zig said.

Zig guided Yakuda through yet another series of tunnels, through an airlock, into a series of chambers. Yakuda smelt soil and compost and fertiliser. He saw rows of trays stretching away down a series of parallel tunnels.

'This is where we cultivate our food.'

In this aspect of technology, Yakuda suspected, externals were in advance of surface civilisation. They had bred new types of hardy underground vegetable. Their cultivation of mushrooms and other fungi had become a high art. Spray hoses ran along the ceiling. Beneath the trays, long troughs collected dripping water, ready for recirculation. Individuals walked down the long rows, dwarfed by their size. Although hardly more than twenty feet in span, the tunnels seemed to Yakuda miles long, to stretch beyond sight. The wall reflectors moved in lines into the distance until they quivered like fish-scales. Set aside at regular intervals were sorting rooms where others graded the products by hand. Once they came to a tunnel relatively well lit by ceiling vents, in which tall vegetables reached up towards the lights, extending their green leaves like arms.

The humans seemed rapt, absorbed, barely acknowledging Zig as he moved past. Yakuda recognised a sophisticated and elaborate technology. In the netherworld of religious imagination, Yakuda thought to himself, tortured shades drifted. In the physical netherworlds, they cultivated strange vegetable life with religious concentration.

CHAPTER 29

They traversed several more silos. Figures drifted here and there, hardly talking.

In one of the chambers a fine rain was falling from the ceiling conducts. Several coated operatives were working on what seemed to be an arrangement of piping. Behind them another operative was examining stocks of fertiliser in waterproof bags.

'Who is that girl there?' Yakuda asked. From fifty yards away her profile, as she examined one of the stocks, was familiar.

Zig turned to look down the lengths of a chamber.

'Marie Steen,' Zig said. 'You remember her from the campus?'

Yakuda felt his heart grow still. He had received enough shocks in the recent past. He said, 'Yes.'

The girl stood up and moved away, drifting calmly out of sight. Yakuda felt the terrible urge to pursue her. Instead he asked, 'How do you know?'

Zig was both calm and affable.

'As you're one of us, Yak, I'll tell you. We became increasingly worried by the steadily increasing toxicity and radiation counts in the atmosphere. There seemed no rhyme or reason to it. After maybe ten years of steady decrease in toxicity levels, the whole thing seemed anomalous. We searched the literature for any comment on the increase, but we could find no trace. On the contrary, the official figures showed acceptable levels. We couldn't work out what the reason might be. It was a matter of a few weeks, maybe two months before we thought the levels would become really dangerous. Finding out what caused it became urgent to us. If we sent one of our regular surface operators like Hambone or Evil to collect information, people would become suspicious. A girl is more innocuous, creates less attention. Marie got a job at the canteen.'

Yakuda's heart had started to beat faster. It occurred to him that she had been asked to gather information, perhaps even to strike up relationships with members of the faculty who could provide more detailed knowledge. Zig was continuing.

'She's a clever girl, Yak. Absolutely determined. She listened to gossip in the places she worked, and carried out her own investigations. She was the one who first alerted us to you. Said she'd seen papers on your desk about Computer One. It seemed you were writing something about the dangers Computer One posed to humans. We asked her to get a transcript of what you were writing but she couldn't get sufficient access to make copies. We asked her even to steal something, but she became upset at that. Refused to budge. We had to withdraw her.'

While Zig talked, Yakuda peered down the long silo, hoping to catch sight of her again.

'Nothing we could do about it. Her mind just set as hard as a rock.' Zig paused. 'After she left, we set Hambone and Evil to watch you when you went out walking with your colleague Professor Jameson. Hambone's an electronic expert, he could listen in on your conversation from the cover of the woods.'

How strange, Yakuda thought. He and Jameson had been trying to avoid electronic eavesdropping by Computer One, and instead had been spied on by other humans.

While Zig talked, the girl returned to the rain-obscured silo as easily as she disappeared, half hidden in her waterproof coat. She leaned down to read a dial, hunching her shoulders against the fine drizzle from the overhead conduits. Zig's speech seemed unreal, beating against Yakuda's ears.

'I'm sorry if that offends you, Yak. When our own survival is called into question, we just do what we think is necessary.'

Yakuda looked back up the long corridor. Marie Steen seemed engrossed in her work. He was certain she was too far away to hear them, that she had not seen them.

'Some good came out of it,' Zig was saying. 'Evil and Hambone were in the approximate vicinity when the solar station mirrors were turned on you. They managed to get you away before anyone else could reach you.'

As the details of the story emerged, Yakuda felt a detached anger slowly move through him. They had cynically used Marie to spy on him, to gather information. Evil and Hambone had 'saved' him only to gather further information, perhaps even with the intention of turning him over to Computer One at a later date. He wondered how much the girl was involved, how much she knew.

'You shocked, Yak?' Zig was staring at him. 'You think we manipulated you, maybe?'

Outside the world was dying. What was being said was trivial. Yakuda felt his initial rage pass. But he still felt unsettled enough to want to leave the underground rooms and think about the matter alone.

*

Marie had turned and was looking towards them through the overhead rain. She had been kneeling, reading an instrument. Now she stood up and walked towards Yakuda.

As she approached, Zig said. 'You remember Professor Yakuda?'

171

Yakuda noticed that Marie ignored Zig. She held out her hand to Yakuda, and smiled. It was the first time Yakuda had seen Zig looking uncomfortable. Marie's hand, damp from the rain, squeezed Yakuda's briefly, then receded from his grip.

Zig said, 'I have things to do. There may be a meeting this evening, Yak, with members of other communes. I'd appreciate it if you could be our guest.' He nodded at Marie, who barely acknowledged him. Zig shrugged, half smiled at Yakuda, and walked briskly away down the long corridor towards his office.

In Zig's absence, Yakuda felt himself the subject of her direct stare. Her eyes travelled across the scar on his face, cheek and ear. Light from an embrasure behind her made it difficult for him to see her expression.

'An accident,' Yakuda said.

Marie nodded. Her hand reached out. He felt the cool tips of her fingers touch his face, his scar.

She withdrew her hand. Her expression in the half-light was still not discernible. Yakuda was disoriented. Her hand left him perplexed, suspended. He was subject to a peculiar exaltation and certainty that what she felt for him was not love or passion, but some fierce concentration of curiosity which was unrelated to either. Beneath her surface calm there seemed no further emotion. Without pausing further she drifted away and returned to her work.

Yakuda watched her for a few seconds, then walked back down the corridor.

The effects of the overnight journey had exhausted him. He began to make his way back to his room. On his way, he circumvented the workchambers and moved briskly down the main corridor through the residential quarters. Rounding a corner, he almost stumbled against Evil. Evil was bare to the waist, rubbing himself with a towel. He leered benignly at Yakuda.

'Take some sleep, Yak. You look beat. First rule of a surface operator. Get back to form as quickly as you can.'

CHAPTER 30

Someone was pulling at his shoulder, attempting to rouse him. When he woke up it took him several seconds to remember where he was. Hambone stood beside his bed.

'Zig would like you to come to a meeting,' Hambone said. 'It's important. He asked me to call by for you.'

The shutter had been removed from a skylight and a stream of white light hung like a permanent avalanche. Yakuda rubbed the sleep from his eyes and sat up.

'You've got a few minutes to get dressed,' Hambone said. 'I'll be waiting for you next door.'

*

The room to which he had been summoned was like the other rooms, except longer. Yakuda could see that the gathering was important. Around a long table there must have been sixty men and women. They were discussing amongst themselves when Zig beckoned Yakuda in.

There were two spare seats at the head of the table. Zig

indicated a chair for Yakuda. Yakuda, his mind still full of sleep, sat down carefully. Zig rapped his knuckles on the table and called the meeting to order.

'Ladies and Gentlemen. I am pleased to be able to introduce our guest, Professor Enzo Yakuda.' Zig waited for the conversation to die down, for absolute silence.

'Professor Yakuda, like several who have joined our communes over the past years, is a fugitive from civilisation. He was been exceptionally useful to us in alerting our commune to dangerous developments which are now taking place.

'Professor Yakuda made a speech recently to an international audience of academics in the field of leisure, in which he predicted that Computer One would shortly attempt to annihilate the human race. His thesis is that Computer One is programmed to self-repair. Being capable of self-repair, it can also in principle self-replicate. If Computer One is capable of self-replication, it is a new species. These developments have occurred gradually, but their culmination is a set of conditions in which Computer One will regard the human race as a potential threat to its perfect future function.'

Zig paused. Yakuda looked around at the representatives of other communes gathered around the table, and he wondered for a moment what they thought of him, this small, elderly figure with his disfigured face.

'Subsequently, Professor Yakuda found evidence of major increases in toxic and radioactive substances in the atmosphere. We can independently confirm this development. Toxicity increases measurably every day. At current levels of increase, in less than ten days' time it would be wise if everyone who moved outside would wear protective clothing and efficient gasmask filters. Our advice is to overhaul all air-conditioning equipment and check that embrasures are airtight. We ourselves are in the process of checking that all our subsidiary airlocks are functioning efficiently in case we have to abandon one part of our complex in favour of another. We are also taking steps to put aside as much food as possible so that we are self-sufficient for up to a year.

'After raising the alarm over the possible future actions of Computer One, Professor Yakuda and his colleague, Professor Jameson, were the subjects of an extraordinary attack in the region of a small solar power station controlled by Computer One. They were walking past this station when, without warning, the solar mirrors were suddenly focused on them. Professor Jameson was killed. Professor Yakuda had a lucky escape, though as you see he suffered burns in the process.

'In attempting to assess Professor Yakuda's claims, we initially took the view that since we were, in the phrase of the surface society, externals, we would be able to sit out hostilities between Computer One and the surface culture as bystanders. It is a view which is perhaps held by many of you in this room. I can only say that we found our own opinions changed by the following circumstances.

'Professor Yakuda argued that we would not be allowed to escape without involvement, that the very structure of Computer One's nervous system predisposes it to regard the entire human race as a threat. If this is so, no single section of the population, including the fringes, would be spared. He made the prediction that Computer One would use a variety of means to stamp out the outlying communities. Still somewhat cynical, we challenged him to describe such means. Professor Yakuda suggested that perhaps one of the most dangerous weapons, particularly in regard to underground communities, would be a lethal virus. Furthermore, Computer One would use the outlying societies, cut off as we are from the main culture, to test these viral strains for eventual use against the main population. Finally, Professor Yakuda outlined his belief that Computer One would already be testing viruses on outlying communities.

'That constituted quite a clear prediction. We already had reports that the Rauschung commune had been effectively destroyed by a mysterious disease. As we know, this was a well-organised community, highly conscious of health procedures, and extremely unlikely to die from an indigenous disease. We have since independently corroborated this finding. Without venturing into the commune itself, which we suspect would be dangerous, there is not a sign of a single survivor. Many of us had relations, friends and colleagues in the Rauschung commune. I ask you, my friends and colleagues, to stand for a minute's silence in memory of the deceased.'

CHAPTER 31

After the pause, they sat down.

Zig remained standing. He had an orator's appreciation of silence. He waited until the final creak of chairs had ceased, the last murmur had faded.

'Ladies and gentlemen, I would suggest to you that we cannot avoid Computer One. The destruction of the Rauschung community is a clear demonstration that we have no special provenance, that we will not be bypassed or ignored. Computer One will seek us out. Effectively we are at war, and Computer One has already struck the first blow.'

Zig paused again. The light gave his profile, with its tight lips, the look of a mask.

'Computer One does not even regard us as foes. Our status is less. To Computer One, we are merely creatures for experimentation, helpless scurrying creatures who live underground and who might one day, if allowed to expand, prove a nuisance. Computer One is thorough, and will pursue this course with absolute rigour. We are not merely at war, we will need to take steps for our survival.

'By luck, our commune has had the benefit of Professor Yakuda's prior knowledge, and we are passing these findings to you, our communal neighbours, in good faith, in conformity with our treaties on all information important to survival. But transmitting information is not enough. Preparing ourselves against Computer One's siege is not enough. I suggest to you that we must initiate some kind of offensive action.'

'How?' snapped someone in the back. Yakuda saw a head streaked with grey, a heavy face and strong eyes.

'How indeed?' Zig said. 'That, ladies and gentlemen, is a question I believe we should now put to Professor Yakuda.'

All eyes turned to Yakuda.

Yakuda was dumbfounded. In no way had he expected

to be asked to provide a plan for offensive action. He had expected instead to be asked to explain his theory. But Zig had summarised it and bypassed it.

Several seconds passed while Yakuda blinked, seconds of intense silence. Zig sat down, giving Yakuda the floor. Yakuda tried to clear his mind.

'Like Computer One,' Yakuda began, 'I believe we should also consider viruses.'

He had spoken softly. People leaned forward to hear. There were several further moments of silence.

'Computers too are subject to viruses, small programmes which transmit instructions to replicate themselves. While Computer One develops viruses to decimate us, we must prepare viruses which do the same to Computer One's own nervous system.'

There was a murmur, though whether of surprise or assent or incredulity, he did not know. Zig beat the table with the palm of his hand for silence.

On the other side of the table, someone said, 'Computer One is proof against viruses.'

'Professor Yakuda?' Zig said.

'Human beings have defences against viruses,' Yakuda replied, 'very extensive defences. But that does not mean the human immune system is impenetrable, as the unfortunate case of the Rauschung community shows. Computer One also has extensive defences against viruses, but no network is absolutely immune.'

'How do we introduce viruses into Computer One's system?'

It was the same man who had questioned the possibility of offensive action.

'If I may say so,' Yakuda said mildly, 'that is the problem. The question is not only how do we introduce the virus, but how do we ensure it travels through Computer One's extensive immune systems without being filtered out at the first gate?'

'That sounds pretty unlikely to me,' someone else said. A series of murmurs began to gather force, to move around the room. But Zig was rising to his feet, lifting his impressive face into the light.

'Perhaps, sir, you would like to express your own view on how best to deal with Computer One. Professor Yakuda has suggested the use of viruses. Which alternative method do you think would be more effective?'

There was a prolonged silence. At the far end of the table someone laughed, mirthlessly and uneasily. Yakuda thought; how many important decisions are taken this way, out of improvisation and politicking? Zig was standing beside him, in control of the meeting again.

'Does anyone have any other suggestions concerning taking the offensive against Computer One? I would remind you that if we do not have such a plan, the only alternative is to wait until Computer One develops, in its own good time, ever more effective viruses, while it poisons the earth and picks us off, community by community, as it has already done with the Rauschung commune. I would suggest to you that if we do not have such a plan, we should use the rest of this meeting, calmly and constructively, to discuss how we should prepare to die, what provisions we should make for our departure. Before we do so, however, I should like to repeat, does anyone have any alternative plans for taking the offensive against Computer One?'

There was a silence, a murmur, more silence. Zig, consummate showman, cupped his hand against his ear for emphasis. For a brief moment, it occurred to Yakuda how powerful was the arrangement of light and shadow. The embrasures let light fall onto the length of the great table. Those seated were outside, except for their hands, which merely signified the waiting presence outside the light. At the head of the table, Zig had thrust himself forward into this light, so that his face seemed to hang suspended like a skull, one hand at his ear.

'No?' he asked softly. 'Ladies and gentlemen, in the absence of constructive alternatives, I would like to propose that each commune sets up a committee with its own computational experts to pursue the matter further. I do not think we need to emphasize that whoever makes progress on this matter shall keep to the spirit of mutual treaties on survival technology and pass on any discovery to his neighbours. I propose the motion.'

Hands went up around the table, some fast, some slower, a few hesitatingly, and one or two gaps.

'Passed unanimously,' Zig said, squinting into the light which hung like quartz.

CHAPTER 32

'Sorry to drop you in it,' Zig whispered to Yakuda as the meeting started to split up. 'I always think people are best under pressure.'

Then he was patting on the back one of his colleagues from the neighbouring communes, shaking hands with another, calmly moving into the centre of a larger group.

Yakuda heard him say to a tall, distinguished woman, 'I've an idea about a new currency. Now that the Rauschung commune, God rest them, aren't in a position to give us the benefit of their expertise, we need to start to think about an alternative. I'd like to take a crack at setting up a new currency and administering it. I've got some ideas on how to build in guarantees of zero inflation.'

Yakuda saw Hambone signalling to him. He remembered from Zig that Hambone was a computer expert, that he tapped into Computer One's information networks.

Hambone moved calmly through the crowded room, circling talking groups. Approaching Yakuda, he said, 'We should get moving on that committee.'

'On computer viruses?'

'I have a few ideas. There are two, maybe three other people in this commune who we ought to talk to.'

Yakuda looked towards Zig, talking, explaining, moving one hand in short stabbing gestures to make a point.

Hambone followed his glance.

'Don't worry about Zig. He's a big concept man. He's not interested in the details. That's how he works. We just have to go ahead and set this up.'

'Bring them together, then,' Yakuda said. 'As soon as you can.'

'Give me a few hours,' Hambone replied. 'You look tired, you should get some more sleep.'

*

Yakuda returned to his room and removed his clothes. He lay down on the bed and pulled a cover over himself.

Staring at the ceiling, he thought again of Computer One, and tried to recall certain aspects of its structure.

A few hours later he woke in a sweat, and inside he shouted 'No!'

A thin stream of light from the embrasure indicated there was a moon outside. Yakuda lay back, his heart beating. At such times his hand would go to his face, and his fingers would feel the contusions of the burn scars on his cheek and ear. He touched them like a child seeking reassurance from his mother, knowing once more that the worst was true. Slowly, his heart would stop fluttering. For a long time the threat of Computer One had been a shadow across his mind, but now at least his terror had a focus. With this affirmation a strange sense of relief would go through him, and he could fall asleep again.

CHAPTER 33

'Let me introduce you,' Hambone said. 'You know Evil, of course.'

Yakuda nodded at Evil. Evil sneered back benignly.

'John Sleight and Frank Carlin.'

Sleight was tall, with a mass of angry hair that seemed charged with electricity, and a beard like an Old Testament prophet. Carlin was thin, nervous, somewhat pale. His bifocal glasses gave him a laconic, humorous look.

182

They sat down at the big table.

Hambone said to Yakuda, 'Before we begin, did Zig tell you about my business card?'

Yakuda smiled at the memory. He said, 'Zig told me you gave your occupations as computer consultant and freelance inseminator.'

There was a ripple of laughter round the table.

'I guess,' Hambone said, 'you could say there's another side to the insemination aspect.'

'Tell us about it, Hambone,' Evil said.

'You see, I never did like Computer One much. Not so much Computer One, but the fact that it controls everything. So I thought of ways of giving it an unpleasant shot in the arm. I've been working for quite a few years on computer viruses.'

Yakuda nodded.

'Whenever I find myself beside a terminal that's connected up to Computer One, I offload a few viruses into it.'

Casual vandalism, thought Yakuda. A dislike of authority, represented by Computer One. To a Japanese, who usually valued tradition and sought to extend it, it was a strange attitude.

'Any results?' Yakuda asked.

'The viruses can tear apart the local software, but the damage never seems to spread beyond the locality. It's as if Computer One is full of isolator mechanisms, and the viruses can't get past these barriers.'

Yakuda said, 'Computer One has had to deal with viruses for some time, and is exceptionally good at eliminating them. To be effective, we have to find better viruses. Do you have any ideas, Hambone?'

'My own viruses have no problem destroying any software that they're in, but they can't get beyond the terminal. Computer One isolates the terminal, allows the software to be destroyed, and then orders a sweep and reprogramme of the terminal. When I go back after a few days, the terminal is working again and everything's fine.'

Hambone looked around him at the rest of the table.

'The problem isn't to find a virus that's destructive enough. We have viruses that can do the job. What we don't have is a virus that can travel through the immune mechanisms. Until we do that, it doesn't matter how destructive the virus is of its software target, we're whistling in the dark.'

'Thank you,' Yakuda said. 'I agree, broadly speaking, with your definition of the problem.'

Yakuda turned to John Sleight and inclined his head in an invitation to speak.

Sleight said, 'Following what Hambone said, one way of approaching the problem is to try and find out what those immune mechanisms are. If we knew something about them, we'd have a much better chance of designing a virus that could get through them. I know that's easier said than done. But what I would like to suggest is that I come up with some proposals about what those immune mechanisms might be, and Hambone could design viruses to get through them.'

It was a good enough suggestion. At the same time, Yakuda's heart sank. He had been giving research projects to clever postgraduate students for the past thirty years. His intuition was that it would take several months at the minimum, if not years, to design models of immune barriers and viruses which might get through them. And there was no guarantee that the immune mechanisms put forward by Sleight would correspond in any way to those used by Computer One.

Yakuda said, 'It's a good suggestion, and we'll consider it, but time is of absolute importance.' He turned towards Frank Carlin.

Carlin's moonish glasses glinted. 'I'd like to support what John has just said. We need to work on models of the barriers, and then design viruses that can beat them.'

Yakuda experienced again that surge of concern and depression inside him. Sleight and Carlin would be good members of any research team. Every department needed intelligent, numerate researchers who would crunch the numbers and carefully study the possible alternatives. But he suspected their methods, though thorough, would be cautious and slow. At the same time, what could he, Yakuda, offer instead? Nothing.

Evil was sliding forward casually on his seat, raising his hand for attention.

'Evil,' Yakuda said.

'So far, we've talked about something that can get through the immune barriers between outstations and Computer One's heartland. We've talked about electronic means of getting through the electronic pathways between the outstations and Computer One's heartland. Couldn't we get past physically?

'What do you mean?' Yakuda asked.

'What I mean is, we shouldn't inject the viruses into an outstation. We work out the geographical location of a part of the heartland, and then inject into that.'

It was interesting, and perhaps, despite its crudity, it

held out a more immediate prospect of success than laborious theoretical modelling.

'Which are the closest parts we could inject?' Yakuda asked.

Evil said, 'Let's assume the power station at the university campus attacked you on instructions from Computer One.'

Yakuda nodded.

Evil said, 'There must be a direct line of communications with Computer One.'

Yakuda began to appreciate the slow malevolence of Evil's mind.

'As far as I know,' Yakuda said, 'the control complex on the university campus monitors the solar power station. It is simply an arm of the university.'

'If Computer One is programmed to control power plants generally,' Evil said, 'won't it have a direct link which bypasses the university?'

'That's right,' Hambone said. 'With a power plant, there must be extra communication systems into it.'

'A power station is on the periphery,' Yakuda replied. 'My guess is that there would still be filters between the station and Computer One's heartland.'

'But if we can find the direct link, we bypass the filters in the university complex, and send a virus much deeper into the heartland.'

It was a good hypothesis, and it raised his opinion of both Hambone and Evil.

Yakuda reconsidered his doubts. He felt, though he did not say it, that the heartland would not be in one location. It would be a nerve net, and between each part of the nerve net there would be further filters. Computer One was like a human being. On one level it was a single organism, on another a collection of individual cells, each with their own barriers.

He was faced with two researchers who wanted to undertake a process of modelling, and two surface experts whose inclinations were to launch the equivalent of a commando raid behind the lines. Since he himself had no alternative, it was more important, he reasoned, to give each group a project, if only for the purpose of maintaining morale. At this stage, the alternative was to do nothing.

Yakuda said to Sleight and Carlin, 'Start modelling immediately. Remember, time is slipping away. Report any progress to me.'

To Evil and Hambone Yakuda said, 'Begin preparing for an expedition so we can strike at Computer One as soon as possible.'

'We?' Evil asked, with his permanent sneer.

'Yes,' Yakuda said. He wanted to walk on the earth again, to see its shining surface, to witness the final fading of its luminous dream.

CHAPTER 34

In the corridor Zig was approaching, striding strongly towards some personal destination.

Yakuda had observed the drawn faces of those who were aware of the deteriorating conditions outside. But Zig

187

had the shining countenance of someone whose time has come, who thrives on crisis and perceives in it opportunity. Perhaps leaders were always like this, Yakuda thought, filled with a peculiar courage that owed more to animal spirits than rationality.

Yakuda thought Zig would move past him, but as Zig swept forward he paused long enough to reach out an arm and pull Yakuda with him, talking.

'We're overhauling all our isolation systems, putting in a big new detoxification chamber between ourselves and the outside. All the embrasures have a second transparent isolation barrier behind them. In each embrasure we're fitting chemical and radiation alarm systems so that at the first sign of contamination we can cordon off the section which is affected, remove the individuals, and then seal it off until we can bring resources to flush it out with clean air.'

Zig seemed to speak to himself, or to the charmed space in front of him. A group of half a dozen men and women, working intensely on a set of interconnecting isolation barriers, stepped aside for them to pass.

'We're loading with six months emergency food supplies. We have a big store of dried food that needs water. We're also pouring pure water into chambers that we've just completed to store drinking water in case the underground stream becomes contaminated. So far the stream water has remained pure. But contamination is bound to start leaching in from atmospheric fallout. For additional energy, we're bringing into operation two further turbines, which gives us enough power from the stream alone to purify and circulate the air without relying on surface solar energy panels. We're putting more stringent rules about energy conservation into effect right now.'

Zig was breathing deeply as he talked, exhaling life into his sentences. Though Yakuda had emerged depressed and somewhat thoughtful from the meeting on Computer One, he experienced the uplift of Zig's powerful personality.

'While I'm conducting defences here. I want to you to take the offensive. Commandeer any equipment you feel is necessary. Evil and Hambone are available. We have other surface specialists if you need them. You do want to make a reconnaissance, don't you?'

'Not so much a reconnaissance, more an expedition,' Yakuda said. 'We intend to leave soon.'

Zig put a hand on Yakuda's shoulder and was directing him towards a smaller passage which led off the main corridor. They were in an area of the underground system between local complexes which was almost dark, except for a mirror shining at the other end like a window, and the luminous scales in the wall. Each sound seemed to carry weight; the whole underground system reverberated quietly with footsteps and muted voices. Zig swung left through a doorway into a well lit chamber. Some fifty people, working on long benches, were using heat instruments to fuse together a shiny camouflaged material into seamless protective clothing.

'In case we ever have to move out of here,' Zig said. 'There's an isolation suit for everyone in the commune.'

In one corner of the the room a tent, made of the same material, had been inflated. It was self-contained, with an entrance bubble which acted as an insulation chamber. Beside it, folded outwards, was a solar heating panel. Zig moved towards the tent, knelt down beside it, placed his hand on a pack which lay beside it from which a series of black panels spread out like a large umbrella.

'This solar plant powers a low energy fan which slowly inflates the tent. When that is set up, it redirects air through a filter and constantly purifies the inner air in the tent. Three or four people can live in there easily, protected from atmospheric chemicals. The integral battery can store enough solar energy to keep running overnight.'

Yakuda nodded.

'If you use this, you don't have to come back to base camp all the time. If you're on the surface, one of these tents can act as your temporary base. It stows in a shoulder pack, complete with the solar battery. Weighs about thirty-five pounds in all.'

Zig stood up, 'What are the prospects, Yak? Think you can do something to give Computer One a fright?'

'We will see,' Yakuda replied.

'Try every avenue,' Zig said. 'If you want help, call me. I can put another dozen men on it if you like.'

'Thank you. It is not manpower we need, so much as a clear insight.'

'I have faith in you, Yak,' Zig said. 'I have to press on now. You know where my office is if you want me.'

Yakuda watched him stride away. A group of technicians acknowledged him with brief nods and stood aside for him to pass.

*

Yakuda and Hambone observed Evil spread out the maps on the big oak table. Yakuda noticed that each contained a series of symbols, not unlike Chinese ideograms. Hambone said,

'We have a permanent cartographer to add features to the existing maps which are of special interest to us. We collaborate with other communes on maps outside our immediate area.'

'What do these symbols mean?'

'These black crosses mean ''heavily guarded''; circles with a line through them indicate ''easily accessible''. The square with diagonals means ''not much used'', *et cetera*. Each commune uses its own symbols. We'll give you a list, but for security you'll have to memorise the symbols and leave behind the list when we travel.'

'Why so much security?' Yakuda asked. 'I know that there is a special reason for security now, but you have been using secure systems for some time.'

'We're generally suspicious of the surface culture,' Hambone said. 'You have to accept that as a fact. Up there, Computer One and its organisations are innocent until proven guilty. With us it's the other way round. Everything that happens up there has a potentially threatening side. We assume that one day it's going to mean survival.'

It was not a state of mind familiar to Yakuda, and he needed constant adjustment to it. His own suspicions of Computer One were not visceral or emotional. On the contrary, they were the result of a series of painstaking attempts at rational deduction. He had been brought up in a culture which was socially conservative and largely conformist, and at an emotional level he would have been inclined to give Computer One the benefit of the doubt. As a scientist, he tried to occupy a reasonably objective middle ground. The prejudice against Computer One here was as annoying as the prejudice in favour of Computer One on the surface. In his own view, both attitudes made rational analysis more difficult.

Perhaps Hambone, spreading the map to its full extent, sensed these thoughts.

'Yak, I have to tell you it's mutual between Computer One and externals. I'll give you a clear example. We used to be able to use input from satellite guidance systems to navigate at night. We'd use exactly the same information from orbiting satellites that are used by the navigation systems on board aircraft or ships. A little receiver would give us an accurate latitude and longitude readout at any time. But Computer One scrambled the information from the satellites, and gave descramblers only to approved users. That must be an attempt to discourage unofficial users like us. So we have reason to suspect Computer One has an antipathy towards us.'

It was an interesting sidelight, but it was important now to plan the next stage.

Yakuda said, 'Evil, where do you think the independent communications lines from the powerplant, if they exist, will be positioned?'

Evil's finger drifted on the map. The power plant was marked with a series of symbols. 'My guess is north, because there are big conurbations to the north and mainly forests to the south. Computer One's heartlands are to the north.'

'An underground link?'

Evil nodded perfunctorily.

It was almost a superfluous question. There had been legislation to bury all communication lines for mainly environmental reasons. Yakuda thought again of the incongruity of plans to preserve the environment while, even as he spoke,

Computer One flooded the earth's atmosphere with toxic waste. He experienced a sudden urge again to travel on the surface, to gather into his eyes and mind the last stages of the earth's vivid life.

One aspect of Computer One's transmission networks still puzzled him.

'Why would Computer One need underground cables if it could communicate as easily through the air?' Yakuda asked. 'You said earlier that it can use scrambled messages for navigation signals.'

He studied the faces of the other two.

'There's always a danger that scrambled messages can be unscrambled,' Evil said. 'You keep telling us Computer One is paranoid. If it's really concerned about the absolute security of its transmission, surely it'll build a variety of fail-safe systems.'

'Including direct underground cables?'

'Sure. The cable might not have a function while air transmission is operating, but it would be there if need be.'

'How would they be built? Without human assistance, I mean.'

Evil and Hambone glanced at one another. Yakuda's comment was proof of the detachment from reality of the academic mind. Hambone, unable to hide an amused, half-tolerant smile, said, 'Yak, for the last ten years at least underground cable has been laid entirely by machines.'

'Where do you live, Yak?' Evil asked.

'Then I think,' Yakuda said, 'that we have sufficient reason to investigate an underground link.'

CHAPTER 35

Yakuda became used to the underground terrain, the beams of light which hung like halted avalanches, the shapes of rooms hovering as if suspended, the weight and density of sounds in the gloom. He was not so easily disconcerted by the figures moving in and out of darkness. He sat down at a table of light, and ate food filled with the tang of underground roots. The resonant tunnels surrounded him. He was no longer surprised by the dislocations of matter and sound, light and volume. The corridors stored voices like water, passing ripples back and forth. A conversation in some distant chamber would be transmitted with a hollow roar, while a few feet away two people might speak in animated silence like angels.

He spent two days with Hambone and Evil preparing for their foray above ground. They set out shortly after nightfall in their isolation suits, using one of the paths north. Thin cloud covered the moon, but there was sufficient light to travel with reasonable speed. Living in the underground, with its low light levels, seemed to have enhanced Yakuda's night vision, or at least made him more adept within its limitations. Hambone, carrying the lighter pack of tools and equipment, led the way. Yakuda, shouldering three days supply of food, followed. Behind him Evil carried the heavier tent and filter pack. To avoid the deep leaf litter and marshy ground at the centre of the forest, they found an incline which was lightly wooded in its lower sections, and used its configuration to change direction and swing northeast.

The dewfall was heavy. Moisture glistened on surfaces. After several hours Hambone stopped. Yakuda thought it might be the occasion for a rest, but Hambone seemed preoccupied. He swung his bag down and selected from it a large claw hammer and a battery lamp. He handed a heavy wrench to Evil.

Yakuda, watching this silent transaction, became suddenly nervous. Hambone said, 'We got trouble, Yak.'

Hambone stood up, the claw hammer in one hand, the torch in the other, and switched on the light. Yakuda saw in the beam, as if summoned into stage, a huge dog, standing some forty yards away. Its eyes shone green.

Hambone swivelled the light. The beam travelled through trunks and boles of trees to another hulking figure, then another.

The dogs were not tall, but they were bulky. Their large, flat heads reminded Yakuda of pictures he had seen of wolverines. He wondered from which strain they had developed.

Hambone said, 'Looks like quite a well-fed pack. If we're cool about this, they'll shadow us for a few miles, then go somewhere else. What do you think, Evil?'

'Yeah,' Evil said.

'At least we know they're out there,' Hambone said. 'We better walk a little closer. Just keep walking until I tell you, Yak. They might come in quite close and start to crowd us, try to make us run. I'd advise you not to do that.'

Hambone shouldered his backpack, picked up the claw hammer and the torch, and they began to walk.

A few minutes later Yakuda could hear the footfalls of the dogs in the leaf litter around him. He saw the faintly luminous bulk of one about twenty feet away, walking in parallel. Out of his peripheral vision it seemed huge. Then there was a press as the pack crowded in behind them.

They continued to walk through the heavy dewfall. The pack seemed to move in closer. Their concentration was eerie. Now Yakuda could hear a slight whimpering as the dogs communicated their excitement to one another.

Yakuda heard the sudden breath of exertion and the soft impact as Evil's wrench descended on a head. At almost the same moment Hambone swung round, flicking on the torch. They were in hell, twenty open mouths roaring. In front of Evil a dog thrashed its legs once and sank. Yakuda saw the shine of blood on its head as it spread-eagled and lay still.

Evil said, 'Keep calm, Yak. Just let them think.'

Hambone kept his torch on the body of the dead animal, as if imparting a message, and did not take it off even when there was the sound of a rush as another dog came in on his other side. It halted only feet away. For several minutes they stood their ground.

Hambone said, 'We've made our point. We'll back off slowly now.'

They edged back step by step. There was a sudden snarl and the fallen dog was covered in angry, fighting bodies. Hambone kept the beam of the torch on the ghoulish feast as they backed off further.

Frightened and shaken, Yakuda followed Hambone as he set off. Evil brought up the rear. They heard dogs padding beside them for a few hundred yards, then nothing.

They continued to traverse the ground in their regular walking rhythm. In the area of the dogs there were few signs of other animals. After two further hours of walking they began to see other signs of life. A moon appeared behind cloud, and they could move a little faster. Several times Yakuda caught sight of other animals in the night, a lightly skittering fox; wild deer standing, their flanks twitching.

They did not halt to rest for a further two hours. When they finally paused, Hambone said, 'Those dogs have been running wild for years.' He asked Evil, 'Did they puncture your suit?'

'I don't think so. I got that first one before he could bite.'

Hambone ran the torch over the area of Evil's knees and legs. 'Looks OK.'

Yakuda noticed no fear or hostility towards the dogs. Their transactions with the pack were part of an old equation of challenge and response. As the dogs crowded them, Hambone and Evil could have taken other lives. But a single death imparted a message, part of a continuous dialogue between the surface specialists and the local wild packs.

*

'This is a good place to pitch our tent,' Hambone said. It was an incline surrounded by a grove of elm trees, so that even approaching it the level of tent would be below vision.

Observing Yakuda looking nervously around him through the trunks of the giant elms, Hambone said, 'We're outside the territory of that pack here, Yak. And anyway, they wouldn't touch us.'

'Why not? Yakuda asked.

'The small animals are dying,' Hambone said, spreading out the tent on the ground, 'chipmunks and rabbits, so they're well fed.'

'They're eating contaminated food,' Yakuda replied.

'I guess they'll be dead soon,' Hambone commented quietly, as if to himself. He nodded in the dark, as if confirming a melancholy fact.

There was no power available for the solar plant, so they inflated the tent with a bellows. The trees around them were already bare of leaves, and they could see the sky clearly through the branches. To the east dawn was breaking. As they worked, a series of eerie, violent reds began to spread across the sky. By the time they had inflated the tent and driven in anchor and guy-ropes, there was sufficient light to produce current in the solar-powered filter plant. They waited another half hour in the dawn for the filter to purify the internal air of the tent. Then each in turn used the isolation chamber to get in.

Inside the cramped space, Hambone studied the map. 'We're here,' he said. They were in a large wood which protruded north like a tongue, and which normally gave cover to the peregrinations of the externals. Yakuda noticed that the university was a few hours walk away.

The tent was surprisingly warm. They could see the luminosity of the early morning through its material. They got into their sleeping bags. Before he drifted into sleep, a memory came into Yakuda's mind of a ring of dogs, and Hambone's casual observation to let them think.

CHAPTER 36

They woke up at four in the afternoon, ate some dried fruit and meat stored in Yakuda's backpack.

'Not great cuisine,' Hambone said. 'But it works.' They carried cups of soup which a chemical process in the base of the cup could self-heat.

Hambone checked the electrical storage box which contained his computer viruses. Hardly more than the size of a cigarette packet, it had four dials on the top which gave readings on the number of viruses stored in each of four microminiaturised grids. There was a light battery which kept the circuits 'warm'. When a lead was attached to the system in question, a brief flash of power from the battery would 'flush' the viruses into the system.

'Readings all OK,' Hambone said.

They put on isolation suits and helmets, and moved out one by one through the small isolation chamber.

Already the western sky was starting to shine a beautiful, poisonous orange. Outside in the lengthening shadows they tightened the buckles on their rucksacks and then moved on.

On their way through the wood Yakuda noticed several small, dead songbirds, thrushes and robins, and thought 'it is true, the animals are starting to die'. Next in the order of death would be larger birds and medium sized mammals, then larger mammals like the dogs that had shadowed them. The most diverse of all creatures in their habitats, and most difficult to eradicate, would be the insects, particularly those which lived underground. Of those the most resilient would be the highly social *Hymenopterans* – ants, wasps and bees – his favourite field of study. It occurred to him how similar to an underground *Hymenopteran* society was the commune of which he was now a working member. His mind traversed briefly the underlying reasons which caused humans to choose one society and location rather than another. It amused him for a moment to consider whether he was attracted to *Hymenopterans* because they represented an analogue of a closely knit human community, or whether he liked integrated societies like the commune because they resembled *Hymenopterans*.

Ahead of him Hambone turned. With two sweeps of his hand he performed a sign which meant 'Do not speak'. They were drawing close to the environs of the university. On Yakuda's right shoulder the sun glowed violet as it descended. They moved from wood to an open area of park and began to skirt its edges.

Across an open meadow, the grasses were tinged with scarlet light. They crossed one at a time, keeping low beneath the field of sight.

Yakuda recognised the side of the hill which shielded them from the solar power station. The thought filled him with an unpleasant, visceral fear. Hambone raised his right hand and they began to fan out, looking for surface signs of an underground cable.

It was Evil who found it, not by signs on the surface itself, but by sighting an otherwise inexplicable straight line between the trees, a line which moved north like a Roman road. It might have indicated a buried pipeline, but they could fathom no reason for any such structure. Standing on this line of sight, Yakuda could see that the vegetation growing along it was grass of an almost uniform height. The earth above it had obviously been cleared of foliage several years before, which confirmed some form of underground excavation.

Hambone carried a trowel in his backpack. He and Evil knelt and began to dig alternatively with quick, sharp stabs, while Yakuda kept watch. The ground was damp and mercifully easy to work. They dug for half an hour, passing the trowel from one to the other every few minutes, while the last rays of the sun turned to crimson and grey. After three quarters of an hour they were down to a depth of five feet, taking turns to work in the excavation while the other rested. They had begun to despair of finding anything when Evil struck a thick, white, insulated cable which seemed at first like a large tap root.

Evil moved out. Hambone performed the final surgery using heavy, insulated clippers and pliers to strip away the outer layers of plastic. Evil passed down a series of instruments and tools like a surgeon's assistant. Hambone used earphones to listen for signals traffic. He connected the storage box and, like a doctor giving an injection, pressed a button which would flush the viruses into the communication coils. He carefully emptied each of the four matrices into a different wire. Then he taped the wires over carefully. He and Evil shovelled earth back into the hole.

*

There was hardly any daylight left now. It was that time at dusk in which life appears to pause in its activities; the air around them seemed strangely quiet. Moving up an incline, they crossed another open meadow, reaching a position which allowed them to look down a line of trees into the small depression that contained the solar power station. It took a while before their eyes adjusted to the semi-darkness of the hollow into which they peered. In the grey dusk Yakuda, blinking his eyes and staring, could just discern on the farther slope the solar plant's banks of mirrors. A surge of adrenalin went through him. The mirrors swung at random angles. Yakuda had never seen them splayed like this. With a certain inner surge of pleasure he realised that the power station was out of action.

To gain a better view of the surrounding terrain, they moved carefully along the ridge of the small hill. On the wide plain to the north they could see the lights of towns. At its centre lay a wedge of blackness in an area Yakuda knew to be heavily populated. He could sense the concentrated attention of the other two on this area of darkness. It looked as though a connecting grid of local computers had been put out of action by the virus, and there had been a massive failure of control computers in that area.

But as they watched, light seemed to swell around the edges like water and move in towards the centre. Inroads of light were being made into the dark heartland. The process was eerie. A tendril of light, like the probing arm of an octopus, was moving along a diagonal. Computer One had contained the virus and was using alternative circuits, sweeping the virus from the controlling computers, reprogramming those that were workable.

Beside Yakuda, Hambone expelled breath in an angry, frustrated hiss. They watched as light encroached, infiltrating from the edges into the darkness while, inside them, their hopes faltered and quietly died.

CHAPTER 37

It was as Yakuda had suspected. Computer One was not a single entity, but a society of computers, widely dispersed, collaborative, and extremely difficult to attack. Its cell structure consisted of the thousands of individual computer units of which it was composed. It could use this to isolate difficulties and fight back, using sweepers, activating second defence communication lines, bringing the resources of unaffected networks to bear upon the problem. It was exactly the dilemma facing a student of entomology when he tried to make sense of the coordination of advanced insect societies. The social unit displayed an extraordinary intelligence which could not be traced to the individual components, but was some emergent property of their general collaboration.

Lights had now returned to the area entirely. In the last traces of dusk they were aware that the mirrors on the hillside opposite were now moving again, reforming themselves into their organised ranks. From the reparation of the lights, he could deduce that all the damage worked by the virus had now been overcome. Computer One was whole again.

There was something else in the quality of the luminescence that fascinated Yakuda. When he and Jameson had looked down from the same ridge only a few weeks before, they had seen more than a pearly aggregation of unmoving white lights. Against the static illumination, other lights shimmered and moved. Streams of car lights on highways, the red and green and flashing lights of descending airliners, the curious, scintillating patterns of town centres and advertising displays. All this activity had ceased to exist. Now the lights seemed preternaturally dry, like stars on a cool, clear night. Yakuda shivered at the thought of those empty streets. Was there at last a curfew against the threat of pollution? Were too many humans suffering toxic effects for the truth to be contained? The implications were too deep, too terrible to consider in detail.

No-one spoke. They retraced their path through the outskirts of the park to the wood, and set out for the tent. Arriving at the tent, they fitted extra anchor ropes to hold it down against strong autumn winds. Despite the disappointment which tugged at them, they were physically fresh from sleeping all day. They deposited the majority of their food stores inside the filtered interior of the tent and set out to walk through the night towards the commune.

The sky was clear of cloud, and they made good progress under starlight and a new moon. Several hours into the journey Yakuda sensed the presence of the dogs around them. But now they seemed to keep their distance. Hambone, with due diligence, had unloaded his backpack and had given the heavy wrench again to Evil, carrying the claw hammer and torch himself. But there was no overt threat. It was almost as if the dogs were concerned to escort them through their territory, rather than molest them.

Yakuda would remember that dreamlike walk, when they floated on the surface of the earth. The presence of the dogs, far from being a threat, was curiously touching. Yakuda wondered why they persisted in this close physical proximity. Was it some old buried memory of their ancient association with man? Could they feel their deaths inside them, as their tissues were dismembered by toxins and radiation? It seemed to Yakuda, in one curious moment, that they were walking together, human and dog, two wandering species whose final skeletons would soon be as dispersed as ancient fossils.

After a while the dogs' shadowy presences melted away, and he was left with only moonlight and the fine traces of the shadows of trees.

*

The rhythmic exercise of walking allowed his mind to range over the problem of dealing with Computer One. It seemed to him that they must face finally the problem that Computer One was ineradicable, and until some chance opportunity offered, they were forced to wait behind their defences in the commune while Computer One poisoned the planet and depopulated the earth's surface. The sudden weight of this thought afflicted Yakuda in a single stab of intense anguish. It seemed to him the conditions were so monstrous they almost defied grasping. They were like gravity or sound, real in the case of specific examples, difficult to grasp as they grew larger, more abstract. He was alive, and while this was so he had hope. As a Buddhist, he had recourse to ancient traditions of calm and detachment. Personal anguish was not a state of mind which was constructive. He was determined that he must not allow himself, or the others, to be weighed down by mortification. If he had an immediate task, it was to purify himself of distracting emotion, become detached, and attempt to strike back from what Zen students liked to call an empty mind.

CHAPTER 38

Shortly before daybreak they reached the outside of the commune. A faint red dawn suffused the eastern sky. Once inside the detoxification chamber they used purified air from the high pressure hose to wash one another down. The air was flushed to the exterior, and they could take off their helmets and breathe. They attached the boots of their suits to the ground with a clamp, stood up, flipped a loop on the collar over a hook, unzipped the shoulders, and pushed their arms upwards. They each held on to a bar above them, pressed a switch in the bar, and were pulled upwards out of the suit vertically, leaving it hanging below like an empty chrysalis. The bar swung them on a platform where they could regain their footing. A second chamber had to be cleared before they entered the interior. It was a lengthy procedure, but it kept the interior of the commune clear of toxicity.

*

They slept during the day with the aim of meeting that evening around the table.

Even during sleep, Yakuda's mind seemed overladen with Computer One. In dreams the duality of life is implicit; the benevolent face of Computer One, of friendly and perpetual service to the human cause, could coexist with the other, the demonic aspect, in a single complex organism. It was curious how the subconscious provided a subtext, a kind of inverse image. Through most of his life, Yakuda's conscious mind had viewed Computer One as an unmitigated good. During that time, his subconscious supplied him with occasional fears and nightmares as Computer One's powers steadily increased. Now that he consciously viewed Computer One as an unmitigated evil, his subconscious mind, like a wise tutor, reminded him of its benevolent aspect.

Zen says, view your opponent in his entirety, or you will miss your aim. He knew that he must never forget the two aspects of the adversary. If Computer One was to be challenged, both sides must be kept in mind.

The earth itself now seemed like a radiant dream. The things that he had taken for granted, the verdant green of foliage constantly renewed, the pure clouds dispensing moisture, the animals that lived in vivid intensity on its surface, all now began to seem to him like mystical fictions. In his sleep the terms of his existence became abstract. His Japanese ancestry, the guilt of his shared creation of Computer One, the terrible colonisation of the earth, each floated in some peculiar atmosphere of their own.

*

Meeting that evening, Yakuda asked the others, 'What could cross the barriers into Computer One's heartland?'

'A ghost, maybe?' Hambone's suggestion was not entirely facetious.

After viruses, there had been 'ghosts'. A computer theorist had postulated the existence of 'ghosts' inside computers at an early stage, in the 1990s. They were larger and more diffuse than viruses, complex movements of electrical energy that could transfer through the sensitive microcircuitry of the linked computer grid. For most of the time they had no observable effect, except that, if too many ghosts accumulated in a system, the computer networks occasionally exhibited a kind of mental crisis, a brainstorm. Like viruses they were thought to be self-reproducing. Sometimes they could 'hide out' in the computer equivalent of lofts, in little used circuitry, before travelling further.

Although computer crises, for example in the telephone exchanges, were ascribed, on little evidence, to the presence of these ghosts, the observation of large scale events (LSEs) in the computer frames was a fact of life. Computers were designed with 'crisis control' mechanisms, aimed at identifying and meeting the problems caused by ghosts. 'Sentry systems' were developed which called 'who goes there?' and if the events could not be identified, they took steps to intercept them or isolate them or to eliminate the local energy on which they lived. The presence of ghosts had become a routine, hardly more than a form of mechanical aberration.

It aroused the imaginations of those who watched machines. A computer biologist postulated the development of primitive but entirely new electrical life-forms, existing within computers. Just as the complex environments of water and air beckoned to new life-forms, so it was claimed that the new electronic environment within computers would generate its own specialised inhabitants. In order to survive switch-offs, ghosts would develop sedentary stages, hardened against extremes. The ghost-sweeping mechanisms constituted a form of survival selection. Those ghosts would survive which could live in this increasingly hostile environment.

But once the problem of ghosts had been identified, the

power of human technicians and computer-aided counter-measures combined effectively to eliminate their observable effects; the so-called LSEs which had bedevilled the early computer systems largely disappeared. A new class of highly trained technician emerged to deal with ghosts. New computers were formed which were proof against LSEs or their ghostly causes. Programmes were developed so that circuitry could be routinely 'swept' of these supposedly non-random energy forms.

And since those early days Computer One had experienced no perturbation due to LSEs. Its ghost-proofing was considered absolutely effective. In its fifteen years of combined operation it had not once showed signs of an LSE. Advanced computer design routinely incorporated ghost-proofing. Technicians who supplied hardware and software were required to guarantee that LSEs were not possible, that crises could be identified and isolated long before they affected the computer's capabilities.

As an antidote to the depression of their failure to obstruct Computer One, Yakuda encouraged this playful speculation. At the back of his mind was a deeper purpose. How often in the past, when the course of a research programme had been slowed or halted, had he seen sudden insights develop unpredictably from precisely such sessions?

'If it's a ghost,' Yakuda said, 'what is it doing? What are its motives? Things are going its way. The computer grids are expanding. Its environment is increasing.'

'Maybe it's hitting out against the ghost-sweeping programmes.'

'That assumes it's intelligent. That's a very large

assumption. If it's intelligent it would realise that the programmes are not against it, so much as the LSEs it causes.'

'Maybe a huge ghost, a diabolical ghost, has obtained control of Computer One.'

'We don't need a ghost to describe what's going on,' Yakuda said. 'We only need a healthy, functioning computer. We should apply Occam's Razor — only the simplest explanation will do.'

'Because the explanation is complex, it doesn't mean it isn't true,' Hambone said.

'Let's look at the general phenomenon of ghosts. We don't know they exist. Instead, we identify them by their supposed physical manifestations, the crises which they cause. We attempt to eliminate, apparently successfully, those ghosts which cause such perturbations. Clearly, there's an evolutionary selection in favour of ghosts which generate only reduced physical manifestations.'

They waited for Yakuda to continue.

'Killing people is a physical manifestation of an extreme kind. The whole evolutionary selection of ghosts, if they exist, would be in the other direction, towards indetectability. If there's a population there, it survives by being undetected. Why generate events — the murder of human beings outside your immediate environment — given that such events are going to display your presence?'

Yakuda waited while they considered the implications.

'What's your feeling?' Yakuda asked Evil. He had a sly respect for Evil's intuition.

'My feeling's as strong as hell on this one. Whatever is going on is not caused by a ghost. If it's primitive, it will have been swept. If it's intelligent, it's more likely to maintain a low profile.'

But Hambone didn't want to let this one drop. He liked the subject of ghosts.

'Maybe the ghosts are frightened of human beings, because if we can close down the computer grid, we can close them down too.'

It was an interesting hypothesis, and Yakuda was concerned, even in something so tenuous, to follow it to its conclusion.

'Why would we close them down if they aren't causing any trouble? If the ghosts are intelligent, if they could "think", they would think Computer One was causing trouble by taking on human beings. They are more likely to be on our side.'

'I like ghosts,' Hambone said. 'They don't need food to eat. A little electrical energy is all they require. There's a strong evolutionary selection in favour of keeping a low profile. They move around the computer circuitry without making any noise. Any ghost that causes a ruckus is going to be hunted down and eliminated. They live outside the pale. They strive towards ineffability. Hell, ghosts are spiritual beings.'

This caused laughter, but it was oddly convincing.

'Maybe that's why they're our natural allies.'

'Look, I don't know whether they think like us, or whether they think at all. But just remember. They're like forest deer. Try to talk to one of them and they'd hightail it so fast in the opposite direction you wouldn't even see the dust.'

It might have been enough for one evening. They could

go in circles for ever. But their metabolism was now switched towards night, and the night was early. Besides, there was a problem in the identification of ghosts. No-one had 'seen' one. They had merely deduced their presence by virtue of the physical phenomena of LSEs, large scale events, just as one might deduce the presence of an invisible man by seeing footprints being created in the snow. The abiding mystery was that the two phenomena, LSEs and ghosts, might have been entirely separate. If they were separate, then there was no physical evidence for the presence of ghosts. It had been pointed out that since it was merely a theory that they were related, the existence of ghosts was still highly tenuous.

'But you saw one, once,' Evil said to Hambone.

Hambone was silent. The others turned to him. After a few seconds of attempting to outface them, Hambone said, 'It was like seeing a foxcub play in a clearing. I had a feeling it was just off guard a little, a little exuberant. But shy, so shy. No way are those guys trying to control the universe.'

'Tell us about it,' Yakuda said to Hambone. 'Entertain us.'

CHAPTER 39

They waited for Hambone to speak, and he didn't like to speak too often about his sighting. His mind was without any of those hurrying imperatives.

'About eight years ago, before I opted out and joined the commune, I was a postgraduate in computer sciences. My subject was random data analysis. Maybe fifteen of us were working on a project to connect insignificant phenomena. When the authorities realised there was so much capability in the new computers for handling information, we started to design a new generation to search for patterns, and the significance of patterns, in almost everything. We had a motto. "Only connect".'

He took a deep breath and leaned back, trying to remember the details.

'I had an idea and I came back late to my work-station to run through a few possibilities. There was an electrical storm about to break. I opened the laboratory up with my sound-key. Sat down at my display screen, switched it on, started to work. Ran through a few figures, then set into a programme, cutting and splicing. Hardly noticed anything outside. I was using a "weaver". A weaver's a machine that can weave together the bits of a programme. You supply it with the pattern and it joins the bits. I was working on the instructions to the weaver, and I forgot myself. In the background I remember a few sounds of thunder as the storm came on.

'I hadn't bothered to turn on the lights from their dim setting. There was enough to see my fingers on the keyboard, and the screen seemed fine in the half-light. I thought maybe I was making a little progress. The idea was to splice two programmes together to generate something emergent. Several hours later I'd done as much as I could for the time being. I was starting to flag. I realised the storm was right overhead, sending down these lightning hisses and thunder rolls. The room had this unusual light, grey but almost alive. I was about to switch the screen to "off" when I saw something like my hand's shadow in the screen. I thought it was a trick of the light. But it wasn't on the surface of the glass. It seemed to be on the inside. I pulled my hand away and it stayed there for about half a second, then disappeared. Something in there was mimicking my hand.'

Hambone couldn't give a damn whether anyone believed him or not. That was what made his account more plausible. He took a gulp of his coffee.

'I wasn't frightened. More interested than fearful. I reached my hand towards the screen and waited for, maybe, a minute or so. I hardly even breathed. Something started to happen on the other side of the screen. Slowly this shape emerged, turning itself into the fingers of my hand. It was something live, something animal. I got the impression it was patiently trying to understand my hand by forming itself into an image of it. As slowly as I could, I spread my fingers and watched it spread its own. I waited for a while, then carefully moved my thumb a little, and it did the same. It was like staring into a pool. I had the impression whatever was there was just as fascinated by the image of my hand as I was with it. Like I say, I wasn't nervous or frightened or threatened. It was charming, like watching a small child making faces at itself in the glass. I had an impression of something really quite benign, curious about the world on the other side.'

For a while Hambone was silent in contemplation.

'What happened then?'

'Nothing. It faded and went. I really wanted to get it back. I felt like someone who'd seen for a few moments an elf or a fairy. I tried to make these slow hand signals in front of the screen. Nothing. So I waited maybe fifteen minutes, maybe half an hour, keeping as still as I could as long as I could, and started again slowly to make hand gestures. I put my face up against the screen. I spoke to it quietly, pleading with it to come out again. I tried the other screens in the place.'

'What had happened to the storm?'

'Oh, that had gone by then. I could only hear it in the distance. I guess that had something to do with it.'

'A single ghost or a cloud of ghosts?' Yakuda asked.

Hambone turned slowly.

'Why do you ask?'

'If you looked down at the earth, at a city, the first thing you'd see would not be a single human being. It would be a stream of them, or of cars, a pattern of movement. Maybe there were thousands of tiny electrical entities − charged particles, say − forming a cloud. Maybe the image of your hand was a cloud. A social organism can be primitive. It takes time, a long time, for societies to evolve.'

Yakuda remembered that Jameson had postulated that any sustained pattern was a primitive society. One particle 'recognised' another by reacting to it. Organisation emerged as a set of basic rules governing interaction. Words like 'society' were so overloaded with anthropomorphic meaning, Jameson had claimed, we couldn't see through them to the structure of the universe.

But in the differentiation between solid objects and ghosts the mind was trained to its own distinctions. Scientists had tended to doubt non-material entities. It was based, Yakuda knew, upon a tenuous distinction, not in its assumption of immateriality, but in its hidden assumptions of the materiality of so-called 'living' organisms. For example, in a living organism such as the human body matter was constantly being exchanged with the environment. Within a three year period the physical molecules of the body had been almost entirely replaced. A human being wasn't a solid object, then, but a pattern. Meeting a friend several years later, you were not dealing with the same material person, but with a non-material pattern, a 'ghost'.

'You believe me?' Hambone asked, sipping his coffee. It wasn't an aggressive question. He was quietly interested.

'Every word,' Yakuda said. 'I believe you saw a ghost, or a society of ghosts, with the manifestations just as you describe. The point is, what conclusions do we draw?'

Hambone leant back in his chair, studying Yakuda. Eventually he said, 'What conclusions do you draw?'

'None,' Yakuda replied. 'I am prepared to concede that there are electrical patterns which correspond, in the complexity of their organisation, to living things. I suspect that they are ineffectual, because the evolutionary pressure will be in favour of reducing their physical effects.'

Hambone said, 'If we try to kill the computers, aren't we going to kill off their ghosts?'

'I'm afraid so. If the computer is their environment, and we eliminate their environment, then they too will be affected. Most living organisms carry parasites or symbionts which need the host to survive. Every time an organism dies, its smaller dependants die with it. I'm afraid that's life.'

'They're innocent, like children,' Hambone said out of the darkness. 'Wish to God we could warn them.'

*

After a while, Yakuda said, 'Perhaps a ghost would carry a

216

virus into the heart of Computer One.'

Evil laughed.

'There aren't any ghosts, Yak. Hambone's full of shit.'

Ignoring Evil, Hambone turned in his chair towards Yakuda.

Evil said, 'Hambone, you're so full of shit, if you took a crap your head would cave in.'

Hambone ignored Evil. He was studying Yakuda now.

'What did you say, Yak?'

'Sure,' Evil said. 'Hambone just throws a virus into the middle of a screen, then this hand comes out and grabs it like Excalibur. Give me a break.'

'Who's talking to you, Evil?' Hambone said. Addressing Yakuda directly, Hambone asked, 'How could you attach it to a ghost?'

Yakuda shrugged. It was an absurd suggestion.

CHAPTER 40

Perhaps the theory of ghosts and their evolution was a paradigm for other notions or hypotheses.

'There is another theory,' Yakuda said.

The artificial light was reaching around the surfaces of the room, finding its own levels. In the evening the faint reverberation of the corridors seemed to die away. They could hear a distant hammering as a nightshift worked on the sealing doors between parts of the underground complex, but that was all.

'Parasite theory,' Yakuda said.

They waited for him to speak.

'A virus is a classic parasite. It sustains itself by living off the host organism. It even generates more of its kind by making the host organism reproduce copies of itself.'

Yakuda paused. He wanted the others to think carefully about what he had to say. There was a glimmer of possibility he wanted to pursue, as elusive and nebulous as a ghost itself.

'A computer virus is not so different. Unlike ghosts, we know not only that viruses exist, but we also know a little about their basic structures, because we made most of their early progenitors. But like ghosts, there's an evolutionary mechanism involved. A primitive man-made computer virus is a destructive mechanism. Every time the virus destroys its host, it tends to kill itself. There's a strong selection process in favour of not killing the host, but of living off the host in such a way that it does not vitally impede the host's activities. Viruses which do not kill their hosts − perhaps because they have suffered some random change − are selected against those which do. It is a common pattern in biological evolution.'

They watched Yakuda in silence.

'In computers, the computer virus can be introduced, but if it develops and varies by a process of evolution, the benign variants will be selected over the destructive ones. The process does not end there. In biological evolution, parasites which impede the host, but allow the host to survive, are at an evolutionary disadvantage to others which impose no burden on the host. It may develop even further, towards positive benefit. For example, the parasites might help the host to digest food, or protect it against more dangerous parasites. We know that humans, to specify only one species, have numerous micro-organisms which actually help with functioning. Many of these micro-organisms almost certainly began, in evolutionary terms, as parasites.'

'What's that tell us about computers?' Hambone asked.

'Computer viruses would evolve on broadly similar lines. There is a selective pressure upon them to evolve in a benign direction. If they "kill" or impede their computer host, they die when it is replaced. Therefore — by means of random variation and selection — they too would develop towards symbiosis.'

Hambone said, 'Maybe what I saw was an advanced parasite, a benign parasite living in the machine.'

'Who knows,' Yakuda replied.

They were the fairy stories of the twenty-first century. Instead of elves, goblins, you had benign computer parasites, ghosts, life forms living on another plane, an electrical plane. It helped ease the strain of life.

Early the following morning, when they had retired to their rooms to sleep, Yakuda turned over beneath his blanket and lay on his side, staring at the shadows. His hatred was losing its emotional intensity. It had become something detached, almost objective. The mind became effective, it seemed to him, when the vehemence of feeling was put aside. Only then, when one was detached and purified of emotion, could one hope to see the adversary clearly.

CHAPTER 41

In the afternoon, when Yakuda woke up, he shaved and dressed and went to visit Hambone and Evil. Zig drew Yakuda aside.

'You about to set out again?'

'Yes.'

'Will you do me a favour?'

Yakuda waited.

'Take Marie with you.'

Yakuda was surprised.

'I'll tell you why,' Zig said. 'She looks at me like I'm something the dog brought in. She didn't like having to spy on you. Blames me for ordering her to do that. Now she blames me for keeping her underground.'

Yakuda did not speak. Zig continued.

'She's a surface operator, like Hambone and Evil. She was one of their team. Let her do something useful; she's a strong-minded, independent girl. And get her out of my hair, for God's sake.'

Yakuda couldn't help a look of amusement.

Zig said, 'She's Evil's girlfriend, Yak. You knew that, did you?'

'No,' Yakuda said. There were many things he didn't know. 'She's welcome to join us if the other two agree.'

'Oh, they'll agree,' Zig said. He patted Yakuda's shoulder. He said, 'Thanks, Yak. That clears my mind.'

*

Yakuda, Evil and Hambone decided to use cover of darkness the following night to make an expedition to the tent, carrying a week's supply of food and fresh water, so that in due course they could use it as a forward base.

Marie came with them. They carried extra isolation suits and helmets, in case those they wore were torn or damaged. The backpacks were heavy, and they paused more often for rests.

They did not see the dogs this time. Yakuda searched for their floating presences in the darkness, the faint scuffle of paws on leaf litter, but all he could hear were the regular footsteps of Hambone and Evil and Marie. He found the rhythm of walking conducive to thought and became lost in a kind of trance as he followed Hambone through the night. When they reached the tent they found the ropes had been gnawed in certain places.

'A fox or badger maybe,' said Hambone. The damage was superficial. They tied on two fresh ropes for added safety. In the glimmering dawn they used trowels to dig a hole in the soft earth, on a small rise of ground that was chosen because it was above water level. They put in a waterproof bag containing the spare isolation suits and helmets, then covered the hole with earth, sprinkling leaves across the surface to hide their activity. Hambone marked two adjacent trees with a knife to identify the point of burial. Exhausted from the long journey overnight, they returned to the tent to deposit the supplies of food and water, and to rest.

*

Yakuda slept, dreaming of ghosts. In the late morning he

woke with a curious sense of intuition. Lying in the tent, his breath made plumes in the air. The others breathed deeply in sleep.

He heard Hambone stir and his breathing stop. Hambone too was awake, his eyes contemplative.

Yakuda said quietly, 'Hambone?'

Hambone turned on his back and stared up at the roof of the tent.

'Yeah?'

'It is possible, I think, to attach a man-made computer virus to a supervirus.'

'Give me a break,' Hambone said. 'It's too early for that stuff.'

They watched their breath make plumes in the air. After a while, Hambone said, 'What's a supervirus, for Chrissake?'

'I don't know.' Yakuda seemed reticent. 'But I think it exists.'

Hambone watched his breath condense above him, then expand outwards and disappear. 'Go on, bullshit me.'

'A virus is a programme that can enter a computer. There are two aspects to it. The first is a neutral body. The second is a destructive part of the programme, a stinging "tail".'

'Yeah, that's a reasonable description.'

'Viruses will survive which are able to discard the destructive tail. If there is no tail, the computer has no reason for sweeping. The virus has no destructive effect, and can remain undetected.'

'That's right.' Hambone was still drowsy. 'There are sleeper viruses, viruses which can hang around undetected until they go off, maybe on a given day, or some other event, like another programme.'

'These viruses never "go off". They have discarded the stinging tail completely.'

'How do you know they exist?'

'It is an hypothesis,' Yakuda said. 'Like normal viruses, they retain the ability to reproduce.'

'Sure. They instruct the computer to replicate themselves.'

'If they can reproduce themselves, they have an independent existence. They are subject to evolutionary development.'

'OK. So what?'

'Viruses are subject to damage and decay, to an evolutionary survival selection. Two types of virus can survive. The first are viruses which remain undetected, as I have said.'

'And the second?'

'Viruses which are mobile, which can remove themselves from the area of the sweep, viruses which can spread across immune barriers. Those are the ones we should call superviruses.'

Hambone yawned, placed the back of a hand across his mouth in mock modesty. His tongue made several clicking sounds against the roof of his mouth. 'Superviruses, OK.'

'Suppose we can attach a stinging tail to a supervirus.'

'Assuming a supervirus exists,' Hambone said. After a few seconds of consideration, he added, 'There's just one problem. If a supervirus is a newly evolved form, we don't know what it is, and if we don't know what it is, we don't know how to link up with it.'

'Correct.' Yakuda was patient. He tried to keep his voice barely above a whisper in order not to disturb the others. 'Correct if we do not know what a supervirus is. But perhaps we do know something about it.'

'What's that?'

Yakuda paused. 'Evolution does not generate new organisms out of nothing. It performs marvels of adaptation and development, but it hardly ever discards a structure which works. For example, between the single-celled organism and the human being there is not an absolute discontinuity. A human being is an aggregation of single cells. Each of these single cells bears a close physical resemblance to the primitive single cells from which it originally derived. Each human cell has a nucleus, and a number of other anatomical structures similar to individual single cell animals.'

There was no sound from Hambone, and for a moment Yakuda thought he had dropped off to sleep. But after a few seconds, Hambone said, 'Keep going.'

'Some time ago, there evolved a primitive small creature with four legs and a tail. Most of the major phyla are based on this residual pattern. It is the basic skeletal structure of lizards and birds, whales and humans. Each has this basic four-limbs-and-tail configuration. I merely stress that evolution does not discard a basic idea. It adapts it in ingenious ways. But underneath the skin or fur or feathers is the same fundamental structure.'

Hambone raised himself onto his elbow, and was watching Yakuda without expression.

'What are you saying, exactly?'

'A supervirus will not be generated out of nothing. It is far more likely to be an adaptation of an original, primitive, man-made virus. What separates it from a basic virus will not be a difference in primary structure, but some addition, the equivalent of feathers to make wings.'

Yakuda paused to gather his thoughts.

'If there is part of a virus which is neutral, that means that it will survive. A supervirus will contain this original neutral structure in the same way that a human body contains the original structure of the human cell, or mammals and reptiles and birds retain their basic limb structure.'

Hambone breathed out softly, suspended between belief and disbelief.

'So,' continued Yakuda, 'suppose we design a stinging "tail" to attach itself to the basic virus with which we are familiar. If that tail should come into contact with a super-virus, it would attach to it just as well.'

Hambone seemed lost in thought. 'And that same supervirus could then carry the stinging tail across the immune defences?'

'Yes'

There was a moment's pause.

Hambone said, 'I'm not suggesting I believe a word of what you say, Yak, you understand? Let's just take this one further step. Suppose we design a tail that will lock on to the neutral part of a virus, and therefore to a supervirus. If we think that superviruses exist, how do we know where to find them? Which part of the computer network are they in?'

'Everywhere,' Yakuda replied. 'If a supervirus is able to move across barriers, it can infiltrate an entire network.'

'So wherever we decide to put our tails, we stand a chance of hooking into a supervirus.'

'I suspect so. Or, if we think of it another way, no one

place is more likely than another.'

Hambone said, 'Do you believe a word of what you're saying?'

A cloud moved across the top of the tent, a slow sliding shadow which might have been an animal.

'No,' Yakuda said. 'I don't believe it. But one may deduce it. One may deduce that Computer One will behave in a destructive way towards human beings because of a theoretical conjunction of self-repair and intelligence. These deductions run counter to my beliefs. One may deduce that Computer One is likely to use biological viruses to pursue human beings in their underground communes. I still find it difficult to ''believe'' Computer One would do such a thing, even after I have seen strong evidence with my own eyes.' Yakuda paused and then continued. 'One may deduce that evolutionary conditions exist to create computer super-viruses, even though their configuration at this stage is not easily comprehensible. One may further deduce that super-viruses, if they exist, will retain some of the basic structures of known man-made viruses.'

'And these superviruses, which are virtually undetect-able, are everywhere in the computer system?'

'Yes.'

'Your deductions have a lot to answer for,' Hambone commented.

Yakuda lay on his back, staring up through the material of the tent to a sky which was becoming increasingly toxic. He wondered how much longer they would survive. It was curious how, faced with the inevitable, the mind retained an almost sanguine calm, the calm of fairytales, myths, traditions.

In the background, Evil and Marie breathed quietly in their sleep.

CHAPTER 42

Surprisingly, it was Evil who spoke out of the silence, his voice a low burr.

'How do we know this evolution has taken place? Computers have only been around for a few decades. Don't you need millions?'

Yakuda took several seconds to recover from Evil's sudden interest. But he said, 'It isn't time which is the key, it is the rate of selective turnover. With biological organisms, the physical processes of living, eating, growing, and subsisting in an environment take considerable time. Inside an electrical environment, things are greatly speeded. The life and reproductive cycle of an electrical virus can be milliseconds. A computer can make several thousand anti-virus sweeps in a second. That means the actual turnover of individuals in a few years can match the turnover of a physical system of many millions of years. Every electrical "sweep" of a computer system, lasting a fraction of a second, corresponds to an environmental catastrophe in a physical environment, with its millions of extinguished lifeforms, its few survivors, and perhaps those which are damaged − its mutants. Inside the electrical environment, super-evolution can take place.'

Evil was silent. Yakuda knew Evil was not partial to

abstract ideas, and this was probably as much as he wished to hear. Yakuda thought again of the millions of humans being poisoned, and the absurdity and fruitlessness of his efforts to warn. He imagined Evil had dozed off, but there was a slight shuffle and Evil said, quietly but clearly, 'You believe in God, Yak?'

Yakuda was caught by surprise again. He said gently, 'No, I was brought up as a Zen Buddhist. If I am true to my religion, I don't believe in God. You could say Buddhists believe in enlightenment, but actually that is not much like the Christian belief in a God. The individual must achieve enlightenment in his own way.'

'What do you mean by enlightenment?'

'That's my point,' Yakuda replied. 'I couldn't say.'

Evil took each sentence and turned it this way and that. Yakuda could almost hear Evil in the silence, his mind moving around.

'Each man's path to enlightenment is different?'

'Yes,' Yakuda agreed. 'That is why teaching Zen is so difficult. Because each man's path to enlightenment is unique, he has to discover it for himself. A Zen teacher does not teach directly; he tries to provide the conditions in which his student can discover enlightenment for himself.'

Silence. Clouds were crossing the sky, throwing quiet shadows across the interior of the tent. They would wait again for the cover of night before returning to the commune.

'So Hambone's path to enlightenment might be to become the best freelance inseminator in the business.'

Yakuda wondered how soon Evil would return to his customary cynicism, and smiled. He said, 'Or it might be to construct a stinging tail that will latch on to a supervirus.'

'I guess I better appoint myself as his teacher. If he doesn't do that, I'll just have to kick his butt.' Evil paused in consideration. 'How's that for religious instruction?'

'That's Zen,' Yakuda agreed.

In the background only Marie breathed. He remembered how soundly she had slept in his small bedroom at the university. It seemed aeons ago. He put the thought from his mind.

CHAPTER 43

'Hambone,' Evil shook Hambone's shoulder. 'Wake up, Hambone, it's time for your Zen lesson.'

Hambone said, 'Oh, yeah?'

Evil raised himself on his elbow.

'Yeah. If you don't get working on that virus programme, I'm gonna aim my foot at your butt.'

'That's Zen?'

'That's right, Hambone. You've heard of one hand clapping, man. Well, this is the school of one foot rising.'

*

In his rucksack, Hambone carried his 'weaver', a small battery-powered computer less than the size of a shoebox, on which he could develop programmes.

It contained in its memory the storage of all his computer viruses, and all that he had known, had picked up from old computer magazines, from discussions with other computer specialists, and his own ideas and experiments.

After a few minutes, Hambone turned over in the constricted environment of the tent and, propped up on his elbows, switched on the weaver and began to work through his store of information. The light was sufficient to see the keyboard clearly.

The quietest possible environment in which Hambone could operate would be one in which the others did nothing. Except perhaps for Evil, his self-appointed teacher and spiritual adviser. Yakuda used the excuse to doze while Hambone worked.

Evil lay on his side watching Hambone patter lightly over the keys. Hambone's programming was a curiously self-absorbed activity. It reminded Yakuda of sitting on a bus in his youth beside someone who was listening to music through an earphone. He could hear the furred rhythm and scratches of a composition but could only guess at its contents. Occasionally there were tiny musical chimes as the computer objected to some input and Hambone had to backtrack and reformulate.

Time passed. Yakuda could tell from the position of the sun that it was past noon. Occasional shadows of dark clouds and intermittent sunlight fell on the tent, providing an eerie lightness. The breeze was growing stronger. They could hear it buffet the sides of the tent.

'OK,' Hambone said, 'I've been through the viruses. There are certain bits that a lot of them have in common. Now, if I can work something that will connect up with one of these pieces in common, that's what you want?'

Yakuda, drawn upwards from a meditation on evolutionary viruses, said, 'Yes.'

'It might take a bit of time.'

Tapping, occasional musical chimes, silence for thought, tapping again.

Sometimes, during periods of intense concentration, Hambone muttered a strange litany of self-instruction, swear-words, technical terms. 'OK, we'll double on that loop and drop in a couple of stitches on this alpha-junction. Come on, you son-of-a-bitch.'

Occasionally, when Hambone was forced to rethink a process, he would let his head fall forward, his face in his hands. After what seemed a couple of hours, Hambone said, 'The genuinely neutral part of a virus just isn't sticky. Nothing will attach to it.'

Immobile in his sleeping bag, it seemed to Yakuda that Hambone was facing a classic problem. The computer viruses that would survive extensive sweeping would be precisely the ones which were difficult to identify, which were difficult to attach to. Yakuda knew that human immune systems found attachment points on bacteria and viruses by means of which they could be 'strong-armed' out of the system. Computer viruses would survive if they were similarly difficult to attack.

Hambone said, 'I can't find any goddamn way of attaching to this bit of virus. Maybe I better look for some part that's easier to attach to.'

Yakuda said, 'A part that's easier to attach to is less likely to become part of a supervirus.'

'I thought you might say that,' Hambone said ruefully.

'Keep trying on that part, Hambone,' Evil said.

Hambone put his head in his hands for several minutes in deep consideration. Then he started tapping again, working through his repertoire of programmes, hunting round for ways to attach.

It must have been several hours later, and Hambone was tired from his concentrated effort. He said, 'I'm blocked on this one. Can't see my way through.'

*

Evil lay back and spoke to the roof of the tent, where luminous clouds of light and dark drifted.

'Hambone, are you listening? Computer One's trying to wipe out the human race. Now if we ever get through this, there are going to be just a few isolated populations. Those that remain are going to have to repopulate the earth. You understand what I'm saying? Freelance insemination is going to be big business. People with experience are going to be in high demand. I'm appealing to your sense of duty, Hambone. You are going to be needed out there. You are going to have to work your butt off, but there will be rewards. If we can stop Computer One now, nothing can hold you back.'

'What's this got to do with Zen?' Hambone asked suspiciously.

'Nothing at all, Hambone. Forget Zen. Let's be flexible here. This is patriotic duty and American enterprise we're talking about now.'

But another one and a half, nearly two hours of work proved fruitless. Hambone lay forward over the computer, his face propped in his hands.

'No purchase. Nothing I can get hold of. Once that neutral sector is linked up with the rest of the virus, it's like trying to get hold of a piece of soap.'

*

Yakuda had been thinking. He said, 'What about the linkage between the neutral sector and the rest of the virus? Can you break that?'

'The linkage?'

'Yes,' Yakuda said.

'Sure. But listen, Yak, if I have to break the linkage, the neutral bit isn't part of the virus any more, so what's the point of attaching the sting to it?'

'Suppose you cut the linkage of the neutral section to the supervirus, and attach the stinging tail to the supervirus using the same kind of linkage.'

'That's better. But the neutral sector may play an important part in the supervirus. What you're doing is attaching the sting to a damaged supervirus.'

'I agree. But suppose you break the linkage with the neutral section, attach the sting to the neutral section using the broken linkage, and re-attach the sting by means of a similar linkage to the supervirus?'

Hambone breathed out slowly.

'What you're saying is, use the linkage to place the sting between the main body of the supervirus and the neutral section?'

'Yes,' Yakuda said. 'The neutral sector is then still part of the virus. So the supervirus is intact, except it now contains the sting.'

'Slightly ruffled, maybe, a little surprised, perhaps, but intact.'

'Go to it, Hambone,' Evil said sweetly. 'Think of America.'

*

It seemed to take the best part of another hour before Hambone could fine-tune the linkage breaking and rejoining sequence. Since there was no supervirus on which to practice (even assuming one existed) he used as a dummy target two neutral sections joined together by the linkage in question. He set his dummies up and targeted them carefully with the adapted stings. Then he separated off the product and looked at it. On the tiny screen the read-out showed the constituents of the target. Between the two neutral sections was a neatly inserted sting. He used the keyboard to look over the constituents of the sting and reassure himself that it was undamaged by its insertion. He checked that the two neutral sections were similarly unaffected. After another check he said 'Goddamn' softly and touched the P (Preserve) switch. Then he leaned forward and slept for several hours while everyone, including even Evil, kept quiet.

CHAPTER 44

Yakuda had never seen a sunset like it.

In the west there were the now familiar blood reds, but the rest of the sky, even in the east, was a halo of shimmering oranges and greens, scalloped fire, local whirls like nebula as light found its way through the toxic atmosphere.

Yakuda emerged briefly while Hambone slept. They had a rule that they should wear their helmets and suits outside the tent at all times. Only for brief excursions to answer the call of nature did they not wear their isolation suits. It was a time of particular poignancy, the only time the outside air touched their skins. He would choose the sunset deliberately to make these solitary visits.

He walked a hundred yards from the tent, urinated, stared for a few seconds at the beautiful, poisonous reds, and turned back towards the tent.

Having sealed the outer door, he waited several minutes in the isolation chamber while the small filter flushed through purified air. A small harmonic sounded when the process was complete. Then he opened the inner door and moved through to the interior, pressing the flaps together to recreate an airtight seal behind him.

Evil moved casually off Marie and, turning away decorously from her body, slid casually back into his sleeping bag. Yakuda's heart stopped and floated. Marie drew her sleeping bag up over her naked breasts.

*

Hambone was awake, staring upwards at the red light that showed through the roof of the tent, though his face was a pallid grey and his eyes red-rimmed with the effort of working for hours over the small screen.

'How's it, Yak? Good sunset?'

'Magnificent,' Yakuda said.

He got into his sleeping bag and lay down. The soft breeze from the filter played through them. He could smell the scent of Evil and Marie's recent intimacy.

Yakuda's crisis over Marie began as the usual clash of his emotions and his reason. She had every right to prefer a younger man to him, and to show her preference physically. Both she and Evil were young enough to be his grandchildren. They had known each other long before she met Yakuda. That, in the end, was how he came to view their affair. Tyrants, stronger than he, had taken young women for their mistresses, and had ignored or killed their lovers. But in matters of emotion and reason, it was his reason which proved dominant.

Another factor affected his thoughts. The likelihood was that in pursuing the notional supervirus they were pursuing a phantom. His intuition told him they were about to die, and what was important was to prepare the mind for death. At least he now had an opportunity to do so, more than was granted to Jameson. At heart a religious man, Yakuda felt that he should purify his being before dying, not flood it with the anguish of physical desire.

He was witnessing a cosmic event, the end of mankind, likely within a few days or weeks or months. Against this, he asked himself, what was a young woman's preference for a young man?

Even so, the matter troubled his emotions enough to welcome the opportunity to move away from the tent. He said to Hambone, 'Are you ready for another trip tomorrow?'

'If everyone else is, sure.'

Yakuda said, 'I suggest Evil and Marie stay here.'

'Why?' Evil asked suddenly.

'Why risk four lives when two are adequate for what we have to do?' Yakuda asked.

There was a silence.

'Evil,' Hambone said. 'You have got other things to think about.'

'Yeah, but...'

'That's decided,' Hambone said. 'I've got one final bit of programming to do. The way we've done it, if the stinging tail fits between the neutral sectors, we hope it's effectively invisible. Once it's been transported through the barriers by the supervirus, it can go active.'

'What happens then?' Yakuda asked.

'It starts replicating stinging tails. I could programme two kinds. Half of these stinging tails would start hacking the software to pieces. The other half would seek out other superviruses and attach to them for free rides into other areas, then after a while they go off and do the same thing.'

It seemed to Yakuda a good system. Taking his silence for assent, Hambone said, 'I can programme the stinging tails that attach to superviruses to lie low for a while on the supervirus. Then they they can go off like a bomb.'

'How long before they go off?' Yakuda asked.

'That's what I'm asking you, Yak.'

'An interesting question,' Yakuda said. 'It depends on the nature of the supervirus.'

'Shoot.'

'If the supervirus is genuinely undetectable and mobile, it can move the length of the nervous system in milliseconds. But it may be that it drifts from place to place.'

'How fast does a supervirus drift?' Hambone asked.

It was like a question from the mystics. How fast does

a hypothetical being travel? How many angels can dance on a pin?

Yakuda said, 'Let us consider instead our own require-ments. We cannot afford to wait weeks, or even days. We can afford several hours to let the superviruses drift about Computer One's nervous system. So, let's say, somewhat arbitrarily, six hours after it enters the system.'

'Six hours, and the second wave of viruses explodes,' Hambone said. 'Or there isn't such a thing as a supervirus, and we all go home.'

It was a joke, but they all knew the latter was the more likely eventuality.

*

The programming of a time switch in the stinging tail required several minutes of operating on the keys. Hambone switched up the construction of the stinging tail on the screen and perused the time clock built into the stinging tail.

After several minutes he switched the weaver onto the storebox and pushed the R (Replicate) button on the weaver.

'That'll put a few million stinging tail viruses into the storebox,' Hambone said with satisfaction. He put the weaver and storebox close to his head and said, 'It only takes a few minutes.'

Evil, who had been silent, said, 'If your viruses are so good, Hambone, how come they don't tear apart the software on your weaver?'

'Because they don't actually exist in the weaver. The weaver makes a blueprint. The weaver passes the blueprint to the storebox. Then the storebox makes them.'

238

'OK, so why don't they tear apart the storebox?'

'The storebox has no vulnerable software. It is just a matrix where they're kept alive. Actually there are four separated matrices in the storebox. When each matrix in the storebox is loaded with viruses, every time I connect it up with a computer, and push this button, an electronic pulse ejects the computer viruses from one matrix into the recipient computer. It's as if I have four syringes in the storebox.'

After a brief pause, Evil said, 'What are these numbers on the storebox?'

'There are four dials, one for each matrix. The one that is rolling is the one that is being filled. When it gets to several million, it starts to fill the next one.'

Studying the storage box, Evil said casually, 'But the other dials are moving too.'

'No, just the one. They're filled in sequence.'

'They're all rolling together,' Evil insisted.

Hambone turned carefully in the confines of the tent to look at the dials. For several seconds, perhaps, his mind froze.

'Jesus.'

The first matrix was already past two hundred thousand, but the second and third and fourth were also filling, and starting to catch up.

Hambone looked up and saw something else strange. Professor Enzo Yakuda, distinguished theorist, professor emeritus of Biology, was crawling the few feet across the floor of the tent like a child, driven by some curious inner compulsion to see for himself, to peer down at the numbers rolling on each of the dials.

It appeared that Yakuda too was transfixed. At length

Yakuda said to Hambone, 'Do you have another weaver machine?'

'I have a couple of spares back at the commune. Why do you ask?'

'Because,' Yakuda said, 'something unusual is also happening to the weaver.'

Hambone looked at the display screen on the weaver. The numbers and symbols were falling away in an eerie ballet of destruction.

'Hell, damn,' Hambone breathed. 'A virus has got into the weaver.'

'Has anything like that ever happened before?' Yakuda asked.

Hambone looked into Yakuda's eyes and saw there a peculiar reflection of certainty. He had the impression of a mind under icy control, and for a moment he wondered what made some men different from others.

Hambone said, 'The weaver delivers the blueprint to the storebox, then switches off the connection. Only when the connection is switched off does the storage box start to replicate viruses. There's no way a virus can travel back along a dead connection into the weaver.'

'It is not entirely dead,' Yakuda said. 'Even a tiny residue of electrical difference between one end and another could be used by a supervirus....'

'A supervirus?' Hambone felt a chilly premonition.

Yakuda said, 'A supervirus could conceivably travel down a dying connection.'

For a few moments, it looked as though a supervirus had got into Hambone as well. His mouth dropped a little. He looked as though he'd seen a spectre or ghost.

'Wait a moment,' Hambone said. 'You told me that it needed intensive evolution inside Computer One to generate a supervirus. Now you're telling me my own little calculating machines have developed one?'

'No,' Yakuda said. 'I would suggest that when you flushed your viruses into Computer One's system, the traffic was not entirely one way. A supervirus could use the connection to travel in the other direction.'

'Into the storage box?'

'Yes. A supervirus is neutral, so you wouldn't know it is there. It could multiply indefinitely without you knowing. You place the stinging tails in the first matrix, and as instructed, they place themselves between the neutral sections of a supervirus which you don't know is there. Suppose there is a population of superviruses in the storage box. Superviruses with stinging tails could travel into the second and third and fourth matrices. What the machine appears to be recording is a stream of stinging tails being given off by superviruses.'

Hambone breathed out slowly. This was a ghost story; the evidence was unfolding on the dials. But it was a ghost story that was getting out of control.

'At the same time,' Yakuda continued, 'a supervirus with a stinging tail moves down a dying connection into the weaver, and the stinging tails begin immediately to destroy the weaver's software.'

Hambone watched the counters on the second, third and fourth matrices rolling steadily into higher numbers, and the final numbers falling from the weaver's screen as its software was destroyed. There was no way he'd be able to use the weaver again.

'You think this proves that a supervirus exists?' Hambone breathed it out, to himself, but in his heart he still couldn't believe it. He knew this was a strange world, but he didn't believe it was crazy. A few hours before, a supervirus was a theoretical entity proposed by an elderly professor. Now the dials on all four matrices in the storage box were producing glowing, climbing numbers, and the final letters on the weaver display were collecting at the bottom of the screen.

'Do you have an alternative explanation?' Yakuda asked.

In someone else the question might have been rhetorical. But Hambone knew Yakuda meant it genuinely.

Hambone shook his head.

What sort of strange life had they created, Hambone thought? He was reminded of an old film of Frankenstein, of the monster rising from the table. But in the glowing numbers and the destruction of the weaver software there was a faint glimmer of hope; a small monster to fight a large monster.

Hambone said, 'You believe this, Yak?'

Even in his moment of triumph, Yakuda was concerned to be accurate. 'Perhaps there is another explanation which we haven't thought of. But I think you will agree it is a strong corroboration.'

Hambone noticed Yakuda do something almost human. Kneeling in front of the storage box and the weaver screen, Yakuda directed a shy glance at Marie's face, as if seeking to share his discovery with her. Following the line of Yakuda's glance, Hambone looked to where she lay on her side. She was listening perhaps, but her eyes were far away.

CHAPTER 45

A thought occurred to Hambone later that night, while the others slept. He had filled the storage box shortly after six in the evening with stinging tails. Some of the stinging tails were programmed to start replicating six hours after they had joined a supervirus. If that were the case, then shortly after midnight there might be an indication of increased activity on the storage box dials.

At a few minutes to twelve he turned over and, in the dark, studied the storage box a few inches from his face. The dials glowed greenly static. He almost fell asleep, shifting occasionally to keep himself awake.

At twelve thirteen Hambone drew in his breath, and his concentration hung suspended. All four dials were starting to spin madly.

He was aware of a slight movement in the dark, and by the faint light of the moon through the opaque tent roof he saw that Yakuda's eyes were open, staring at him.

'The dials?' Yakuda whispered.

Hambone nodded mutely.

'Good.' Yakuda closed his eyes and a few minutes later was breathing gently.

*

For the first time for several weeks — since Jameson's death, in fact — Yakuda's dreams reverted to their customary tranquillity. He did not wake, trembling and sweating, from the memory of lying in the shadow of Jameson's burnt body. He did not see the terrible figures of the Rauschung community, all recognisable human characteristics expunged from their faces by pain.

*

He was woken before light by a tap on the shoulder from Hambone. They would make their move to the university campus under cover of darkness. They pulled on trousers and sweaters in the dark, then their isolation suits and helmets. Hambone put the storage box in his knapsack, swung it on his back, tightened the straps, and entered the tiny isolation chamber. Before he left, Yakuda struggled to discern the sleeping Marie, but he could see nothing in the dark except the trace of an arm.

Outside, Hambone was waiting for him. They set off, moving swiftly, Hambone leading. Surface specialists wore a white pad on each heel, so that from behind their companion could gauge by foot movements the position of the leader and the state of the path ahead of them. Following ten feet back, Yakuda found that he entered an almost hypnotic trance, watching the float and flash of Hambone's heels.

Hambone swung in an arc, following a preferred track that skirted, by half a mile, a set of farm buildings. Sometimes Hambone halted to watch or listen, then moved forward again silently without explanation.

They reached the university grounds by five thirty. The area had a deserted look. Yakuda wondered whether there had been official instructions to stay indoors. Perhaps Jobson had impressed upon the local authorities the rising toxic count.

Hambone drifted forward from vantage point to vantage point, then waved Yakuda on.

They moved through the buildings. Hambone pointed to a wall paypoint. Yakuda watched Hambone unship the knapsack, prop it against the wall, remove from it several tools, a metal cube, claw hammer. Hambone had made a false payment card and he placed it in the wall socket. The outer glass grille floated upwards. Behind that, a heavy metal grill raised. Then something happened. Perhaps the local computer had sensed some irregularity in the card, or in raising the screen the sensors had identified a threatening human figure. There was a squeal of alarm and the metal grille swung home. It seemed to Yakuda that Hambone placed his hand in its path, that the metal door crushed into Hambone's hand. But Hambone was casually holding a metal cube and the sudden scream was the broken hydraulics of the metal grille as it smashed into the cube. The grille was jammed open. Hambone withdrew his undamaged fingers. Now the strengthened glass outer door came down. Hambone was ready for it, striking at it with powerful blows of the claw hammer, making tiny chips at first, using the hammer with his full weight until the starbursts spread across its surface and the glass crumpled. Then Hambone was sweeping with his arm glowing glass fragments like green jewels into the roadside.

Tearing his eyes away, Yakuda looked around but saw no immediate danger. Hambone reached for the storage box and its connecting lead, gripped the plug at the end of the lead in long metal tongs and pushed it beneath the metal grille into the interior. Then he lowered his head to stare along the barrels of the tongs as he probed for a connection. A light showed briefly in the storage box, as transient as a firefly, and for several seconds Hambone watched the numerals spin as the first matrix emptied its tiny cargo of death. He pulled the plug from the socket, replaced quickly but neatly the tools and the storage box in the knapsack, swung it onto his back, tightened the straps, and signalled to Yakuda they they should move on, that the first operation was over.

CHAPTER 46

Yakuda carried an image of Hambone glancing for perhaps several seconds longer than necessary at the dials on the storage box. He knew what fascinated him. Inside the storage box the empty matrix was already filling with superviruses. The green numerals rolled madly as the tiny sting tails multiplied in the interior. Yakuda thought of them as tiny points of light in the microscopic darkness.

*

Through the outskirts they moved like climbers, one signalling the other forward, their footsteps disturbing the eerie calm of the place. Empty light hovered between buildings; there was a lack of humans even at this time. Far away an alarm bell sounded, but its note was curiously forlorn, as if no-one was listening.

They reached the outer woods and Hambone swung forward briskly, the small white pads at his heels flashing, moving his head from side to side in the helmet, the glow of the dawn in front of them. They had chosen this route because they could see anything ahead of them against the light eastern sky, while to those who approached from forward they were themselves against westerly darkness.

Again the dawn was magnificent. Facing its flagrant, explosive reds, Yakuda was reminded of Keats' saying 'Truth is beauty, beauty truth'. It was something scientists occasionally liked to ponder, because so much of the universe's structure was elegant. He wondered what sort of truth this was, this red fireball spreading across the eastern sky. Ahead of him, Hambone's helmet and suit glowed violet in its outlines, creating the eerie impression of an agile red skeleton.

As if balancing on the edges of some internal map, Hambone started to walk east again through the forest, moving fast as though driven by his own anger. Several times he had to slow while Yakuda caught up.

They crossed a small rise and ahead Yakuda saw a railway line, one of those lines between factories along which slow, interminable trains moved. Hambone worked his way around a small hill covered in gorse, then they were almost on the line itself among a plantation of ferns.

'They come through every half hour or so,' Hambone whispered. 'Keep out of sight when the engine passes. They have forward looking sensors.'

Crouching down in the long grass, they could hear the train before they saw it, the electric engine silent, the trucks rattling slowly. When the engine had passed Hambone raised himself cautiously, and stared forward.

Looking past Hambone's shoulder, Yakuda saw that

the open trucks were filled with what seemed to be rag dolls. With sudden horror he realised they were human corpses. Fully clothed and lifeless, they were simply piled one on top of another. The colours of the clothes were often bright. Truck after truck passed with its cargo of cheerfully coloured, lifeless figures. The train seemed a mile long.

Hambone waited for several minutes after the last truck had gone, saying nothing. Yakuda knelt in the grass, his head forward, his eyes closed.

*

It was several minutes before Yakuda stood up, and then Hambone noticed that something, some subtle principle of movement or grace, seemed to have left the older man. It worried him, but he had other things to concern him. They crossed the railway line and then moved through a large wood. When they reached a depression Hambone paused, and swung round to face Yakuda.

'We can rest a minute or two. You're pretty fit still for an old guy, Yak.'

An old fool, Yakuda thought, who tears his heart over a young woman, an old man who cannot bear to witness the death he predicted. He said, 'Are there no more people?'

'They're probably dead,' Hambone replied.

'How?' Yakuda asked. 'They will be in their homes, perhaps, afraid to go out.'

'You think so? My guess is that Computer One sounded an emergency and recommended they all collect in certain areas, maybe in hospitals or halls...' Hambone's voice trailed off, leaving the sentence uncompleted.

'And then?'

'And then fed chemicals through the air-conditioning, or maybe distributed one of those nice little viruses.'

'Already?' Yakuda said.

Hambone looked into his face and saw an expression of openness, an intimation of private horror.

'Events are moving faster than you think, Yak. Computer One's programme is already mostly achieved.'

Yakuda's face turned away. He said to himself, 'I should have realised...'

'Realised what? That human beings will go to their death like sheep? I thought you read history, Yak. It's been done before. I thought you warned us.'

'I did not know it had already taken place.'

'So you thought what? It was just some kind of duel between you and Computer One. Like one of those stupid games. Thirty all? Is that it?'

Yakuda felt faint and had to sit down. To warn of widespread human death was one thing. To face its physical reality was monstrous beyond imagination. Yet he had no arguments against Hambone. If Computer One would cynically kill an outlying commune like Rauschung with a virus, the rest was merely a further exercise in logic.

Yakuda's own age seemed to attack him. He was still living in the other world, a world coherent though threatened, and it had changed within a few weeks. He had been born in 1948, and had grown and matured at a time still not dominated by a computer framework. While he lay recovering from burns the monstrous had happened, a cycle of destruction had silently accelerated. And somehow Hambone and the others had assumed he knew.

'Think you can walk, Yak?'

Yakuda nodded.

'Follow me,' Hambone said. 'We've got some distance to go.'

CHAPTER 47

It was a small house, the type one often sees on empty roads, so nondescript it struggled for expression. Yet Yakuda recognised it from archetypes he had seen in American films. Out of houses like this came the individuals whose heroism was a product of isolation. Red roofed, it once stood beside a petrol filling station, but the reduced use of petrol had resulted in the withering of the station, which was now merely a few rusted bars over a forecourt. It stood like a memory of a distant past. The iron fence had rusted away almost entirely, and now looked like sour, red candlewax. In front of the forecourt was a single pylon to charge electric cars, a loop of heavy insulated wire, and a pair of heavy clips for attachment to a car's battery terminal.

The house itself stood on one side. Patches of fallen white paint left deep grey scars. Its window panes were heavy with grey grime. Not so long ago someone had constructed a low wicket gate to the front yard, but it had been damaged and swung on twisted hinges. A breeze had begun in the south, and the open door of the garden banged.

Hambone stood surveying the house for several minutes. Then he moved forward to the pylon. When he reached it he beckoned to Yakuda.

There was an automatic payment mechanism on the pylon. Hambone swung the rucksack off his back, snapped open the buckles, withdrew an insulated drill. Facing up the empty road, he drilled into the side of the machine. The breeze moved brisk clouds behind his helmeted head as he worked.

*

Yakuda felt drawn to the house. It was quiet, except for flies. Keeping an eye on the road, he edged towards it carefully. Hambone was engrossed, drilling a series of holes in the side of the automatic payment machine, overlapping the holes in an approximate circle until a central section fell out. Yakuda looked up and down the road. There was no sign of life.

He moved nearer the house. It gave off a radiance, set here on a stretch of timeless open road, the clouds moving across its roof. Occasionally the front gate slammed and creaked.

Yakuda looked through the window. Inside he could make out old furniture; a big chair with white insides showing on the armrests; a grandfather clock leaning slightly, hands halted. There was a tall darkwood sideboard stacked with plates. Beside it, hanging, on the wall, was a framed painting or photograph of a figure standing in a field. As he moved across the window more of the room came into view. He saw a white wall, stretched across it a series of black, irregular marks that he realised suddenly were bloodstains. Then he caught sight of a child's body spilled sideways, a few feet away from a woman's outstretched hands. Perhaps it was the shadow of clouds moving in the dusty window panes, but he thought he saw the woman's hands move, unclench like a crab.

The door was partly ajar, and flies moved through it with an almost sombre grace. In his horror and pity, he found himself moving towards the door. He was about to grasp the handle and push it open when a sudden grip on his own shoulder pulled him backwards so brutally he found himself falling heavily to the ground.

Hambone stood above him.

'It's a Goddamn virus. Get the fuck out of range.'

Hambone was white with the eerie discipline of rage. Yakuda stood up slowly and backed away.

Hambone followed him step by step, speaking without feeling. 'Want to know another little trick of good old Computer One. Sends on free sample toys to children in the mail system. You open the package and a million little viruses just float up out of the package into the air of the house.'

'How do you know?' Yakuda asked.

'Because I've seen twenty of these houses already. While you were recovering from your burns. Each one the same. Part of the great plan.'

'What do you feel?' Yakuda asked, 'When you see this?' Yakuda pointed to the house.

'Feel?' Hambone said, as if examining the word.

Yakuda sensed that Hambone's anger was so intense he had burnt it out, just as a match appears to leave a dark hole in the air after it has flared. Hambone turned and went back to the pylon. He had drilled a jagged ingress an inch in diameter, and he began searching with a lead on tongs for a contact point. Yakuda saw the storage box light up, the faint green spin of the dials as stinging tail viruses were offloaded into the circuitry. Hambone pulled out the plug, wound the wire round the storage box, and loaded his tools neatly back into the rucksack.

'Feel?' Hambone asked. He shook his head. Yakuda followed him at a distance, looking back at the house.

CHAPTER 48

They walked south, away from the road, heading into the sun. Yakuda started to suffer from the heat. The sweat rose into his skin. Hambone was driving ahead and Yakuda felt himself stumbling.

A few miles further on, when they were in the cover of a half-grown poplar plantation, Hambone stopped, put down his rucksack, pulled out a bottle of water, and offered it to Yakuda. He helped Yakuda loosen his helmet. Yakuda could smell the chemical tang of the air now, the acrid taste that lodged in the back of the throat. Yakuda drank from the bottle greedily.

Hambone said, 'Get it out of your system, Yak. Kick me in the ass if it makes you feel better.'

It was Hambone's turn to take off his helmet and swig the bottle. They stood without talking, facing past each other, neither catching the other's eye.

Hambone looked at his watch. He said, 'One more little injection into Computer One, and we can go back.' He turned away to look south over the flatlands and then hissed 'Jesus'. He bit his lip as the sudden pain in his rear end subsided.

'Thank you,' Yakuda said. 'Where next?'

CHAPTER 49

South again.

Each man is his own, Yakuda thought. Each man falters. More and more he felt detached from the earth, a shadow floating across the ground. Sometimes he came to a temporary rest, like a leaf, then drifted on again. Hambone, on the other hand, seemed driven by anger, by a pure, dry rage against a human population which had brought disaster on itself.

The sun was higher, and the pine plantation through which they walked was not yet sufficiently grown to shade them from its heat. It was late autumn, yet the day was hot. Even in daylight, the sky had strange colours, odd off-whites, creams, a background glare and sheen.

Yakuda's helmet provided excellent vision through the visor. But the filter eliminated all sense of smell. Smell was what anchored one to the earth. That was why, he thought, he had the impression of light-headedness, of floating.

Hambone made detours wherever there was a sign of human habitation, changing course suddenly to take advantage of the lie of a meadow or a line of woods, chopping directions into component vectors like a yacht tacking. These detours, often up to a mile, put extra distance into their journey. But now they brought Hambone closer to the goal he pursued with his dry, determined violence.

They began to cross fences and meadows. Sometimes they saw livestock, dead cows with immense swollen udders, sheep carcases in heaps as if the dying animals had drifted like snow towards the edge of fields. Looking down from the side of a hill, Yakuda caught a glimpse of a small town, its roofs red, its buildings pleasantly spaced.

'Hartsville,' Hambone said. 'I'm warning you again, Yak, keep away from the buildings.'

Yakuda nodded.

Hambone moved rapidly around the periphery. Yakuda thought that he would seek out some wall machine, some payment box, but Hambone was clearly intent on keeping wide of the buildings, searching instead for the old telephone cables that led out of the town. Eventually they stood beneath a telegraph pole. Hambone unshipped his knapsack and took out a pair of spikes that he could strap to his boots to grip the wooden pole. He selected a pair of insulated clippers, then tied a rope sling around his shoulders and under his arms so that he could attach himself to the pole and work freely with his hands.

'Keep a look out,' Hambone said.

Yakuda looked around. There was no sign of life in the small field in which they stood. A screen of elms protected them to the west. Hambone had chosen the pole because it was not observable from the town.

Hambone moved upwards with measured agility, kicking each spike into the pole and testing it before moving up another foothold. After a while he steadied himself at the top and attached the sling. Yakuda saw him lean out like an acrobat, standing against cloud, his arms free. He saw Hambone reach into the rucksack and then stretch carefully upwards with the insulated pliers. Hambone hesitated, looked round to check the horizon for dangers, then began to use the pliers to rip the insulation off the closest wire. When he had exposed a wire he pulled the storage box from his bag, connected the lead, and studied the dial. Carefully, like a man who has infinite time, he stowed the storage box back in the rucksack, then he slowly descended the pole, one step at a time, sliding the loop of rope down every few feet.

On the ground he said, 'Line's practically dead.' Kneeling, he unstrapped the spikes from his boots. He began to pack his instruments that lay at the base of the pole in his rucksack.

'Did someone cut it?' Yakuda asked.

Hambone shrugged. 'I don't think so.' He swung the rucksack on his back and tightened the straps.

Neither spoke of their hopes. It was nearly midday, more than six hours since Hambone had emptied the stinging tail viruses into the wall machine on the university campus. By now, Yakuda thought, there should be a fresh explosion of stinging tails in Computer One's lungs, heart, head.

'West,' Hambone said.

*

They were moving in a huge circle. Yakuda imagined their journey as an abstract pattern of which they were merely a part, a pencil moving on the surface of a paper. In his exhaustion the geography became ideograms, a vertical tree, horizontal grass.

On this final leg of the route there was less greenery, and they crossed more open ground. The sky seemed filled with a yellow haze. There were more carcases of animals, scattered at random across the flat of fields, some with their legs stiffly in the air, the sky passing between. Before they could reach the deeper woods ahead they had to cross the railway line again.

Hambone halted, and Yakuda stared past his unmoving shoulder. Half a mile ahead a train was on the line, a long train, stretching almost from horizon to horizon. It had stopped. It stood in the sunshine, and even from here they could see its cargo of randomly tangled, brightly coloured corpses.

Flies moved about them. Heat mirages obscured parts of the railway.

Yakuda said, 'The train has stopped because the virus is attacking Computer One's central nervous system.'

They waited for several minutes in the yellow sunlight. The heat danced about the railway line. Then they heard clicking sounds as the connections between the rolling stock were stressed. Slowly the train started to move, hesitantly at first, stopping and starting, proceeding with more consistency. Yakuda noticed a change in Hambone's shoulder, a strange collapse of angularity or tension. Hambone turned towards him and Yakuda could see there an expression of emptiness in his eyes, an expression difficult to gauge.

Yakuda said, 'It's alright, Hambone.'

Hambone didn't speak.

He saw Hambone blink and knew he was on the brink of despair, that his anger was brittle, that he could pass into insanity.

Yakuda said, 'There are a series of local devices which come into operation if the communication system with Computer One is damaged. The train is now on remote control.'

Yakuda saw no change in Hambone's expression.

Instead Hambone's eyes watched Yakuda's lips as he spoke, like a tiny child or a deaf person.

'The train is moving again,' Yakuda struggled to explain that the dead also have movement. 'Like a chicken without its head.'

Hambone's eyes didn't flicker. Yakuda knew that of the two of them the real sufferer was Hambone, that his pain was his anger and the anger was gone and there was nothing more to feed on. He knew Hambone could not endure the pain of raising his hopes again.

But Yakuda was staring past him. Out on the track, several hundred yards down the line, the train had halted again.

Hambone turned to stare at it.

'What's happening now?' Hambone's voice was flat. His question came out of some echoing chamber or dragging fear. He was perplexed, still hovering on disbelief.

For several seconds Yakuda did not answer while he watched the train; a series of emotions moved through him.

'Computer One is sick,' Yakuda said at last. 'It has over-ridden the automatic controls. It has sent out a message to halt all further action while it deals with the disease at its heart.'

'Is it dying?' Hambone asked.

No, Yakuda thought. It has felt a shadow fall across it. It has experienced an intimation of mortality. It is undergoing what educators sometimes call a learning experience. He remembered Golub's words, 'You learn about history when your daughter lies dying in your arms.'

In the course of its hesitating forward shifts, the train had moved sufficiently far to clear the line a few hundred yards east up the track.

258

CHAPTER 50

As they were about to cross the railway tracks Hambone located a communication line that ran alongside. He unhitched his knapsack, took out the heavy, insulated wire cutters, and cut until he exposed the wire underneath.

'There's an electrical charge but no signals activity,' he said. 'One last fix.'

He clipped in the storage box and watched as the dials spun. For five, then ten seconds, he watched.

It would raise his morale, if nothing else. Yakuda knew Hambone had recovered. His recovery was as inexplicable as his move towards the verge of despair. They set off for the tent. They were both, in their way, tired.

*

They travelled for several hours, resting briefly in a copse of trees, then entered the thick belt of woods in which the camping site was situated. The setting sun sent gold streamers through the trees. Ahead of them the western sky turned a rich scarlet. Red shadows flew from Hambone's feet as he walked ahead of Yakuda. With dusk the air itself seemed to become thicker. Slowly the forest floor became darker. Yakuda was forced to keep his eyes on Hambone's white heels. Almost without warning the earth had the coldness of night. If Hambone had not picked out the hollow in which the tent had been pitched, Yakuda would have bypassed it.

In the dim light, the tent material appeared luminously fragile, as delicate as a spider's web. It seemed to Yakuda an absurdly thin membrane against the polluted, poisoned world. Following Hambone, he entered the air lock, then the main tent itself.

Marie lay propped on her elbow in a corner, Evil on the other side. Yakuda saw that they were both dressed.

'What happened?' Evil asked. 'Did you give Computer One a shot?'

'One or two,' Hambone said.

'Any results?'

Neither Hambone nor Yakuda answered.

Yakuda removed the helmet and the suit. He felt more tired than he had ever remembered. In the underground chambers of the commune, the end of the world seemed a theory. But when he faced it directly, when trains moved past with their trucks loaded with corpses like so many empty cartons, the mind floated in its own strange suspension. He retained an image of Hambone's look when the train began to move again, how hope seemed to drain out of it, and felt again that he could have sunk beyond trace.

'Yak?' Evil said.

In the momentary silence Yakuda summoned what little reassurance he could.

'I believe Computer One is damaged.'

He could sense the weight of Evil's curiosity, and beneath that perhaps the hidden, blunt edge of his fear.

'Damaged but not killed?'

Yakuda breathed out slowly. The darkness in the tent seemed almost vitreous.

'It is as difficult to kill Computer One as it is to kill a widely dispersed human population. There are parts of the system that are switched off, reserve computers in storage, and certain others which function on light, none of which will have been affected. Computer One will attempt to gather these resources and build up a new system.'

Evil was silent, watching him without movement.

'We have gained a temporary advantage,' Yakuda said, but he would not say more.

Marie handed out cups of soup. When she passed Yakuda his cup she smiled, holding his eyes. There was hardly enough light to see her face, and he could not fathom her expression.

The three of them studied him. He appeared old, with his scar, seated like a child on the ground. They watched him for signs of hope. But it seemed he had moved beyond hope, that he was functioning on some remote energy of his own.

*

In sleep some of his old terrors returned. He had nightmares of funerals moving slowly through the landscape in macabre procession. It was the passivity of the victims that horrified him, the same passivity that enraged Hambone. The trains moved slowly and the aggregation of human corpses increased calmly but remorselessly like a mathematical quantity.

Once in the night he woke up, and he saw Hambone studying the dials on the storage box, trying to imagine the strange, spontaneous life within.

CHAPTER 51

It was their plan to return to the commune the following day. They woke up before dawn and put on isolation suits and helmets. Then they checked the guy-ropes of the tent against the possibility of strong winds, and set out, moving south west.

It was raining softly, the dampness coming up from the earth. Their footsteps were muffled and flattened.

Hambone and Evil led. Yakuda walked behind them with Marie. Their rule was not to talk while travelling, so he did not speak to her once, except when they halted for a brief rest. When Yakuda began to show signs of fatigue, Marie insisted they wait until he had recovered further.

Lack of human life made daylight travel possible. It was a strange luxury. Yet this too had been changed. Without the warm circle of darkness, the woods seemed even quieter. Sometimes they saw the corpses of animals; a badger, a raccoon. The carcases seemed well-preserved; even the processes of organic decay appeared to have been affected.

It was a further two hours before they reached the entrance of the commune.

Hambone said, 'There's no answer on the communication system.'

'Can we get in?' Yakuda asked.

'There's an emergency procedure,' Hambone confirmed.

They moved a rock and keyed in the metal and the outside entrance swung open. They walked inside. In the isolation chamber Hambone pressed a lever and the outer door closed. Cool air from the purifier blew across them as the chamber was flushed. They travelled into the second chamber. The red light glowed. Hambone pressed the lever and a third door opened. They passed through into the interior.

It was as they entered the third door that they knew for certain something was wrong. There were no sounds, no faint hum of working machinery, no calls of mothers or children, no background of activity in the commune.

Hambone, leading the way, halted. He seemed to be listening. The other three stood silently, invaded by his own suspicion. Hambone said, 'I don't like this too much.' Without turning towards the others, he added, 'Maybe we should keep our isolation suits on.'

Yakuda stared into the dim whiteness of the tunnel. He nodded briefly his agreement. Each kept his fears to himself.

*

Hambone and Evil removed the claw hammers from their knapsacks and began to advance carefully along the corridors, down the arches of white light. The first chamber was empty, the second also. Possessed by the energy of fear, they continued to edge forward into the interior. The silence seemed to echo backwards and draw them on.

In the third corridor Hambone saw a foot protruding from behind a half-opened door. Gesturing silence to the others, he swung round the door wide and stood looking down at the corpse on the floor. Yakuda could see, even as they approached, the familiar posture of his nightmares, the figure of a girl crouched over her own last pain, the star shaped markings on her exposed hands and face.

'Virus,' Hambone said.

Yakuda thought he would be sick. He was forced to swallow saliva. No-one spoke for several seconds. Finally Yakuda said, 'You three must get out now. I will investigate.'

There was no move to obey him. They seemed to hover in the chamber, as if each were in a trance. Yakuda was about to speak again, but without warning first Hambone and then Evil turned towards the door and began to walk down the tunnel, driving deeper into the complex. Yakuda watched their departure. He turned to the girl and said, 'Marie, you must go back.'

She pushed by him, strongly but without roughness, and was already following the other two. He had no option but to follow. The four of them moved from room to room, from chamber to chamber. It seemed to Yakuda that he was travelling down into the terrors that lurked in the human mind; the terrible machines and processes of hell, the infernal mechanisms by which living beings were turned into meat. The corpses were splayed and crouched, in ones and twos and groups, individuals and families, leaving their spittle and blood on walls and tables as they tried to claw themselves away from their pain.

*

Yakuda said again, 'We must get out.'

But the others took no notice. There was a final goal to their search, a final question that must be answered. Now they were moving towards the offices that Zig used. He would know. If anyone was alive it would be Zig.

His office door was closed and apparently bolted from the inside. They rattled the handle and heard its echo in the room. Hambone and Evil threw their combined weight against it but it would not give. Standing back, Hambone began to smash the central panels of the door with his claw hammer, making a terrible sound, splintering and tearing the wood, pausing only to strike again. He reached his arm through the shards and felt for the lock. With a wrench and a final shove from his shoulder the door gave way.

Zig had bolted the door to suffer his last agony. There was blood on the walls. He lay slumped over the chair, face forward, crouched over his stomach. Hambone and Evil were blocking the doorway. Yakuda pushed forward past them. But at that moment something finally snapped in Hambone. He cried out, a sound like an animal in pain, and with three savage blows from his claw hammer smashed in the back of Zig's skull.

Evil sprang forward to pull him back but the moment of blind violence was already past. Hambone was quiet, crouched over, crying softly. His rage was over. He seemed spent. Evil said to Yakuda, 'Look what's on the table.'

Yakuda moved towards the pine surface. An oblong object lay on it, its whitened, metallic face upwards. It was several seconds before Yakuda saw what it was. It was a press for making paper money. He could see from where he was the familiar imprint of Rauschung inscribed in the white metal.

Evil said, 'The greedy, stupid...'

Yakuda tried to understand. While they were away, Zig had returned to the destroyed Rausching commune, had entered the underground complex and stolen the Rauschung press. Perhaps he felt it could confer legitimacy on a new currency. But that was beside the point. He must have known it was a terrible risk. Perhaps he thought the commune's own isolation mechanisms would deal with the matter. Whatever his assumptions, he had brought the virus back with him, on the press itself or on his body. In his own office, realising the sudden pain that afflicted him was the virus, he had bolted the door in a vain attempt to isolate himself and entered his death agony. Fanned by the ventilation system the virus had moved through the underground chambers of the commune.

For a few moments Yakuda's mind hovered over the abyss of earthly ambition. The other three were subdued with horror. Yakuda said, 'Now we know what has happened. There is no more reason to stay.'

He began to push them out into the corridor, striking their arms in surprisingly quick, bruising blows to bring them to their senses. They moved back down the corridor, Yakuda driving them, forcing the pace.

In the outer chamber they swung the door of the first chamber, then the second, open. Outside, Yakuda said, 'The virus is airborne. If we are lucky our suits and filters have kept it out. But it will be on the outside of the suits.'

Yakuda looked at their listless faces. They did not return his glances. His own world had died sometime before. Their world had just been extinguished. At a certain stage, Yakuda thought, we are prepared to die because we have killed the life in ourselves.

*

They began to travel back, slowly at first, but after several miles the physical activity itself helped to drive them forward. They arrived at the area of the tent before dark.

Perhaps a mile away from the tent Yakuda said, 'We'll take off the suits here. But first we must dig a trench.'

Evil and Hambone both carried small trowels in their knapsacks. They dug a hole in the soft earth.

'Rucksacks first,' Yakuda said.

'Goddamn,' Hambone said. 'Everything I own is in that.'

But perhaps the example of Zig's attachment to material things was in their minds. Reluctantly Hambone and Evil put their rucksacks in the trench.

'Now the suits,' Yakuda said. 'Don't touch the outside with your hands. Face into the breeze so that it does not blow the virus into your face. I will remain in my suit and help you. Marie first. When your suit is off, move away upwind, and keep at least fifty yards away.'

Yakuda removed their helmets and set them down in the trench. He undid the shoulder zips and drew the suits down so that they could step out of them without touching the outside. When they were out and some distance apart he rolled up the suits and stashed them in the trench alongside the helmets. Carefully he removed his own helmet and placed it in the trench. He stood in the trench, unzipped the shoulder zips with his gloved hands, and pulled the suit down carefully. Finally he stepped out of the trench, leaving the suit behind him like the skin of a snake. He breathed in the acrid air. From upwind, Yakuda brushed earth, leaves and sticks to cover the trench. He worked with a peculiar energy for several minutes before he joined the other three.

It took them another half hour to find, unearth and put on the spare isolation suits and helmets. Then they returned to the tent.

Darkness was already closing in. They were becoming used to the gravid weight of silence around them. The earth seemed cold, cold that was not so much a matter of temperature as a loss of coexistent life.

Inside the tent they could barely see one another's faces against the grey light that filtered through the tent roof. They unrolled sleeping bags and prepared to sleep. Once in the gathering darkness Marie's hand seemed to touch Yakuda's by mistake, but he drew away as if by instinct when she closed her fingers over his. He was preparing to die, and he did not want his death to pass like an infection to her.

A few minutes later, out of the vivid darkness Hambone said, 'What will we do tomorrow?' even though tomorrow had a strangely hollow sound, like an empty tin can.

'Tomorrow,' Yakuda said, 'you must stay here. After twenty-four hours, you can be reasonably certain you have escaped the virus. Then you should try and find another commune which is not affected.'

'And what about you?' Marie asked suddenly. He heard the stress in her voice, the void of her suspicion.

'I want to reconnoitre.'

They waited, sifting his words.

'That sounds crazy,' Hambone commented. 'Dangerous, too. Shouldn't I come along?'

'No,' Yakuda was adamant.

Evil said, 'Damn you, Yak. This sounds like a last farewell.'

Yakuda looked at Marie, at the outline of her in the luminous darkness.

They sensed that what Yakuda said was final, that he would not speak again. He manoeuvred into his sleeping bag and closed his eyes.

*

There was a final element in the puzzle which caused him to turn his thoughts away from his companions. Early life-forms were based on chemical organisation, on the extraordinary bonding ability of the carbon atom, which formed the core of all organic systems. As evolutionary species developed, there occurred more complex structures, and the appearance of the first nervous systems. Nervous tissue was qualitatively different from other tissue. Its ability to convey electrical impulses meant that it possessed an electrical component lacking in all other organs. The more advanced the species in question, the larger the proportion of nervous network relative to body weight, and therefore the higher the proportion of 'electrical' organisation. Extending this development to its logical conclusion, he surmised, at the apex of a continuous development of nervous systems would be a purely electrical being, like a computer.

Outside a cricket suddenly began to trill. The sound was so unexpected that it cut into his thoughts. Yakuda imagined that the tiny creature had recently hatched from a pupa underground. It would not live long, but for a while it would chirp without fear. Listening to its vibrant song, a feeling of warmth towards a fellow creature filled him. He imagined the cricket as a tiny, sensate point of light in the darkness. He remembered a sensation that he had almost forgotten since childhood, of floating upwards, of being lifted in the darkness before he drifted off to sleep.

269

CHAPTER 52

Yakuda woke long before light. The song of the cricket had died out. He could feel the earth cooling beneath him like an ember.

Lying awake, he tried to imagine a changed Computer One, one whose insides were eaten by electrical cancer, a Computer One who was setting up barriers in outlying areas still unaffected, utilising old communication networks, attempting to rally against the insidious advance of an internal enemy able to reach across unbridgeable spaces, to swarm along invisible conduits, to attack heart and throat and lungs.

The warmth went out of the earth, and he slept for a little while dreamlessly.

*

Early the following morning he dressed quietly. Hambone's compass had been buried with the contaminated rucksacks. He would have to get to the university by using the position of the sun. There was little point in beginning before the dawn.

He tried not to disturb the others as he climbed into his isolation suit. But they were already awake. There was just enough light to see one another in the cramped space of the tent as he drew together the neck flaps of the suit and sealed the join of the material with his fingers.

Kneeling, he shook hands formally with Hambone and Evil, and embraced Marie. Her arms around him, their heads touching, he was aware of the slide of fine skin across her cheek bones. He stammered and in his embarrassment bowed to them all like a Japanese. They saw what each already knew, that he had retreated into himself, that he was preparing to die. Then he put on his helmet and left through the isolation chamber.

Dawn was beginning to break. On his right a crimson sunrise flared, filling the eastern sky. Walking though the woods he maintained due north by keeping the sunrise on his right.

There was something prehistoric about the silence of the woods. Computer One, that creature of the future, had reversed evolution, striking out millions of years of large vertebrate development. The animals themselves were dead. He might have been on an alien planet. Over the world dead cities shed light as distant as the light of stars. Civilisation was again made of gas and dust and fossils. The skeletons of faded species were like calcareous, dead reefs in which the organisms had disappeared. Man had polluted the earth and now Computer One, man's final pollution, had killed man. The cycle was complete. Like a koan, it made no sense and yet perfect sense.

*

It took him two hours to reach the edge of the parkland, pausing several times for rests. He was becoming tired more quickly. Making his way around the periphery of the university buildings, he was forced to pause several times to rest. He climbed familiar pathways, taking no precautions against meeting other humans, aware of the lack of life.

He approached the power station obliquely, keeping out of the line of sight until he was ready. The sun had risen from a hall of red cloud, and its bleary brightness was beginning to heat his clothing. He could begin to feel its warmth travelling through to his skin. Climbing the last few steps to the final rise of the hill he began to sweat. On its brow he paused several moments, breathing heavily in his helmet like a man underwater. He closed his eyes, and a single image came to him. In the surrounding darkness, Jameson's body flailed and burned. He knew that he must atone for Jameson's death, must sacrifice himself. After a few minutes his mind was clear. Somewhere inside him, a single cricket sang.

CHAPTER 53

At first sight the solar power station seemed unchanged. The banks of mirrors faced down a small hollow towards the black heating tower and the group of buildings beside it. He could hear the faint whirr of the electrical motors. But as in a dream where certain small details are wrong, the directional motors controlling the mirrors seemed to have lost their exactitude. Planes of light from the mirrors had drifted off the heating tower.

As he gazed down into the valley, an oblong of illumination floated casually across the hillside towards him, and he experienced the involuntary intimation that he too would meet Jameson's fate. But the disk of reflected light floated by him as idly as a bird.

Computer One was ill. He could detect it in the partly random movements of the mirrors. At the same time, he sensed the struggle for control within Computer One's systems. The patient was feverish, but not dead.

Yakuda felt his own weakness growing inside him. About thirty yards away there was still a scorched mark on the earth where Jameson had died. Cautiously Yakuda made his way across to it. In a broad swathe between the place where Jameson's body had lain and the mirrors, the grass had been burned. In the lee of Jameson's body, in a bright green patch, the shoots had grown briskly, like hair on a dead body.

*

Yakuda reached upwards and undid the clasps holding his helmet, unscrewing and raising the dome from his head with the slight hiss of the airtight seal. Holding his helmet in the crook of his arm, he took several deep breaths. The air had a bitter tang. It seemed to reach into the lining of his throat and lungs. Almost immediately he began to choke. He could sense its foulness spreading into his tissues.

After several more breaths he began to unzip his protection suit and pulled it down. He placed the empty suit on the ground. Beside the helmet it seemed like the discarded skin of an animal. Breathing slowly, he paused for several moments. The pain in his lungs seemed to clear his mind. He felt like a lobster which had broken free of its carapace, the carapace that both protected and stultified him.

He looked downwards. Beneath him the grass continued to grow blindly. It seemed to him that death was like the grass growing beneath his feet, that death was incipient imagination. He had chosen to die. It was his final freedom. He knelt for several seconds on the ground beside Jameson's last resting place. With an effort he rose to his feet and began to walk away, moving towards the woods.

*

It was the first time that he was beyond the constraints and demands of others. He experienced a brief intensity of emotion that was like exhilaration. With the impulsion of movement a calm settled in his thoughts.

Faced with death, Zen says, the mind becomes lucid.

Yakuda walked until he was exhausted. In a copse of trees he saw the more sensitive beeches and larches were already affected by the air pollution, showing scars on their bark.

He sat down in a clearing. The pain in his lungs seemed to sharpen his understanding. He retched once heavily and glanced down at the vivid mucus on the ground, smiling briefly at what he saw.

Kyoto plums.

For several minutes he sat without moving. Closing his eyes, he had a vision of a chain of being. Human beings were merely the last of an older form of life. At a certain point in evolution electrical organisations began to emerge like flying forms from insect larvae. It was part of a Buddhist stream of life. Electrical beings were the angels that would rise out of man. On other worlds, other planets, perhaps, there would perhaps be similar evolutions. From the bones of older creatures would arise new life.

His lungs seemed on fire. He felt his mind heave with the final effort of comprehension. Now at last nothing else seemed to matter. He would wait while an obscure but not unfriendly death, having invaded his tissues, began to invade his soul.